Also by Victoria Heckman

In the Elizabeth Murphy Animal Communicator Series:
White Fox
Wet Work
Burn Out

In the K.O.'d in Hawai'i Police Procedural Series:
K.O.'d at Banzai Pipeline
K.O.'d in the Rift
K.O.'d in the Volcano
K.O.'d in Honolulu

In the Coconut Man Mysteries of Ancient Hawai'i Series:
Kahuna
Kapu

Stand Alone:
Pearl Harbor Blues

1

White Fox
Animal Communicator Mystery #3

Victoria Heckman

In Memoriam

"Skinny"

For all my sons

Zach
Liam
Kyle
Trevor

This is a work of fiction, a product of the author's imagination. Any resemblance to events or persons living or dead is entirely coincidental.

2018 Revenge Publishing
Copyright 2018 Victoria Heckman
All Rights Reserved
Published in the United States by Revenge Publishing
ISBN 978-0-9970880-4-5

Cover by Liam Heckman
Author Photo by Dennis Eamon Young Photography

Acknowledgements

Thanks to so many people who helped see this book through. My family first and foremost, my editor, Sue McGinty, and my beta readers. And of course, Freya.

WHITE FOX
ANIMAL COMMUNICATOR
MYSTERY #3

VICTORIA HECKMAN

One

Elizabeth Murphy had just gotten settled for a quick nap. Since she was still in her first trimester of pregnancy, she didn't understand how she could be so tired all the time. 24 hour morning sickness would do it, she figured. She wasn't throwing up often, but felt nauseated much of the time. She had decided a morning rest would be helpful. Her firefighter husband Tig was on night shifts now, but he was gone much of the time with his second job, as the owner of a pond company, doing design and maintenance. When the baby came, they'd agreed she'd need him much more then. He was saving days off and hurriedly upping the training of his assistant, Karl, to run the business.

Elizabeth sighed and tucked a pillow between her knees. She didn't look very pregnant, she knew, but she was so excited, she wanted to run out and buy maternity wear. However, she *felt* pregnant, bloaty and uncomfortable. She drifted off with visions of tiny Tigs and Elizabeths. They had decided to be surprised about the gender of the baby.

Mom! Mom! she heard her Tabby cat Teddy cry in her mind, just as the cat flap banged. Followed by the pounding of small bison-like feet down the faux wood hall to where she almost slept. The patter of a second set of hooves signaled smaller, younger Edward's entrance.

She refused to move. *What?* she answered in that mind-speak she shared with most animals, particularly with her own. She sounded crabby to herself. *Just so tired.*

Mom! You know those guys next door? Teddy referred to the college students renting the neighbor's house. The question was accompanied by a thump as Teddy leaped onto the bed, jarring her. A smaller, more delicate bounce as Edward joined them.

Yes? She remained on her side and Teddy slithered over her. Unusual since he loved to be petted, but wasn't a lap cat. *Remember how you said it's been so quiet over there?*

Elizabeth sighed and opened her eyes to find Teddy inches from her face. *I was trying to sleep. Is it really important?*

Teddy thought his kibble bowl being only 75% full was an emergency, so who knew?

I know why!

She couldn't resist his beautiful green eyes with black eyeliner and black lines of 'jewelry' as she called them, draped around his neck. She leaned in and kissed his nose, which he hated. Punishment for waking her. She smiled. Edward, on the other hand, loved being cuddled and rubbed for as long as any victim could be trapped into doing it. Tig was his person, so Edward was often carried around like a football, lying boneless purring in ecstasy. She pulled Edward into her, rolling him on his back. Pure black, except for a few white hairs on his chest and tummy, he closed his eyes and purred while she stroked his belly.

Affronted, Teddy pulled back. *Mom, I'm serious.*

"Okay, I'm up. What?" she said.

They moved. Those people moved. And you know what else? They had a baby with them! And they left it!

"A baby? What do you mean? We would have heard it. I think." Elizabeth was wide awake now. Teddy was excitable, that was true, but he was not inaccurate.

She and Tig had spoken of how quiet and well-behaved the Tech U students had been. When the 'kids' had first moved in at the beginning of the school year, they were worried about the noise. Tig had friends in the fire department from Tolosa, the 'big' city ten miles away, who spoke of many police and fire calls to the housing near the university. Noise, accidents, injuries, parties, the stories were unbelievable. She and Tig owned their home, okay the bank did, and were concerned they'd never get another night's sleep. Moving was out of the question, so they just waited to see what would happen.

Not much happened; the occasional sports night, when a few of their friends showed up and watched some game and drank beer; a few barbecues. Their hot tub in the back yard aligned with Tig and Elizabeth's bedroom made for some interesting sounds, but on the whole, they'd been excellent neighbors. But a baby? For sure they'd have heard or seen it. The houses in this development were only ten feet apart.

Elizabeth continued to rub Edward. His paws kneaded the air, his eyes mere slits. Teddy had moved out of kissing range but gazed at her intently.

"Tell me more," she told him. Elizabeth was an animal communicator by trade. Her last few jobs had gotten her noticed on social media, and she had more pet owners wanting her services than she could visit. She had gotten better at 'phone' communication, out of necessity. She preferred face to face 'discussions' with animals and owners, but now those were saved for the more serious cases. With the baby on the way, both Tig and Elizabeth were working extra hours. She could still do phone consults after the birth, but in-person visits might be difficult for a while.

Teddy and Edward were her 'children' and she could converse with them almost like a person. While they understood a lot of English like most household pets, more difficult concepts were done by sending feelings and images. She would speak along with sending pictures and emotions, they would respond silently, and she would hear or see it within her mind. She had done it since she was a child and hadn't realized until almost adulthood that everyone didn't do this, or even know about it.

I know they moved because all their stuff is gone, Teddy said.

We checked, added Edward, eyes still closed.

"How did you check?"

A big van came, and they loaded it and all their cars with things, Teddy said.

"When did this happen?"

Yesterday. Or before. I forget.

"Teddy, this is important. When?"

Two night times ago. Maybe three." Teddy squirmed. Telling time wasn't his strong suit. When they traveled overnight, or if just Elizabeth would be gone, she would tell the cats how many nights they would be alone. Overnight was still a clear case of pet abuse as far as Teddy was concerned. Even with neighbor and friend Janie to check, and full bowls of food and water.

Elizabeth started to get a sick feeling that wasn't morning sickness. "Tell me about the baby. How do you know they didn't take it?"

I told you, we checked. Edward opened his eyes.

"How did you check?"

You know the big window-doors? Teddy asked.

That's what he called sliding glass doors. "Yes. You saw it through those?"

Yes, at first. But then it came out, well, she did. Edward rolled onto his stomach.

"I'm confused. The baby came out? Of the house?" Elizabeth reached for the phone. "I'd better call someone." She wondered about calling Tig or 911. His station was less than five minutes away.

17

Yes. She's so cute! She looks like Teddy, a little.

That stilled Elizabeth's hand. "It's a she, and she looks liked Teddy?" Pregnancy hormones were making her loopy. Too quick to react. Now she had an idea of what might have happened. "Show her to me."

Instantly a little gray tabby kitten picture appeared in her mind. She stood with her front paws on the slider and silently meowed.

"Okay. I see. How did she come out of the house?"

Another picture, of a pet door arose. "Can she get out of it now?" Elizabeth asked.

Yes, but she's afraid. Her people are gone and she doesn't want to. Edward sat up, expression serious—only his eyes visible. Mouth closed and black whiskers left gorgeous green-yellow orbs glowing in the dim bedroom.

"Maybe they're coming back? Did they leave food or water?"

No, she didn't find any, Teddy said. He should know, she thought.

I told her she could come here. She'd be safe here, right Mom? Teddy said.

That surprised Elizabeth. Teddy was the dominant cat, and he graciously allowed Edward to stay after Tig rescued him from a fire. Edward was smaller, frailer and gave into Teddy most of the time. He had begun to show some independent spirit, though.

"Edward? How do you feel about another cat? Even temporarily?" Elizabeth wondered how

Tig would feel about another cat. Tig had surprised her by keeping Edward. Edward had won his heart. Plus, Tig had saved his life, so there was that. But a female cat. What if the neighbors came back? What if Teddy was exaggerating about her being abandoned?

Edward sat solemnly. *I would like a sister.*

I know I might be wrong about the nights she's been alone, but it's still a long time, Mom.

Elizabeth tried to recall any kind of moving hubbub and couldn't. It's hard to move in or out quietly. So they must have meant to be sneaky. Maybe because they were abandoning their animal? She knew students did that regularly at the college housing areas.

"Okay. For now. How do you suggest we do this? I'm not breaking into their house."

It's okay, she's here. I told her to come over. Teddy plopped off the bed, tail waving.

Wow. Like a play date or something. "Where is she?" Elizabeth slid on house slippers.

In the back yard. Yes, I warned her about the pond, Edward added.

She says she's hungry and thirsty. Teddy's rotund shape swayed right and left as he led the way to the back door.

Elizabeth felt she could only follow. She reached out to the kitten to soothe her, but the kitten felt confident. Apparently Teddy and Edward had been communicating with her long enough to make friends.

Elizabeth opened the back door and there she sat. A gorgeous gray tabby, with glittering green eyes, tail wrapped neatly around her, looked up and into Elizabeth.

"Oh, my!" Elizabeth said. "So tiny!" She was perfect. Elizabeth had been working with animals her whole life, and this kitten was barely weaned. She reached down to pick her up, and the kitten flopped over onto her side, exposing her belly.

"Oh!" Elizabeth repeated. She couldn't resist another second. She scooped up the kitten and cuddled her close. She draped her tiny self over Elizabeth's shoulder and purred. Elizabeth felt something click in her heart and fell absolutely in love. She didn't think she could give this kitten up even if the people came back. Who did that, anyway? Leave a baby! Well, Teddy got that right.

"Okay, you. Food and water." If the kitten was as young as her size indicated, she probably needed wet food. She didn't have any kitten food, but she would get some.

Us, too, Mom?" The two handsome boys sat like bookends on either side of Elizabeth. *We saved her, right?*

"Yes, you did. You get a reward for that." She bustled around opening a can, getting three small dishes, all the while cradling the kitten, who was most content.

To the boys' credit, mostly Teddy's, they didn't try to steal any of her wet food. Teddy was food-motivated and had the waistline to prove it. The kitten ate and drank delicately and then explored a bit.

What do I do now? Elizabeth thought. She's far too small to go out at night. She had emergency supplies in the garage for rescue animals and sick days. The litter box would be far too big for her, so she fashioned one with low sides out of a cardboard soda tray. She called Dr. Otis, her amazing vet's office to schedule a check-up and get her micro-chipped. All this without texting Tig. She was nervous about that part. Should she wait and tell him in person? He usually came home after pond work and before his evening shift so they could have an early dinner together. *Guess what honey? Dinner is salad and sandwiches and a new kitten!*

Elizabeth did feel that once he saw her, he would fall in love, too. But with a new baby coming and other expenses . . . those were legitimate concerns. If she took more clients, she could cover any vet charges.

First things first. Her name. The boys had taken her on a tour of the house and Elizabeth put her little litter box and separate food and water in the laundry room, near the door where she'd come in. The house wasn't very big. She found all three of them asleep on her and Tig's bed. A kitten sandwich.

Elizabeth did a mental check. Apparently, the boys had known about her for a while, but kept it a secret from her. *Hmmmm.* That was new. Their minds were lighter now that they'd come clean. They had also made it seem as if the kitten were in imminent danger, but again, not true. She didn't know what to do about that. She probed the kitten and saw she was exhausted. It did seem she'd been alone for closer to three days. A dripping sink had given her a little water, but no food. Elizabeth felt herself getting angry. Did adults really think a kitten this small would just go outside and fend for itself with all the predators around? She could never outrun a coyote or bobcat, even if she stayed close to the house.

The kitten seemed healthy. She assumed she hadn't had shots or any other real care. The kitten's eyes opened, and when Elizabeth focused on them, she saw they were highly intelligent. A little startling.

Hi, little one, she began.

Hi, Mom, the kitten said.

Elizabeth laughed. *You are something else. What is your name?*

They called me Baby. That is stupid. I'm not a baby.

You kind of are. But you're right. You won't be for long. You will grow so fast." Elizabeth couldn't help it. She had to pick up the kitten once more. *You are such a love. What should I call you?*

I have a name. I came with a name.

Elizabeth had never heard of this. She supposed animals had names for each other. Maybe in the wild, but domestic animals? Oh, well. She learned something new every day.

What is your name?

Freya.

Two

Elizabeth checked the time. Tig would be home soon and she hadn't started dinner. It was a little strange eating so early, but a nice time to catch up on each other's days. He could eat at the fire department, but if they got a call, a meal might be postponed for hours.

She put the kitten back on the bed to nap with her brothers. She chickened out on texting Tig about it. As she made a big salad, she rationalized it was better to tell him in person. She whipped up a quick vinaigrette dressing and tossed it together. She made some sandwiches, tuna salad with potato chips right in between the bread. Added a nice crunch and some salt.

She finished placing everything on the table and heard Tig's truck pull into the drive. He came through the door like a whirlwind. She received a quick kiss and he disappeared down the hall.

"Gonna take a shower. Be right back," he called.

"Uh, oh." No chance to warn him. *Or Freya,* Elizabeth thought.

An unusual name. She'd have to look it up later. Somebody was a creative namer. Not the previous owners, obviously. Who, then?

Elizabeth poured tea in tall, ice-filled glasses and sat down to wait. His showers were fast when he had to go to work. Again, he could shower at the station, but he preferred to start the shift clean after a pond job, if possible.

"Elizabeth?" he called from their room.

"Double uh, oh." She stood up, but he was already coming to meet her.

"Look what I found." He was dressed in a tee and jeans and cradled little Freya, who looked extremely smug.

He didn't look too mad, she thought.

"I didn't get a chance to tell you," she began quickly. "I didn't want to text you, but I knew you'd be home for linner," what they called this in-between meal. "The boys found her," she added weakly. As if that absolved her. Speaking of which, two satisfied cats followed Tig out of the hall.

Tuna? Edward asked.

Tuna, Teddy confirmed.

I like tuna, Freya added in sweet, feminine tones. She lay relaxed in Tig's grip, but had rolled so most of her fit in his palm. Her back legs dangled, straddling his wrist.

Elizabeth melted. *Have you ever eaten tuna, little girl?*

I like the smell of tuna, Freya corrected.

"You guys are doing it, aren't you?" Tig asked, referring to her inner conversations with the cats.

"Yes," Elizabeth said aloud for Tig. "Her name is Freya and the boys told me her story. She's like no kitten I've ever seen. She acts like a mature cat in a lot of ways, but she's so tiny."

"I was getting out of the shower and there she was, sitting on the edge of the tub. Not worried about me or the water. Like a little Egyptian statue."

"Let's eat. I know you don't have much time."

That's my spot, Edward said. Tig had kept Freya in his lap, traditionally where Edward sat. He was much smaller than Teddy, but nowhere near the size of petite Freya.

"Edward would like his regular place, please," Elizabeth told Tig. They looked down to see Edward politely waiting for Freya to be moved.

"Here, you take her. I don't want her to get stepped on or anything."

Elizabeth placed Freya on her thighs as Teddy watched all of this with surprising calm. "Are you okay, Teddy?" Elizabeth asked.

Yes. I don't like laps. But I like tuna.

"I know. After we eat, okay?"

I know. Rules. He flopped onto his side, unperturbed that a new ball of fluff might usurp his role.

Edward, what do you think? Elizabeth asked him.

I'd like a sister. She is smaller than me. That's good. He purred from Tig's lap, and they could both hear it over the crunching of tuna-potato chip sandwiches.

Between bites, Elizabeth told Tig the strange story of the college kids next door and Freya's odd behavior. "She said her name was Freya, that she came with the name. The students called her Baby, which she did not like, but whatever Freya is, it fits her. I'm going to look it up later."

"Maybe it's Egyptian?" Tig suggested. "She acted like she was queen of the world when I first met her. They worshiped cats, right? Maybe she's used to being worshiped," he joked.

"Certainly not by those people next door. They neglected her. They don't deserve her."

"We can keep her for a few days, I guess. If they come back for her, some kind of misunderstanding, we have to let her go."

"Sure, I know." *Over my dead body,* Elizabeth added.

No, Freya said. *I waited for you. I am staying here.*

She's our sister now, Teddy said.

What do you mean, you waited for us? Elizabeth asked Freya.

You. I waited for you. I'm supposed to be here.

Elizabeth was nonplussed. *What do you mean me? Why me?* She had never heard of an animal waiting for a person it had never met. Teddy was 'her' special boy, and Edward was

Tig's, but they were all one family. She felt confused.

Freya oozed complacency and superiority.

Fortunately, Tig was focused on his food and sneaking bites to Edward in his lap and the occasional bit to Teddy on the floor. Strictly illegal and a bad habit, but if no one complained, she wasn't going to.

She needed more information but had no idea where to ask. *Boys, how do you feel about Freya being here? Staying here?*

It's like she said. She's supposed to be here, Edward said.

Teddy, aren't you jealous, or anything? Elizabeth was puzzled. Teddy was pretty territorial, and he knew he was special. He wasn't fond of Buster's visits, maybe because he was a dog? She blew out a sigh.

Jealous of what? I'm still your boy, right? Edward's a baby, and he likes dad.

But, Teddy, she's a baby, too, and she's going to take up time and effort. Maybe food? Aren't you worried about not having enough? Elizabeth was worried about saying the 'f' word to Teddy.

No. She's a hunter. She is the one.

Aaagghhh. Elizabeth didn't know what to say. She gave up for now. She just had to convince Tig.

Elizabeth finished her salad. Tig plopped Edward down and cleared his dishes. "I gotta get going. Shift starts soon."

"So, I should call the vet, maybe? To see if anyone's missing her?" Elizabeth grabbed the salad bowl and her dishes.

"Sure, and maybe you should get her checked out. She looks fine, but we want to make sure our princess is healthy."

"What? Princess?" Elizabeth was stunned. From thinking he would be angry, or at least hesitant, to having a princess?

"Look at her. She's obviously regal." Tig came to stand at Elizabeth's chair where she had set Freya after the meal. The kitten lay, back half on her side, the front of her body up and straight, front paws extended and crossed.

What did you do? Elizabeth demanded.

I told him I was supposed to stay here. He needs me, too.

He can't understand you. How did you do it?

I can make creatures think and feel things. He feels he needs me now. And he does. You both do.

We do too, chirruped two other little voices.

That's not going to work on me. Whatever it was. Elizabeth was a little worried. Things were moving too fast. Freya *was* adorable. Maybe she was a little wacko. Animals had mental issues just like people. Maybe Tig just thought she was cute. But no mention of extra work, the baby coming, the additional bills. That was odd.

You will find out that you need me. But in the meantime, I am just . . . yours.

What do you mean, mine?

"I gotta go, babe. See you tomorrow. I'm working on a pond with Karl." Tig mentioned his assistant, a college-aged family friend who worked on jobs too big for one person. He'd started getting his own clients, too, and Tig helped him out too.

"Okay." Tig kissed her good-bye as Elizabeth stood stunned by her chair.

The boys stretched and headed toward the back door. They had their own cat flap from the living room, but they liked a door person at this exit, which led straight to the patio and pond. Freya also stretched her front paws, humping her back up like a Halloween cat.

I think I'll go, too. Mom.

"Oh, my gosh, you are so cute." Elizabeth picked her up and cuddled her. She melted against Elizabeth.

It'll be all right. You'll see.

"Be careful. You don't know this area yet. Stay with the boys. You may be a princess, but you are a tiny one. We have owls—she showed Freya an owl in her mind—and they love to pick up things and fly away with them." She kissed Freya firmly. "That's something else you have to get used to around here. Kisses."

I know about kisses. Teddy and Edward told me all about you when I arrived. That is another way I knew you were the one for me. I give kisses, too.

"You do? How?" Elizabeth was curious. Teddy rarely gave kisses, and Edward was more of a hugger, going limp so he could be worn as a scarf.

29

Freya squirmed around until they were face to face. She put her nose against Elizabeth's nose, very gently. Then she raised her head and carefully licked Elizabeth's forehead.

Those are my kisses. Almost no one gets those. She said it just like a teenaged girl.

Elizabeth smiled. "Those are great kisses. Oh, one more thing. What did you mean when you said you waited for me?"

I can be seen, or not seen. As I wish. When those other people left their house, I hid. I was not seen. I waited for you. Through the boys. I told them what to do. Now I am here.

Mind blown. Now she would really have to keep this from Tig. They did not keep things from each other, not on purpose. They both had terrible memories which didn't help. Tell each other the same thing three times, and forget other things completely.

"Okay, what do you mean, you can *not* be seen if you choose? Like invisible?" Elizabeth couldn't believe she was asking this of a cat. Of anything.

Freya tilted her head in a very human-like way. *Yes. For lack of a better description.*

"So, those people did not abandon you like I thought? You left them?"

Yes. But they did not leave food or water.

Point taken. "You didn't want to stay with them anyway."

No. That does not excuse good manners.

Come on, Freya! Teddy.

We have to show you where the mice and lizards hide! Both Teddy and Edward sounded excited.

Elizabeth carried her up the back steps and propped the gate open to the 'outback' as they called the wild area behind the house.

"Be careful. I still have to teach you about the dangers we have here." Elizabeth set her down. The boys had already gone out the small door in the fence Tig made.

And I have to teach you too, Freya added as she leapt lightly away.

Three

Elizabeth kept an eye on the back gate as she finished cleaning up after dinner. She began to feel a bit nauseated and wished she hadn't finished her salad. For some reason, this baby liked tuna, so they ate a lot of that. She made a cup of mint tea, which often soothed an upset stomach or headache. Now that she was pregnant, about eight weeks was the doctor's estimate, she'd given up lots of fun things. She still had a cup of Peet's coffee in the morning, but decaf. Herbal tea the rest of the day. She wasn't a big drinker, but now any was off limits.

She took her tea out to the pond and checked the koi. They burbled to the surface, and she returned to the kitchen and brought back a handful of diced tofu. She could talk to them too, but it was more work and so she usually waited for them to speak to her. The matriarch, Princess Keiko, was the best 'speaker.' If something was amiss, she would tell Elizabeth. "Tofu," was the usual request.

Freya sat at the edge of the pond watching. She was a quarter of the size of the giant fish.

Don't fall in, Freya, Elizabeth said.

I won't. She looked comfortable despite the deep pond and the sea monsters at the surface.

"Do you know how to swim?"

Yes. I don't mind it. I haven't swum for quite a while, though.

Nothing weird about a kitten saying it hadn't swum in a while. "Uh, those rings in the middle are in case you fall in. You can paddle to one and get in. We'll come get you."

Very good idea. Freya bounded up the steps and sat on the wooden loveseat that Tig and Elizabeth called 'the viewing port.' It had a good view of the pond and the yard. Elizabeth still felt a little queasy, so she joined Freya.

As soon as she sat and placed her tea cup on the arm rest, Freya crawled into her lap. This was nice. Teddy was a next-to cat, not a lap cat, and Edward was really fond of Tig, although he did love a cuddle from her, too. But having her own lap cat would be nice. If Freya stayed this way.

Oh, I will.

What?

Stay this way. Do you feel better?

Elizabeth concentrated. No nausea. *Yes, I do. Did you have something to do with that?*

Freya simply purred.

Oh, boy. "Don't you want to play with the boys? I'm not going to let you out at night. You're too little. Too many dangers." She sensed a rebuttal coming. "I know, you are strong and brave, and uh, ruled your own kingdom or something, but you're still small. When you're bigger, you can stay out longer."

Freya remained in her lap, but a distinct *humph* feeling was her response.

"If you don't want to play, I'll take you in with me."

I'll go with them. For a while.

"You come when I call. You may be tiny, but if you don't listen, I'll lock you in the bedroom."

Elizabeth put her down and took her tea mug to the kitchen. She did feel much better. That would be her last food for the evening, she figured.

She closed the front blinds and locked up for the night. It felt weird when Tig worked overnights or his twenty-four hour shift. She was fine alone, but still she missed him.

In the little room off the bedroom she called her office, she checked her email. A few new clients wanted consults. Nothing she wanted to tackle tonight. She emailed responses for future contact and decided to run a bath.

As the water filled, she went to the back door to call the cats. The boys were microchipped, and the cat flap could read them and allow them access, but Freya wasn't chipped yet and she needed to get her inside. Right. Vet tomorrow.

She did a mental scan for the boys and saw them chasing lizards. Edward was doing most of the chasing. Teddy sat on a big fallen log and watched his progress. She didn't see Freya with them, and the evening had become decidedly darker.

She called out to her and Freya responded. She sat atop the six foot fence and surveyed her new domain. She really was beautiful.

"Okay, guys, everybody in. NetFilms!" Elizabeth called.

Teddy and Edward loved cuddle time on the bed, but Freya sent a question mark. "Freya, you too."

As the boys picked their way through the yucca and agave jungle, they sent Freya jumbled pictures of the TV screen, popcorn and the bed. No wonder she was confused.

Elizabeth knew Freya could outrun her and hide so she simply waited. Freya skittered down the fence onto a bamboo leaf cushion. The backyard that wasn't pond had various types of bamboo and a litter of leaves under all for fertilizer and ambiance. She landed softly and made her way to Elizabeth.

"Good girl." Elizabeth saw the looks on Edward and Teddy and added, "And boys." They each got a head scritch and a pat, but Freya waited at Elizabeth's feet. Elizabeth picked her up. "I guess your magic does work on me, doesn't it?" She snuggled into the kitten, who again draped herself over her shoulder and purred.

Hearing the bath water still going sent Elizabeth running to the bathroom to shut it off. "Just in time!"

Teddy and Edward had stopped in the laundry room for a snack, but she still carried Freya. *Are you hungry, too?* She probed Freya and found her stomach full. Of mouse. Ick.

I took care of it. But I do like those crunchy things you have. Can I have some back here where we sleep?

Somebody's sure of herself. I guess that'd be all right. After bath time since you are not too hungry.

Elizabeth carefully got in the bath. Perfect temperature, if a little full. She noticed her bump. Not really a bump. Sort of a bulge. She didn't look pregnant at all. She wanted to look pregnant!

One thing bothered her. Although her tests came out fine, she had not felt anything from the baby. She knew it was the size of a lima bean, or a lentil, but she thought she, of all people would be able to feel an essence from the baby. She worried about it but didn't tell Tig. When she tried in her mind to mention it, it sounded completely ridiculous. Her specialty was animals. Maybe that was it? But her own baby? She could talk to bugs for Pete's sake. Not very well, but still . . .

Elizabeth opened her eyes. Freya sat on the edge of the tub, like the Egyptian statue Tig saw.

Why are you worried? Freya asked.

No eavesdropping. If that's what you were doing. Man, she was going to have to shut her mental door to her own animals. Teddy and Edward could just drop in like that, too, and she had told them it was rude. She'd met another animal who could do it, but that was rare. She thought she could let her guard down at home, but maybe not.

Freya sent a question mark.

No listening in on my head without letting me know you're there.

That's what I do. I'm very good at it.

It's rude. But you're right. I am worried. The boys know I have a baby inside and you might as well, too.

I knew a long time ago. What are you worried about? It's fine.

How do you know it's fine? I mean, I know, but how do you?

It is alive. I can see it. It is happy to be with you. Just as I am.

Okay, back up. How do you see it? Can you talk to it?

It is too small to talk like we do. But I see it the way you see us when we are not with you.

Why can you do it when I can't?

I don't know.

Elizabeth soaped and rinsed and thought. *Let's go back a bit. What do you mean, a long time ago?*

Edward told me.

Okay, this is too weird. How did Edward tell you?

He saw I was needed. That I was coming. I had to come, for my sake too. He told me about your baby and that you might need my help. He is strong, but not strong enough.

For what? This was getting crazy. Maybe the little kitten was unstable. She would need to watch out for her.

Freya laughed. That was the only way to describe it. She opened her mouth like a yawn, but the cutest set of squeaks came out.

"I'm done with my bath. You'd better move if you don't want to get wet." She let the plug out of the drain and stood. Freya remained at the edge, watching the water swirl away. Just like a regular cat.

Elizabeth wrapped herself in a towel and grabbed PJs from her dresser. The boys were crashed out on the bed in their movie-watching spaces, ready for her. As she tucked in with Freya on her chest, her cell phone rang. She checked the ID. Tig.

Four

Elizabeth answered her cell without disturbing Freya. "Hey, there."

"Hey, you. How are you feeling?" His voice was warm and sultry.

"We are all settled about to watch some NetFilms. Wish you were here."

"Yeah, me, too. How's the little one settling in? The boys still okay with her? She's so small."

"They're passed out next to me, and she's on my chest. She seems to grasp the pace of the household already," Elizabeth joked.

"That's great. The last thing we need is a territorial dispute."

Somehow Elizabeth felt Freya would win without trying. "I don't think that will happen. You still okay with keeping her? I mean if the neighbors don't come back, of course?"

"You have something in mind already, don't you?"

She heard the smile in his voice and again wished he was here with them .

"I did overhear something."

"And by overhear, you mean an animal told you, right?"

"They are reliable, you know."

"Okay, which one?"

"Freya. She told me she waited for me. That she hid in the house intentionally, and Edward had been in contact with her." Elizabeth did not add how long ago that had been. She'd been thinking about it. Edward had said some strange things to her just about the time she found out she was pregnant. Freya had spoken to him that long ago? He did mention a special connection to Elizabeth. In all the craziness, she had forgotten about it, but now his little wizardy comments came back. At any rate, Tig, understanding as he was, might not be ready for full disclosure.

"That settles it." Now Tig sounded mad.

"What?"

"If those people were so cruel to her that she had to hide herself until we could rescue her, then we are keeping her."

Oh. She had not expected him to interpret it that way, but yay. "So, it's okay if I take her to the vet tomorrow for shots and a chip and say she's ours?"

"She is ours now."

"Tig, you never cease to amaze me." Freya also, apparently because Elizabeth sensed her listening in to the conversation and a sudden rise in purring and kneading matched the comments.

"As long as our boys are okay with it, I am, too."

She wished he was here because it was things like this that made her love him even more, and she wanted to hug him. And maybe have some private time. Ha. No chance now. Private time happened less and less lately.

She put her free hand on Edward, and he immediately purred. Teddy was out of reach without dumping Freya, so she contented herself with the smaller two. Teddy was adorable, as she continued to chat with Tig, she watched him smile in his sleep. She was tempted to 'listen' in on his dream, but she was a little too tired.

"Just wanted to remind you," Tig began, "Karl's starting back to school to work on his business degree so he won't be as available to help me."

"Full time?"

"No, just a couple classes, but he still has his own pond clients and Stacy." Tig mentioned Karl's girlfriend.

"I did forget. When does he start?"

"Soon. Summer session."

"I have to applaud him for going back. It's gotta be tough. And Stacy is sweet, so he can't neglect her."

"Nope. I've already warned him of the perils of neglecting your female," Tig joked.

"Very funny. If you think I'm a lot of work now, just wait 'til we have this baby."

"I can't wait." His voice grew soft and she knew he meant it. They had waited a long time for this, saving money, finding the 'right' time.

"Oh, before you go," Elizabeth added, "Freya sat on the edge of the tub with me while I had my bath. Just like you said. She says she doesn't mind water and can swim."

Tig laughed. She loved his laugh. "She's going to be our challenge, isn't she?"

"I think so." Elizabeth knew so. She just didn't know how big a challenge.

*   *   *   *

Elizabeth awoke early and alone. The cats had abandoned her. Not unusual. They could go out the cat flap at 6 AM when the timer opened it. She felt a little hungry. Tig would be going straight to his pond job. She wouldn't see him until around 4 PM. She had to admit, as smart as they thought they had been, it was harder than she thought to be separated so often.

No reason to dress this early, so she put on her moose slippers and shuffled out to the kitchen.

Freya sat in the middle of the kitchen floor eyeing her sternly. *You forgot about me, didn't you?*

She had. Sort of. She felt guilty. "I'm sorry. I'm just waking up. Breakfast for you, okay? I promise, I will get you food today and we have to get you checked by the doctor."

Elizabeth quickly opened a can and tried to be stealthy. Teddy did not need to eat as often as a kitten, but she didn't want to have to argue with him about it every day. It had been tough enough with Edward's kittenhood.

I don't need a doctor. I'm fine, I told you.

"It's kind of a rule here. You have to have certain shots and I need you to have a microchip so if you're ever lost, I can find you."

I can always find you.

"If we are ever separated, anyone could find us and get us back together."

Elizabeth watched her eat and knew she could not explain to this little creature how things were done. She couldn't bear it if Freya got an illness that could have been prevented.

"Do you want to go out with the boys for a while? I have to make an appointment with Dr. Otis first."

Fine. Freya sashayed to the back door and looked up at the handle.

"You're not getting out that easy." Elizabeth picked her up and Freya flopped over her shoulder. She could feel the fine bones of her ribs rise and fall with a slight rattle as she purred.

Forgiven? Elizabeth asked.

She felt a slight kiss on her ear as an answer.

Elizabeth opened the back door. Gray summer fog sat low over the yard. The eucalyptus trees dripped their morning mist and all was still. Chilly, but she left the door ajar for Freya. She had a feeling this kitten would be doing a number of extraordinary things. Better not give her the ATM password, Elizabeth thought as she headed back to dress.

43

After her morning meditation, she brewed a cup of tea. Her daily meditation was her grounding, a habit she had formed as a way of anchoring herself to the house and land. It allowed her to do many things, like the readings she did for animals, and not just pets. Wild ones, too. The connection remained with her all day. When she wanted to contact an animal, she just reinforced it as needed. She also used it for protection, if she needed to do something she was worried about. Public speaking was one.   Sounded silly, but it helped her get through a speech about what she did for Career Day at the local elementary school.

She had risen to fame after a case of reuniting a wild mama deer and her baby, and the social media storm had been fast and furious. It had settled down, but she had a Facefriend page now and often got requests through that. However, the most terrifying was the speech in front of a hundred elementary students.   Janie, her across the street neighbor and best friend, had suggested a slide show too, which had been a life saver. Along with grounding. It didn't help her not want to throw up, but she survived. She could have used Freya then.

Dr. Otis' office was open so she called and got an appointment for early afternoon which gave her time to grocery shop.

She recalled her conversation with Tig from last night. Something didn't seem right. What was it? To do with Freya, but they hadn't been talking about her.   She got her purse and a sweater, readying to head to the grocery store when she remembered.   Karl, their assistant, friend, helper, was going back to school. The spring term had ended weeks ago. Why did the college students move out now? Mid-month, so long after term and also before new classes began? That felt like strange timing. They couldn't have gotten complaints as bad tenants. They were practically invisible tenants. *Perfect if I was the landlord,* she thought. She knew the home owners to say hi to, but they were on sabbatical in South America somewhere, and she wasn't the caretaker or manager. They had arranged this all before they'd left. She didn't really know the neighbors; they were gone more than they were here. Teachers, she thought.

As she turned these thoughts over, a ruckus came from the backyard. She ran toward the screaming and all three cats poured in through the laundry room door.

A complete cacophony assaulted both her ears and her mind. The boys were excited and Freya was in the lead with something in her mouth.

"Great. What do you have?" Elizabeth asked over the screaming, which turned out to be coming from a baby rabbit Freya held. She set it on the floor, still in her mouth, but set a paw over its back. Elizabeth did not know rabbits screamed that loudly.

I brought it for you, Freya said.

Look what she has! Edward hopped back and forth.

It was very fast, Teddy added.

What did you do to it? Elizabeth asked.

Me? I didn't do anything. I found it. You can fix it.

"What's wrong with it? Why does it need fixing? Are you hurting it?"

No, I'm holding it. It might get away and if I have to chase it again, then it might get hurt. They, indicating Edward and Teddy, *might not know we're helping it. They got kind of wild the first time.*

"Okay, okay. Let me get a carrier. Just . . . don't do anything. Any of you." She sent calming waves to the baby rabbit who was having none of it. It was terrified, but as Freya said, she wasn't hurting it, just keeping it on the floor.

Because Elizabeth didn't know what was wrong, she didn't want to pick it up yet. She ran to the garage for the smallest pet carrier. Ironically, the one she was going to take Freya to the vet in later.

She lay a towel in the bottom and got on the floor with Freya. "Boys, maybe you should go out. This can't be good for the rabbit."

Mom, they both complained, but she mentally shoved them toward the pet door.

"Shoot. I should close the door," she chastised herself. Getting up and down from the floor was getting a bit more difficult these days. Before she could move, the door swung shut.

She looked at Freya, who still held the rabbit. "Whatever that was, save it for later," she said to herself.

She again sent calming waves to the bunny, who was frozen with fear. She reached over, and

Freya released her hold on the rabbit as Elizabeth took it. Almost like they had rehearsed it.

It was tiny and beautiful. It was a sage rabbit, smaller than hares or others of their species. As a baby, this one was even smaller, though perfectly formed. The eyes were clamped shut, but the nose and mouth looked clean and free of discharge. The small ears were covered in ticks, but she could take care of it later. As she held the baby, its heart rate decreased and it relaxed. It sent her fear and pain. It looked okay, but as she turned it, she saw a huge flap of skin was torn off the side and rear leg and dangled. As far as she could see, it had no other wounds or injuries. The flap would have to be cleaned and stitched.

"Tell me what happened Freya," she said as she carefully bundled up the rabbit and tucked it in the carrier. "Tell me the truth because I'll know if you're lying." She didn't really know if she could tell or not. Freya was too new, and very capable. Of what, she hadn't learned yet.

I found it like this. From what it said, an owl tried to get it but didn't have a good grip. It tore this skin off then dropped it. It hid last night in the log pile and I found it. It was afraid of me, and the boys, and it ran. It should have listened. I wasn't going to hurt it.

"Gee, I can't imagine why it wouldn't listen to you and two other giant predators. Besides, why would you talk to it? *How* did you talk to it?"

Like we all do, Freya said in that teenaged girl, duh, voice.

Another new thing. She would have to ask Teddy and Edward if they talk to other animals. It made sense, but it was confusing. Edward had talked to Freya a long time ago, and Teddy had also talked to her, supposedly when she hatched her plan to leave the neighbors. But talking, like people? As in, "Hey, how are you?"

"Okay. I have to go now. I'm taking the rabbit to the wild life care center. I'll be back in a little while. Then we'll go to your doctor for your check-up."

Fine. Can you leave the door open?

"Can't you just open it yourself?" Elizabeth said a little sharply.

Not all the time. I'm still young and learning. Closing it was easier.

Oh, wow. Why did I ask? "Yes, I'll leave it open, but please don't go far. I will worry about you, you know."

I know. Thank you for not locking me in another room. Or a cage.

Elizabeth didn't know what to say. She washed her hands thoroughly, opened the door for the cats and gathered her things.

Five

The Central Coast Wildlife Center was only about a fifteen minute drive so she figured she could stop for groceries and kitten food on the way back. She hoped the baby rabbit didn't go into shock. And why would a rabbit talk to a predator? A question for later.

She pulled into the dirt lot. Not too many cars. Probably the doctors and volunteers. She knew it was a non-profit that ran on donations and grants. Over the years she had brought a number of injured animals here and it was certified for exotic animals too, so as animals were found or turned in, they were rehabilitated. Many could not be returned to the wild and were used as education animals at schools and libraries.

She pulled the carrier from the car and sent more healing and calming waves. The baby was not in shock but needed medical care. The wound caused it a lot of pain, and it was still scared.

Elizabeth pulled open the door to the pre-fab trailer that served as the office and approached the empty desk. Since she'd been here before, she grabbed the clipboard and began filling the form calling, "Hello?"

An older woman in a puppy print smock came out of a hallway. "Hello," she greeted Elizabeth. "How can I help you?"

"My cat brought in this baby rabbit. I don't think it has major injuries, but it does have quite a tear in its skin."

"Wow, lucky your cat didn't kill it."

"Um, yes. I guess it was a present. Here's my info." She handed the woman the clipboard.

"I'll take it back and have it checked. Can you wait a few minutes for your carrier?"

Elizabeth nodded and sat in the orange vinyl chair against one wall. Aged and tattered posters of animals and wildlife warnings papered the fake wood paneled walls.

She texted Tig the newest development. As she hit send, the woman came out of the double doors with the carrier.

"He seems like a healthy little bunny from our first exam. Here's your carrier."

Elizabeth handed her a check as a donation. She always donated when she brought a creature in. She felt it was the least she could do for the great work they did. "Is it possible for me to come pick him up when he's healed so I can return him to where he came from?"

"We have volunteers who do that."

"I know, but I know exactly where and I'd like to help." Elizabeth always imagined some creature's relatives all wondering where Uncle Jim got to, or some silly scenario.

"I'll note it on his chart. We'll keep him a few days and see how he's healing up in case anything else is wrong."

"Thank you." Elizabeth slung her purse over her shoulder, her mind on the grocery store and Freya's vet check-up. She swung open the door and almost crashed into someone entering.

"Oh, I'm so sorry," Elizabeth said.

"Elizabeth?" It was Karl, Tig's assistant.

"Karl! What are you doing here? Did you find an animal?"

"No. I, uh, got a part time job doing data entry and some research here at the facility."

"I thought you were going back to college?"

"That, too."

"How will you have time?"

Karl shuffled past her. "I didn't want to tell Tig, but since the drought and the county making everyone use less water, I've had trouble getting pond clients. So, I've had to explore other ways to make money."

"Oh, Karl, I'm so sorry. I guess it's good you're going back to college. Tolosa College?" she asked, mentioning the local community college.

"Uh, Poly Tech. I got a grant." Karl looked uncomfortable.

"Congratulations! No shame in getting free money. Free government money!" She laughed.

"That's a tough university. Best of luck. Okay, gotta run."

She gave him a quick hug and jumped back in her car for a fast trip to the store. She would be cutting it close for Freya's appointment, since she had to clean the carrier first. She never put an animal in the carrier unless it was sanitized. Particularly a wild animal.

She whipped through the grocery store getting a variety of things, including some kitten food. She didn't know where a live mouse rated on that scale, but she'd do her best. At least Freya hadn't eaten the rabbit. Gross.

At home, she washed the carrier and called everyone in for a wet food treat. Dirty trick, but she was in a hurry. She closed the back door and Freya looked up at her.

I know what you're doing, she said. *You made it clear about your laws; you can just tell me. But do I have to go in the cage?*

"I suppose not until we get there. You can sit on the seat, then. I'll figure out a seatbelt later if this becomes a thing. The doctor's office has all sorts of animals who are not as smart as you, and they all need to be controlled. Fair's fair." Elizabeth had no idea how to negotiate with this cat.

"Be good boys. We'll be back soon," Elizabeth called as she tucked Freya under her arm and locked the front door.

The five minute trip to the vet was interesting. Freya stood on the passenger seat with her paws against the side window, watching.

At the vet's office, they had a little wait because an emergency arrived. Freya watched a Great Dane from her carrier. *Are you all right?* Elizabeth asked her.

Yes. I've seen dogs this big before.

A cat across the room was not so easily mollified and hissed periodically, clearly at Freya, not the giant dog, who was well behaved.

Elizabeth sent calming waves to the other cat. It didn't listen. All Elizabeth got from it was a loop of *not a cat, not a cat.*

Their names were called and she was taken to an exam room by Tony, one of her favorite vet techs. Elizabeth had already explained to Freya in the waiting room what would happen, but when Tony took Freya away from her to be weighed, Freya finally sent out waves of concern.

On the outside, she seemed fine, but because Elizabeth was probing, she noticed her distress. *It's okay, it's okay*, she sent over and over.

A few moments and Freya was back with Dr. Otis. Dr. Otis was calm and exuded positive energy and vast knowledge. Elizabeth had been bringing her rescue animals to him for years, and he was nothing but kind and professional. He was quite familiar with Teddy and Edward.

"So, this is Freya?" He gently looked in her eyes and ears, checked her mouth and palpated her, feeling her feet, checking range of motion. "Where did she come from?"

Elizabeth hated to outright lie, but she didn't know what else to do. "The boys found her in the outback and brought her home." Not a complete lie. "She seems healthy, and they have agreed to keep her, so we just need her to be checked and get her shots and a microchip."

"Tony scanned her when he weighed her, and no previous chip. So you don't know if she's spayed?"

"No. I checked for lost kitten ads and no one's responded. I'm not taking her to Animal Services."

"She's lucky you found her. All the coyotes out there."

Elizabeth was holding her breath and she knew Freya felt her anxiety.

"She looks healthy. We'll get her started on her first set of shots and then you can bring her back for a spay."

"Sounds good."

What are shots and spay?

I'm sorry little one, the shots are going to hurt a little, but they will keep you safe from sickness. The spay, uh, is to keep you from having kittens.

I suppose it's best. At least for now.

Elizabeth decided not to tell her that spaying was permanent. Freya could never have kittens. Sigh. She hadn't had to have this talk with either Teddy or Edward. They had not had any awareness of *it* before they'd already been neutered. Is this a version of the conversation she'd have someday with her child? Not spaying it, of course, but, oh, boy.

She stayed connected to Freya after they took her in back to give her shots. It did hurt. Her little legs were so small. The microchip was as big as a grain of rice which hurt, too. Poor Freya.

As soon as they got in the car, Elizabeth put Freya on her lap and concentrated on pulling the pain up and out of her. She knew Freya might have trouble doing it herself, particularly once the pain had already started. This was a technique she was learning and had done successfully a few times. A mild pain in herself, she could lessen, but it was a skill to work on like any other. She could not reduce her own nausea, but Freya did that for her.

She felt a snap, like a rubber band released as the pain went down a notch. She felt it leave Freya's body. Now it was just manageable discomfort.

"Let's go home little girl, okay?" She let Freya stay on her lap the five blocks home. The vet's office was next to the fire station and she remembered she should check her phone when she got home to see if Tig responded. He wasn't at work yet, but any fire-related thing reminded her of him.

Speaking of which, she'd better get a wiggle on and make some dinner. Maybe he'd want to barbeque some burgers. Those were fast if she got them all ready for him and lit the grill. It was also relaxing for him to grill, have a beer, and water their bamboo. With Edward's help, usually. When Tig was home, Edward was near.

No beer tonight, of course, but she could toss a salad and get the patties prepped along with sliced onions and tomatoes.

At home, Freya got a thorough sniffing, which she allowed, from her brothers. Freya was feeling much better, just tender at the shot sites.

She checked her phone. Tig had texted a rabbit emoji and a happy face. Must have been a busy day with the pond. Wasn't Karl supposed to help him today? Or he to help Karl? She wasn't sure. They'd catch up over dinner.

The truck pulled into the drive. "I'm out here," she called as she pre-heated the grill.

"Coming!" Tig came out to the patio and hugged her, finishing with a warm kiss. "So your day was busy," he teased.

"Sure was. How was yours?"

She watched as Edward magically appeared, and Tig scooped him up. "Where's the princess?"

"She got her shots and a microchip today, so she might not feel so hot."

"Poor baby. My day was pretty good. Karl said he had to leave early to register for classes, so I was on my own. Not too hard. I wanted him to help me get the plants from the nursery, but we can do that tomorrow and then put them in. We're almost done with this new pond. Then we have some maintenance jobs. We're keeping busy. It will slow down as we get into the fall, but man, it's been a busy summer."

"Do you want to barbeque burgers or water? I can man the grill if you want."

"I'll do it, thanks. I can water tomorrow."

Elizabeth went in to grab the plate with the burger patties and thought about what Tig said. Almost the opposite of what Karl had said about his schedule. Maybe it was a mistake? Registering for classes and working at the rescue center were two different things. Hard to mistake one for the other.

She didn't want to accuse Karl of anything. He might have registered first and then come to the rescue center. Maybe his classes were full. Any number of things. She shouldn't stir up trouble. She decided to enjoy dinner with her family.

It was Tig's Friday, so tomorrow he would only work on the pond and have several days off from the fire department.

Six

After dinner, Tig took off like a whirlwind for the station and Elizabeth cleaned up. Before Freya went out again, Elizabeth dragged out the cat door manual and wrestled with adding Freya's chip to the door. A very patient kitten was thrust against the panel over and over again until it read her chip properly. Because she was a cooperative kitty, unlike a 'normal' cat, she got Freya to go out and come back in again right away to confirm the test.

Teddy lay on the floor and Edward posed on the arm of the couch to better enjoy the show.

"All right, all of you. Go out for a while. You have some time before it gets dark." Elizabeth shooed them all out the pet flap. However, she did leave the patio door open.

She had made a phone appointment with a client and just had enough time to reground herself and let go of the stress of the day.

She stayed in her meditation chair near the front window and enjoyed the new landscaping she and Tig had put in over the summer. It was mostly Tig and Karl and a great crew led by Francisco. Tig hired Francisco and his landscape people on the rare occasion that a job was too big for him to handle alone; a big property to landscape with large rocks or other issues. Elizabeth and Tig had waited until the community sewer lines were complete and had looked forward to finishing the front for years. Now it was a semi-Japanese style rock garden with one of Tig's special torii water features. It trickled to a cobblestone dry 'river' that dropped to a lower level 'pool.' They had had fun picking out the rocks and cobbles and the few plants. Because Tig was gone so much and did landscaping as a second job, he really didn't want to have a high-maintenance front yard. The back was different. It was their tropical paradise sanctuary.

She admired the parts she could see around the Japanese boxwood hedge they kept for privacy: the Mexican bamboo, one of her favorites, with its feathery boughs and the top of the torii as water trickled peacefully over the stone Tig had made and hung.

She felt completely centered as she dialed. The woman picked up right away.

"This is Elizabeth Murphy calling for your session. Is this Maria?"

"Yes, thank you so much. Did you get the picture of Tilly?"

"Yes, I did. A Pomeranian?"

"A pom mix, but she takes after her mother."

"You said her behavior has changed recently. Can you expand on that?" Elizabeth asked.

"As I mentioned in the email, we think she's about five now. A rescue we fostered and then just kept. But that was several years ago. We spent a lot of time training her, and she's been a doll. We walk her daily, and on weekends we take her to the beach which she just loves."

"Is she acting ill at all? Still eating and drinking?"

"Yes. It's more her behavior, I guess. She's always been pretty good to respond to commands, but she's started bolting out the front door, barking her brains out. She's never done that before. Our street is very busy and I worry she'll get hit."

"Is she escaping from the yard?"

"No, nothing like that." Maria sounded like she was about to cry. "If I open the door for the UPS driver, or to go out myself to water or get the mail, she squirms through and just runs down the drive or out into the yard. I'm so worried."

"Are there any animals or people around when she does?"

"Sometimes, but not the same ones, you know?"

"Okay. Let me talk to Tilly. It will be quiet on my end of the phone for a few moments, okay?"

"Okay."

Elizabeth tuned into Tilly, using the photo as a target, focusing in. *Tilly? Are you there? It's Elizabeth. I came to talk to you, okay?*

Sure. This is neat. Mom doesn't talk. I mean, she does all the time, but just words, you know?

Yes, I know. She's worried about you.

Why? I'm fine. Oh, that dog. Yeah, he's a bad one.

Tell me about the dog. Is he why you're running out of the house now?

Yes. He comes every night and marks my yard. He's very mean and sometimes scratches up Mom's flowers. She loves those. We water them together. I can mark the yard. I'm supposed to. It's my yard. Not his!

How do you know he's mean?

We go for walks every day, and then his people moved in. He barks when we go by and growls. I could take him if Mom would let me.

Is he there when you run outside?

No. But I can smell him. The odor's so strong and I have to cover it right away.

Your mom is worried about you crossing the street and getting hit.

I don't usually go that far. Sometimes I guess I do.

Can you show me a picture of the dog? Have you seen it on your walk?

A little through the fence. A picture floated into Elizabeth's mind of a German Shepherd-mix dog, maybe with some Husky, very aggressive. No match for little Tilly. It barked angrily through wide slats in the fence.

Show me the house. A picture of a run-down house attached to the fence. No grass or plantings in the front yard. No maintenance had been done on the house. If there wasn't so much junk in front, she'd have thought it was vacant.

Do the people walk it at night? Have you seen them?

No. I think it gets out. Or maybe they let it out. It poops too. I smell it all over the neighbor's houses. I try to tell the neighbor's animals, but I don't know if they listen to me.

Okay. Can you please stop running out? It scares your mom.

I don't think so.

How about if you promise not to run into the street?

I can do that. I'll try not to forget.

I'll ask your mom if she wants to find these humans and see if they can keep the dog in at night. Would that be okay?

If it doesn't come and mark my territory. I will guard my house and my humans.

She knows. That's why she's worried. You don't know this, but the other dog is much bigger than you, and if it's really mean like you think it is, you could get hurt. Your mom is worried about that, too.

I'm strong.

I know. I'm going to talk to your mom now. Thank you for talking to me.

This was fun! Let's do it again.

Tilly's bubbly energy popped like a burst balloon.

"Maria?"

"Yes. I'm still here."

"It's a bit complicated." Elizabeth explained the situation and added that she thought the house was close to theirs, which is why Tilly knew what the dog looked like and how it came every night. "There's a possibility the owners don't know it's escaping the yard. Perhaps discuss it with your husband and see if you can find the house. If you feel comfortable, maybe let the owners know what's going on. The dog could get hit by a car or attacked by coyotes too. Tilly has promised to try and stay in the yard, but she can't stop herself from overmarking. We made a deal she could protect you and the yard, but she would stay away from the street. She didn't sound sure. She seems impulsive, so I recommend you find that other dog."

"Oh, thank you so much! I think we can find the house after a few tries."

"I tell you what. If you can take a picture of it, maybe find out the dog's name, I will try and talk to it, too."

"If I can't get the name can you still do it?"

"Yes, but it's harder that way. I can try."

They signed off. Elizabeth was tired. Communicating with animals other than her own was always exhausting. Talking to their own cats was almost like talking to a person. Buster, Janie's dog across the street, was easy, too.

That reminded her. They had a baby. Garrett. He was walking, well, toddling and eating some people food, and gabbling. He had never tried to talk to her inside her mind. She'd never given it much thought, but perhaps that was why she couldn't talk to her own baby. She just couldn't do people. But her own baby!

She closed the front blinds and called for the cats to come in. Surprisingly, they all arrived, albeit slowly at cat speed, tails waving. She had begun a habit of adding dry food to the bowl in the evenings as a bribe to bring them in. The cat flap locked at 6 PM. She didn't want them out after dark with so many predators. Teddy was getting older, and was not thin, so she was afraid he'd be a target. Edward was young and sleek, but Freya was an infant compared to them.

Teddy got diet food, which he complained about daily. Edward got full-fat food, but she had to hide it from Teddy. Now a third dish she'd have to hide from both of them. Apparently kitten chow was ambrosia and the best thing ever. Both adult cats shouldered their way to her tiny bowl.

"You guys. Stop. She's coming with me. Knock when you're ready," she joked. She picked up Freya and the bowl and took both back to the bedroom, closing the door behind them.

Freya ate undisturbed while Elizabeth showered. By the end of the shower, Freya again sat on the back corner of the tub rim.

"You are a funny, amazing girl." She picked Freya up with slightly damp hands.

I know.

"We'd better let those guys in." She toweled off and put on PJs. The bowl of

64

deliciousness was placed out of reach and the door opened again for two cranky cats waiting to jump on the bed.

After a bit of NetFilms and a short chapter of a new mystery novel, she turned out her light.

Seven

As usual, the cats slept immediately and she couldn't resist pulling Freya close as she drifted away. She had to turn her brain off despite how tired she was. Growing a whole person inside her was exhausting despite its lentil size. She sent out feelers to the aggressive dog, but as she suspected, got no answer. It was the equivalent of standing in a crowd and expecting the correct person, whomever that was, to recognize and respond to her.

She didn't know how long she'd slept but it didn't feel very long before she slipped into dreaming. She didn't feel fully asleep so a dream was odd.

Frigg! Frigg! Answer me, called a voice from an unseen source. *It is near time and you are not ready. Folkvang will have more residents. You must care for them.*

It was cold in the dream. Winter with snow covered mountains and a chilly-looking bay beyond a thin strip of beach. A stream warriors wearing furs and carrying primitive-looking weapons ran from the hills toward the beach, which Elizabeth could now see had a small dock and some strange looking ships.

Prayers have been said, and I have commanded you guide these souls, came the voice.

I am not ready, answered someone who sounded remarkably like Freya when she "spoke" to Elizabeth.

That matters not.

I am in danger and in hiding. It must wait.

You will do as I command.

The connection was broken as Elizabeth awoke to find Freya on her chest, front legs stiff and slight whimpers accompanying her tremors.

It's okay, baby, Elizabeth said as she stroked Freya gently into wakefulness. *Was that your dream or mine?* she asked.

Mine. Freya oozed off the bed in the dark and Elizabeth heard her lapping water.

An amazing dream for a cat. However, Elizabeth had had visions provided by a koi fish before, so it was not unheard of. Strange maybe, but perhaps better to accept it until a different theory came along.

Freya jumped back up and snuggled close. Teddy and Edward slept on, oblivious. Elizabeth fell back into sleep, trying not to think about what had happened. Dawn was a long way off.

*   *   *   *

Morning came and she woke alone. Tig would be working at home today and on the one pond. She stretched and padded out to get a cup of herbal tea. Decaf coffee wasn't the same. She was pretending she liked it, but today she felt like tea instead. Anything for the baby Murphy to come. No cats so they must have figured out the cat door. Freya could probably open a safe at this point. The usual fog had given way to sun, heightening her disposition and lessening her worries about the cats.

She brewed her tea and took it to her meditation chair near the window. Grounding done, she heard the truck pull in. Tig must be coming home before he set off for his pond duties. She waited until he had hugged her good morning before she asked him about food. He was always hungry but maybe he'd eaten at the station.

He hadn't. "Just wanted to get out of there today and spend some time at home. I'm meeting Karl in a few hours to work on that job."

She began making blueberry pancakes, the fresh berries a fortuitous purchase. "Coffee?"

"Sure. I keep trying to get them to get Peet's at the station, but no go."

Elizabeth smiled and made a small pot for Tig. The smell was about to drop her, it was so delicious. She opened the back door and called, "Daddy's home!"

Moments later three excited cats exploded through the back gate.

Hi dad, Teddy greeted.

Up dad, Edward added and Tig complied.

Freya sat at his feet, tail curled delicately around her. Tig picked her up, too.

Elizabeth looked for jealousy or anxiety in Edward, but there was none. Two limp cats left no hands free for coffee, so Tig sat while she finished the pancakes.

She brought everything to the table so the cats weren't disturbed. *Sure, we're going to be firm parents,* she thought.

She plopped Freya in her own lap; Edward was at his usual post. She tried to imagine a baby seat at the table, too, but couldn't. New seating arrangements would have to be made.

I'm good, see? Teddy could read Elizabeth as he lay on the floor, smug and fluffy.

Yes, you are. She sent out waves of love to him, and his cheeks puffed in his version of a smile.

Elizabeth felt Freya snuggle deeper into her lap and knew she also felt loved and secure. Edward's complete relaxation and rumbling purr attested to his comfort level, too. All was well in the household.

"What's new? Anything? How's the bunny Freya rescued?"

Elizabeth chose not to share the dream until she had more information. "I have to call tomorrow and see when he can come home. I want to place him back where he came from." She sipped her tea.

"Do you believe Freya was saving it? That it wasn't an attack gone wrong?"

Elizabeth felt Freya stiffen. *Relax. He doesn't know.*

"Yes. I'm sure. If she'd have wanted to kill it, she would have. She also didn't have to bring it to me. She could have left it in the outback."

"True. Okay, quick shower and I'll throw my tools together, then I'm off." Tig poured Edward onto the floor and took his dishes to the sink.

Elizabeth sighed. She felt a bit abandoned lately. They'd agreed to do this, but it was harder than she imagined.

The house was quieter again after he left. As always. She scrolled through her social media to check for new clients and was brought up short by an article on a young man who'd died in a surfing accident the day before. She clicked on his profile to see his photos. A young life lost always made her sad. A picture he posted with his mom made her gasp. She knew her. She'd gone to college with her. They'd stayed in touch off and on, and Elizabeth now realized her son was the young boy she'd met a number of years ago. She felt even more melancholy.

Tears rose to the surface as she sent a message of condolence. She absolutely could not imagine losing a child. She thought of Garrett across the street and her own growing stomach and began to cry. She wasn't much of a crier, but now it felt like the right thing.

She felt the cats probing. *Are you okay, mom?* Teddy.

Should we come back? Do you need us? Edward.

Freya was just there, at her feet. Elizabeth picked her up and draped her over her shoulder as she'd become accustomed. A hug of sorts.

No, don't come back. I'm okay, she sent.

I'm staying. Freya squirmed down into her lap and Elizabeth sat like that for quite a while. She felt her sadness lessen, much like the nausea had, and allowed her mind to drift.

Tell me about your dream, she asked Freya. *What place was that?*

Home. One of my homes.

You're just a kitten. Where is it?

Far away.

It looked like a frozen wasteland.

That place is. I am not always there. I have other domains.

Domains? How do you get there? Do you mean you dream of these places?

Of a sort.

Elizabeth sighed. She didn't know if the kitten was ill or just had odd dreams. Most animals she 'talked' to had dreams based in some sort of reality. Food, prey, illness, family. But, it was not impossible to think animals had strange dreams they could not interpret, just as people did. She had read an article on dreams rats had, by scientists at MIT. They thought the rats dreamed of the mazes they ran previously, based on their brain waves, but really, how could you be sure? Maybe that gorilla Koko, who could talk in sign language. She decided to think about it later.

She glanced at the wall clock. Already noon. She didn't feel like eating, but the nutrition counselor she'd met with after she became pregnant was adamant about a good diet.

Maybe soup. She threw some veggies into a tomato juice broth and brought it to a boil with some spices. Then she turned it down to simmer for an hour. Maybe she'd feel like eating by then.

She did some cursory cleaning to use up that hour. She really felt like a nap, but would wait to eat first. Maybe she was depressed, too.

"Frick!" she cursed as the hot pad slipped and she burned herself on the soup pot. She was attempting to swear less because of the baby. Not that she or Tig swore a lot, but she welcomed the challenge.

That reminded her of something. She ladled soup into a bowl and grabbed some crackers. Two cats crashed through the cat flap as they sensed a meal coming.

"I'm sorry, guys, you won't like it. Vegetable soup. Have some kibble."

Ick, or the equivalent.

Freya jumped lightly into her lap. "You'd better stay small if you think you'll be in my lap all the time," Elizabeth said.

I will.

The voice. Swearing *Frick.* She remembered the dream. "You were called Frigg, right? Sometimes? That was you in the dream, right? Someone was talking to you and called you Frigg."

The boys wandered out again.

Yes. I have different names at different times. Frigg is one. I prefer Freya.

"Me, too. It's pretty. But that was just a dream, right?"

Questioning waves from Freya.

"Never mind. I don't know what I think." But she couldn't shake the feeling there was more to this. Suddenly, she worried Freya would leave as quickly as she'd arrived.

"You're not leaving, are you? You said you came to be with me, you chose me. So, you're not going to leave?" The thought of losing Freya was unbearable now.

I'm not truly leaving. I may have to go from time to time, but I'm not leaving.

Elizabeth was even more confused. Freya sounded like a wise old woman, not a kitten. She'd done enough rescue work to know what that was: *Food, bottle, nurse, poop.*

"I am overtired and stressed. I'll figure it out later." Her phone buzzed with a text. Tig would be home for dinner and stay. Elizabeth's emotions rose way up. "I must be hormonal," she mumbled as she carried her dishes to the sink.

Nap? she asked Freya.

Outside, I think, was the response.

Okay. Be careful.

Elizabeth put herself to bed and didn't awaken until she heard the front door slam, heralding Tig's arrival.

Eight

A nap, longer than she'd anticipated, and her husband arriving home did much to raise Elizabeth's spirits. As she heard Tig move through the house, working his way back to her, she realized she had no dinner plan. Freezer? Her mind was blank. What else had she gotten at the store? She sat up just as Tig came in. He bent to kiss her hello and she drank some water. Less groggy now, she asked, "How did it go?"

"I don't know. That kid. I know he's trying to go back to school and has a lot on his plate, but sheesh." He ran a hand through his dark hair, making the curls stand up in tufts.

"What happened?" She felt around with her feet for her slippers. Was her stomach bigger than before her nap? That couldn't be.

"He agreed to work with me today, but then, half-way through, he says he has to go. We only have a day of work left and we'd be finished if we'd done it together. Now I have to go back tomorrow, and he says he has class."

Elizabeth stood and stretched. "I'm sorry." She put her arms around him and held him. Hugs were so therapeutic; a hug always made things better. Cats knew that, too. Tig relaxed and hugged her back. "What's left for you to do? Can you finish by yourself?" she mumbled into his shoulder.

"Probably. It's just the principle. You say you're going to do a job, you do a job."

She rubbed his back. "I know. I'm sorry," she repeated. "How about a beer and some watering? You were going to do that anyway."

Hey, guys, come help dad, she called. She immediately felt Edward move toward the back fence from the outback. Teddy was much slower, and Freya sat in her new spot, atop the rail on the fence, six feet up. How she got there was a mystery.

"Sounds perfect." He kissed her and led the way out of the bedroom. Her brain spun for dinner options as she watched him meet the cats in the back by the pond. Out the picture window over the chest freezer she watched the procession of Tig, the hose, Edward-the-football, Teddy resting like a tea kettle near the viewing port so he didn't get wet. Her eyes swept the yard for Freya. Where was she? No longer on the fence, she was so tiny and camouflaged that when she merely held still, she was impossible to see in the striped sun and shadow of the bamboo forest.

Elizabeth wasn't worried, but she realized she was extremely attached to the little cat after only one day. Perhaps more than she was to Teddy, since he was grown and quite large and Freya, however mature she sounded, weighed not quite six pounds. A predator would make one bite out of her.

Her musings and concern yielded a sound she'd only heard once, but already recognized. Freya laughing. She sat atop the gargoyle's head. For one of Elizabeth's first birthday presents after she and Tig got together, he'd gotten her a large piece of outdoor statuary, a big, black gargoyle, she named Fluffy. He was the guardian of the garden. Teddy was too fat for Fluffy, and Edward had shown no interest in him, but Freya balanced perfectly on top of his head, a branch of bamboo hanging down far enough to hide her or for her to bat around.

Freya's wide mouth and squeaks of obvious enjoyment made Elizabeth laugh, too. *You!* she called to her. Yo*u're so funny.*

You're so funny, came the reply. Freya hopped down from her perch and trotted to the back door where Elizabeth caught her up in a tight hug. The softness of the kitten's down, yet the sturdiness of the small body immediately relaxed her. Elizabeth kissed the little head.

Tig and company were oblivious to the whole exchange.

"What should we do about dinner?" Elizabeth asked Freya.

Freya flashed a picture of a bird. "Ew," said Elizabeth.

You asked, came the reply.

Yes, I did. Elizabeth put Freya on the window sill and opened the chest freezer. "Seems like we'll both get what we wanted." She pulled out a package of frozen chicken.

She left Freya on the sill watching the men and took the chicken to the sink to defrost it.

The evening passed in domestic comfort, and the family called it an early night.

*   *   *   *

They were all up early the next morning, Tig wanted to finish that pond job and recheck all the hose connections and the pump plus planting a few more landscaping touches. Without Karl to double check everything, it would take longer. Tig had some maintenance jobs he'd postponed until this new build was complete, and he didn't want to keep his regular customers waiting longer than necessary. He sailed out with the sandwich she'd hastily made.

Elizabeth hadn't slept well and woke nauseated. She made some peppermint tea and after her grounding meditation, Freya jumped up to work her magic. The overcast day had the boys wandering aimlessly. They went outside, but immediately came back in, complaining it was too wet. The mist hung in eerie banners low to the ground, the strands dripping as they bobbed through the trees. In this coastal desert, that's how most plants got their water, but it still made for creepy mornings and evenings. On days when coyotes got all wound up and yipped and howled as they chased some poor animal, Elizabeth told the boys, and now Freya, to stay inside. When it got really bad, she'd bribe them with a tiny bit of wet food and lock the pet door. She just couldn't bear the thought of a coyote springing at them from the depths of the trees, hurting one of them or carrying it away.

She braced herself for a battle with Freya about it, but she agreed all too easily, Elizabeth thought. She brought her tea back to bed and turned on NetFilms. Elizabeth really wasn't feeling great by now, so she sat up with her tea and Freya again climbed aboard. Warmth spread from the little body to Elizabeth's abdomen and the queasiness passed, and she dozed.

When she awoke, the TV was still on, but bright sunlight slanted through the blinds. She had slithered down on the pillows, and although the boys were gone, Freya remained. She sat higher up on Elizabeth's chest so they were almost nose to nose. When she again opened her eyes, Freya did too, their green depths probing into Elizabeth. Just when she was sure Freya was going to say or do something profound, she opened her tiny mouth in a vast, yawn, accompanied by a squeak.

Elizabeth laughed and kissed her head. "I feel better. Perhaps we should do something." Freya stood and stretched one delicate hind leg after the other before dropping to the floor and leaving the room, tail waving. Elizabeth's phone rang. Caller ID showed the Central Coast Wildlife Center.

Elizabeth picked up. "Hello?"

"Mrs. Murphy?"

"Yes?"

"You can get your rabbit now."

A moment before she put the thought together. "Great! I'll be there in half an hour."

The day had become beautiful while she'd dozed. The boys were out and about, and Freya had disappeared too, she assumed to join them. Elizabeth put on her jeans but they were too tight! She'd gotten a little bigger. She didn't really need maternity wear yet, but she put on some stretchy yoga pants, not that she did yoga, but they were comfortable.

She washed out the pet carrier again since Freya had been the last user. She didn't want to pass any domestic animal germs onto the wild population. But really, she thought wryly, Freya probably did it herself carrying the rabbit around in her mouth. Oh, well. One tried.

She was still in no mood to eat, except for a few soda crackers. She'd figure out more meals when she got home and released the baby bunny.

She sent a message to the cats about her location and told Freya she'd need her help returning the bunny to where Freya had found it.

Freya didn't respond directly, but Elizabeth got a sense of acquiescence. The kitten was so hard to read! She probed further and was confused by the return. She could see and feel Freya on a physical level, she was there in the outback on a fallen log, but she wasn't in her body. Her personality was absent.

Freya? she called. *Don't sleep out there. It's dangerous. You have to pay attention.*

I'm not sleeping, came faintly and from far away. Much farther than the log behind the gate. Elizabeth didn't have the time or energy to pursue it. She'd have to trust Freya was being truthful. She sent quick messages to Teddy and Edward to watch out for her, that she was inexperienced. Teddy sent back a big question mark and a picture of Freya sitting on the log like Elizabeth had mind-seen her. Edward was a little more aware and sent back a picture of her in the same position, but transparent, like people portray ghosts, and then another version of Freya far away and smaller. Elizabeth had no idea what that all meant, but the boys were babysitting, Freya was responding, so for the moment, that was all she could do.

She popped the carrier in the car and mulled this over while she made the short return trip to the wildlife rescue center in Cove City, fifteen minutes away. She came to no conclusions, except she would have to spend more time with Freya to figure it all out.

Her little Honda bounced over the rutted road to the office trailer. She entered the reception area, empty again, and called out, "Hello, rabbit pick up!"

A different woman came out this time, clad in squirrel scrubs. One of the vets? As the swinging doors opened, she heard snatches of muted conversation between a male and female. She couldn't make out the words.

"Hello, thank you for coming!" the scrub-clad woman said.

"My pleasure. You folks do such great work here, it's the least I can do besides donate."

"Your little bunny is in excellent health. We gave him some antibiotics with his stitches. They're healing nicely, so if the flap doesn't get yanked off again, it should be a clean patch. He's very young, but weaned, so he's good. You're sure you know where he came from?"

"I'm sure." *I know where Freya found him,* she silently amended.

"Okay, let me get him then. This your carrier?" She pointed to the carrier Elizabeth had set on the office desk.

"Yes, it's clean."

Squirrel Lady nodded, took the carrier and pushed through the swinging doors. A few moments later, a woman with two small children entered the trailer. The children jostled to balance a cardboard box. "Our cat got a bird!" the little girl who looked older cried.

"It's gonna be okay, right?" the little boy added. His blond hair fell into his eyes as he implored her.

"I don't work here. Let me get someone for you," Elizabeth said. She pushed through the swinging doors calling, "Hello? Someone's in reception for you."

She had never been behind the swinging doors before. Maybe she should have looked at the bird first?

The hall was dark and extended in both directions. She took the left, poked her head into an empty office and kept going. The next office wasn't empty. Karl sat at a computer terminal punching keys.

"Karl!"

He glanced up, startled. "Oh. Hey, Elizabeth. What are you doing here?"

"What are *you* doing here? Tig said you had classes so you couldn't help him finish the pond today."

"Yeah, uh, that's right. This is for a class. I have a biz-add class I have to do lab hours for. So, this is it." She assumed he meant Business Administration.

At her blank look he said, "I have to put in so many hours to get class credit."

"Oh." Now she felt silly. "Sure. I was just surprised to see you. I came to pick up a rabbit Freya rescued."

Now he looked blank. Since he hadn't been working with Tig much, he probably didn't know about their new addition. No need for a lengthy explanation. "The college kids next door moved and left a kitten. We adopted it."

"Hey, you're not supposed to be back here," the vet said, holding out the carrier.

"I know. I was looking for someone to help the family out front. I ran into—" she saw Karl's quick shake of the head and stopped. For some reason he didn't want her to mention they knew each other. Maybe he wasn't supposed to be chatting on company time since it was for class credit.

"I ran into this young man who just told me the same thing. That you'd be right out. Thanks." She took the carrier.

The vet followed her to the double doors. As Elizabeth pushed through she saw the receptionist with the family, all gathered around the box.

She returned to the bright sunshine, the big, landmark rock at the cove just in front of her. She carefully set the carrier on the passenger seat and belted it securely.

"Gonna take you home, little guy," she told him, and sent out waves of security and healing. Other than its rapidly beating heart, he didn't give much back. Maybe it wasn't the brightest of rabbits.

Back home to the eternal question, what's for dinner?

Nine

A dinner miracle did not reveal itself on the way home, so she brought the carrier with the rabbit through the house to the pond area.

"Hey, guys. Guys? I'm gonna need some help, here," she called to the outback. Small rustlings, probably Edward. He was always so good about coming. Teddy would eventually, but that was not going to happen unless there was food involved. She felt an immediate reply from Freya and realized the kitten always responded to her. She didn't understand it until now, but the kitten was connected to her and had been for some time. Knowing Freya, she might have been doing it before Elizabeth realized it, or was aware of the kitty. She didn't put much past the little striped wonder.

Elizabeth likened Freya to Tig in a way. Tig was always there, in her mind, in her heart. She didn't have to worry or wonder, he just was. Freya was there, too. Like someone holding your hand, but you don't realize it for a while, until the warmth builds up, and you think about it.

Freya's smile rose to the surface of Elizabeth's mind and Elizabeth called to her. *Where are you? I need you to help me return this rabbit. Without giving it a heart attack.*

Mom? Mom? Edward's sweet voice matched his pointed face peering through the Plexiglas door in the back fence. Tig had wanted the cats to see if there were predators before they went out.

I'm coming Edward. Where's your brother?

I'm here. Teddy sent a picture of himself sitting on the fallen log. He'd been spending more time out there lately. Cats rarely do something for no reason. Since Freya had arrived, he'd been out here more.

Elizabeth opened the back gate and took the carrier through, leaving the passage open. *Freya? Where do I go? Can you lead me?*

We wanna come, too, added Edward.

No, we don't, said Teddy. *It's too far.*

How far is too far? asked Elizabeth. *You can come Edward, but stay behind so the little rabbit doesn't get the life scared out of him.*

I would never do that! Edward was indignant.

It was true, he was the sweetest cat in the world, and not much of a hunter. In fact, he might cuddle it if given the chance. He was very loving. But a big—compared to the bunny—black cat with long fangs and claws was scary.

Teddy, although sturdy, round and also sweet, was quite a hunter. Many a day the front yard was dotted with headless mouse corpses or just a sheaf of feathers. Elizabeth could not break him of the habit. She told him to put the bodies someplace else, at least. He refused. The heads were the most delicious part, according to Teddy, and he saw no reason not to leave the rest, since he didn't want it. *Ick.*

Freya materialized under the yucca leaves, her brown-gray stripes blending with light and shadow and the dirt of the path. She was a quarter of Teddy's size and could hide in a bedroom slipper if needed.

This way. Freya hopped her way along the fringe of the trail, just under the hang of sage bushes and salt-cedar.

Elizabeth followed, trailed by Edward. Elizabeth checked on the bunny. He seemed all right at the moment. Maybe he was unaware he was escorted by two hunters, however well-meaning they might be. She tried to reassure him, but she got no feeling, no vibe. Hmmm. Unusual. She did not get fear, so that was good. In fact, the bunny was watching out the small slits in the plastic carrier. His nose twitched and he raised a paw just as Freya said, *We're close now.*

Where exactly did you find him?

I found him under this tree, Freya indicated the leaf litter of a towering eucalyptus, *but he had run from there.* She turned and looked farther up the mountain. *His den is in the sage with the others.*

What others?

Lots of bunnies, Freya said succinctly.

Where should I let him go? Elizabeth felt a little frustrated, mostly with herself. What was she thinking offering to return a wild rabbit exactly to his den?

Follow me. Freya started up a game trail, bunny-sized, winding through the sandy dune that made up the whole area. Walking was difficult in the soft sand. Elizabeth doubly regretted her promise. She had never been one for 'long walks on the beach' if the sand was soft, and here she was, following a kitten up a two-inch wide bunny trail to release the world's dumbest rabbit to his relatives who might not have realized he was gone. Sweat trickled in her hair and down her back. She wished she'd brought water. Or worn a hat. Or—

We're here. Freya sat with her tail curled around her tiny body in front of a sage bush that looked exactly like every other sage bush for miles.

Edward, true to his word, sat in the same position, but ten feet down the trail.

The rabbit crashed around the carrier, eager to escape. He must have smelled home.

She tried once more to calm him. Perhaps impart some last words of wisdom or caution. Like, don't rip out your stitches and you'll be fine. But no one responded when she reached out, like a big void. Too scared? She didn't think so. She sighed and opened the carrier. He shot out in a blur and vanished into the sage. It was so fast, she wasn't sure she'd truly seen him move.

The hill was silent except for the breeze rustling pygmy oak leaves fringing the sage field.

That was anticlimactic. Elizabeth latched the carrier and looked at the cats. *Well, guys? Shall we head back?*

Freya smiled, but it was a little wan. *I'm tired.* She sounded like any kid after a long day.

Oh, baby. Of course. Elizabeth had forgotten how many steps Freya had to take compared to Edward or herself. *You did a very good thing. I don't suppose you want to ride in the carrier, do you?*

If Freya could frown, she did so. Her whole face pulled down in disgust. Elizabeth didn't know how she did it, but the message was clear.

I didn't think so. I'll carry you in one hand and the carrier in the other, okay?

What about me? Edward asked.

You'll have to walk. I don't have any more hands.

I'm tired, too. Dad wears me. Edward sent a picture of himself draped over Tig's neck like a scarf.

I can see I'm not winning this one. Okay, how do we do this? Edward first. She draped him around her neck. He was completely limp and surprisingly comfortable. Next she picked up Freya, who fit mostly in one hand, and tucked under her arm. Then she carefully lowered herself to pick up the carrier by the handle without dropping everybody.

"This must look amazing," she mumbled as she slowly started down the track toward home. "At least it's downhill." After only a few steps, she felt herself being watched. She turned to look back toward the sage field and saw nothing. However, as she stood staring, she could make out faces. Lots of faces in the bushes. Bunnies everywhere, up in the sage branches, down on the trails, all holding very still. She opened to them and felt a huge wash of gratitude and joy.

Both Edward and Freya saw the faces, too. Edward was intrigued, but Freya seemed to expect it.

Did you know all these bunnies were here? Elizabeth asked her.

Of course I did. This is my land now.

Your land?

One of them, certainly. Freya closed her eyes, and Elizabeth knew that was the end of the discussion. For now. At least she didn't say 'domain' again.

By the time they reached the back gate Elizabeth was exhausted. She'd had to put Edward down a few houses away, but Freya, however ancient inside, was still a baby in body, and could not walk anymore. She got royal treatment all the way.

"A cup of tea, and I just might make it to the bed."

A treat? Teddy asked.

You didn't even do anything, Edward admonished.

I didn't go. That was a big help. Right, Mom?

Technically, he's right. I had all I could carry as it was. Treats. Elizabeth got a small can of wet food and gave ascending order of amounts.

Teddy only got a bite, and he knew it, but he also knew he had no argument. Edward had walked and was also quite slim, so he got almost half, and Freya got the other half. Elizabeth knew the boys would muscle in so she took Freya's dish back to the bedroom and closed the door. Her tea water heated and she took her cup of peppermint along with Freya who had not allowed herself to be put down.

"Guys, I need a lie-down, okay? I'm going to close the door for a bit."

Both boys made their mouths very small in silent disapproval but watched as she reclosed the bedroom door, not attempting to rush her.

Elizabeth closed the blinds and lay on the bed. She got one sip before she fell into a heavy sleep, Freya tucked on the pillow next to her, safe from rolling, but within reach.

Ten

Elizabeth awoke disoriented and stiff. The dark room didn't help. Freya still slept, now upside down on the pillow. Elizabeth slowly rose and opened the blinds. The mist had returned and covered the sun, making the day darker than usual. She sipped her cold tea. Still delicious. Her calves hurt from the trek up the sand dune. Recalling the many bunny faces staring at her was a little surreal, but she'd experienced weirder.

Just glad it's over. She fumbled her slippers on and turned on the nightstand light. Freya stretched and slowly opened her eyes, still upside down.

Hi, Mom.

Hi, Lovie. Are you feeling okay after that long walk? Elizabeth sent out her cat-checker senses. It was a quick evaluation she did practically on the fly for the boys, anytime they acted off or disturbed. Freya was tired and sore, too, but satisfied at what she saw as doing her duty in her 'land.' A flash of snow and a bitterly cold beach raced across Elizabeth's mind. *What was that?*

Freya, still upside down but fully awake, said, *Home.*

Wait, what?

One of them. Don't worry. It's like a dream to me, too sometimes.

Okay. Time to get up. For me, anyway. You can stay here if you want.

I'll come too. Freya flopped off the bed and stretched again.

Elizabeth opened the door and was greeted by two disapproving cats, glaring much as they had when she'd shut them out. She knew they hadn't waited there the whole time, but she let them think she didn't know.

We've been waiting.

I know. I have to come up with a plan for dinner. I hope without going to the store again. How do we eat it all so fast? Or how do I not buy enough? I used to be a great planner, but since this baby, I can't seem to do more than one tiny thing at a time.

She shuffled out to the chest freezer to see what might have appeared since the last check. It was already past lunch time, but she wasn't very hungry. Just sore.

We're hungry, Teddy said.

Fine. Elizabeth poured fresh kibbles, which didn't fool anyone. Teddy wouldn't deign to walk over to the bowl.

She grabbed a yogurt from the refrigerator and stood with the door open hoping for inspiration. Tig was off from the fire department today, but he was working hard to finish the pond by himself.

Thinking of Karl bailing on her husband made her mad all over again. Karl was sitting in a cushy office at a computer, not only *not* helping Tig, but lying about it. That might be a harsh assessment. He was trying to get an education. Usually she wasn't so crabby. *Maybe take a step back*, she scolded herself. *You don't know what's going on, really. Just relax. It's fine.*

Then she checked the clock. Her many tasks and then her nap had eaten up the whole day! Dinner.

She pulled out salad makings and chopped and tossed. She made her red-wine vinaigrette dressing Tig loved, and threw in some garbanzo beans for good measure.

She dug to the bottom of the chest freezer in desperation and found a package of frozen shrimp. Victory! Shrimp with pasta and lemon butter. Saved. Tomorrow the store for sure.

The overcast day made it feel later and darker than it was, and she was tired enough for it to be over. She parboiled the pasta so all she had to do was dunk it in hot water to finish. She gently sautéed the shrimp and turned off the heat before they were done.

She sat at the kitchen table with her reheated mint tea and realized her legs ached awfully, even with the nap. She glanced down and saw swollen ankles. That can't be good. She also noticed her baby bump was actually sticking out! Freya climbed aboard and Elizabeth saw the kitten had less room.

Tig's truck backing into the drive heralded his arrival. She didn't get up, but that was okay. She figured there'd be a lot more days where she couldn't get up so they both might as well get used to it. She smiled down at her tiny baby bump and waited for Tig.

He blew in, dropped his stuff by the door and gave her a kiss while picking up Edward. He assessed her elevated feet and haggard expression. "Everything okay?"

"Yes, just so tired." Elizabeth was comforted both by the bump as she'd taken to calling it, and Freya. She realized she had a hand on each.

"What can I do? Something smells good." Tig opened a beer.

"Turn up the heat on the water and when it boils again, dump the pasta in. The shrimp should be done and the salad's made. I think there's bread, but I didn't make garlic bread," she apologized. He loved his bread. She felt like she'd been slacking off in the wife department, but really, she just wasn't able to do as much. What would happen when the bump was a huge ball, not some lima-bean sized critter? She sighed.

"What's up?" Tig asked. "I got this." He smiled, and his eyes pulled up at the corners.

She studied him. "I know. But you shouldn't have to." She felt herself tearing up and refused to let it go. Silly.

"Are you kidding? Now I can impress you with more of my mad skills." He dropped the parboiled pasta in the swirling water, then began to set the table.

"I'm afraid it's going to get worse before it gets better," Elizabeth said. "I feel exhausted and now my feet are swelling, and I'm only at the end of the first trimester."

Tig sat next to her. "Look. You're healthy, right?" She nodded. "Baby's doing great, right?" She nodded again. "The boys are fine, we've got a princess now, too, and I'm fine. I have a steady job with health insurance and a second job that's just rolling in the dough, right?" he joked. The pond company did well since there was next to no overhead. No office rent, supplies were bought as needed by the job and referrals steady, so mostly profit. He complained about Karl working less, but that meant less payout, too, so it wasn't all bad.

Tig rose and scooped out cooked pasta and shrimp onto a serving dish. He put it and the salad on the table. "Dare I say, hormones?" he asked. "I really think we're fine. Making a person is harder than we thought, that's all. I'll do whatever I can to make it easier. The kids will, too." He indicated the cats. Teddy lay on his side in the center of the kitchen, exactly where anyone would need to go. Edward kept Tig's chair warm, and Freya still sat on Elizabeth's lap.

Elizabeth smiled at her family. "You're right. I'm overwhelmed, but it's all good." She decided not to mention seeing Karl again today at the rescue center. What if she'd misunderstood and caused a rift between the two friends? She also decided not to mention Freya's conversation about this being one of her 'lands,' and the flash of icy beach and sea she'd seen in her mind.

She did regale Tig with an elaborate Return of the Rabbit tale and how amazing Freya had been, especially when all the bunnies thanked them, in their bunny way. Teddy, not part of the adventure, lay unmoving on the kitchen floor, only the end of his tail flicking up to show his displeasure at this exclusion. Elizabeth figured there'd be a headless corpse in the front yard somewhere to reflect this.

The little family cleaned up and headed back to the bedroom for some NetFilms and an early night. Elizabeth sighed and wished she had some energy for private time with Tig. As usual, he sensed her feelings and squeezed her hand, kissing her cheek with understanding.

Tig's phone ringing woke them sometime in the wee hours. Karl. His house had caught fire. Although he'd been cleared medically, he had no place to go. His family did not live in the area and Stacy, his girlfriend, was out of town. Could he stay with them?

Eleven

Tig jumped out of bed. "I'll be right over to get you." He changed clothes as fast as if he'd been on duty as he explained the situation to Elizabeth.

"Did he lose everything?" she asked.

"I don't know. I think his car's safe, but he shouldn't drive. A fire is devastating emotionally, too. I want to be sure he's okay."

"Do you want me to come, too?"

"No, I'll bring him right back here. He sounded as if they'd already taken his initial statement. Poor guy. The investigation could go on for a while. I hope he had renter's insurance. Even if it's ruled an accident, he'll still need a place to stay. I don't know if he has a key to Stacy's place, but he shouldn't be alone right now. She's visiting her folks and can't get back in a hurry."

Tig grabbed a jacket and his wallet, kissed her goodbye and she was left in a bubble of silence. A glance at the clock told her it was nearing 5 AM. She felt awake, but the cats still lay amid the covers.

"Should see about the guest room." She shuffled down the hall to the extra bedrooms. One was a sort of office for Tig, and the other was starting to look like a nursery. The office/junk room had a daybed, so it would do. If Karl stayed longer than anticipated, and they needed to work on the nursery, she wanted it free. She pulled files, pond tubing and connections, manuals and invoices off the daybed and piled them on the little desk and floor.

"Another day, we'll organize this." She indicated the piles. "Preferably before tax time." She was soon joined by three curious cats who were almost never allowed in this secret room.

Freya immediately jumped atop the desk, and Edward and Teddy began a game of chase under the bed.

Elizabeth got fresh linens and pillows. She took her time remaking the bed. A small chest of drawers would do for his belongings. She felt for him. Even if it didn't all burn, smoke and water damage would ruin almost everything else. She put clean towels in the front bathroom.

Feeling like she'd done all she could for now, she put on a pot of coffee and made herself a cup of tea and a piece of toast. As she buttered the toast, she heard two cars on the quiet street. It was almost six, but not many people were up. A few dog walkers and the early commuters just beginning.

I love toast, Freya said.

You do?

It's my favorite. We don't have toast where I'm from.

That's a topic for another day. Tig and Karl are back. Here's your toast. Elizabeth pinched a bit from the middle, juicy with melted butter. She had just gotten extra mugs and cream and sugar when the men came in bringing with them a strong smell of smoke. The cats disapproved and evaporated, probably to the master bedroom, as far as they could get and still be in the house.

She hugged Karl. "I'm so sorry, Karl. I'm glad you're okay. Were you hurt?"

He shook his head. "Just scared. I woke up and the house was already on fire. They think it started in the electrical panel somewhere. My granny unit is far enough away from the main house and the neighbors' that they weren't damaged. Fast response time from our boys and girls." He smiled at Tig.

"Lucky for you. Were you able to save anything?" She poured him a mug of coffee and guided him to a chair.

"No. Some stuff was in my car parked on the street and far enough away. I had a few things at Stacy's, but the apartment's a total loss."

"Anything valuable? Family photos?"

"Not really. My place was so small. I had my phone by the bed so I grabbed it. My school stuff was in the car for the most part. Those texts are expensive."

"Have you called Stacy?" Elizabeth nibbled her cold toast.

"I'm waiting until she's up. No point in waking her and worrying her for no reason. She has a few more days with her parents, and there's nothing she can do even if she comes home early. I'll be talking to insurance companies and the fire investigator, so. . ." he trailed away. His face had a thin veil of smoke stain, with streaks where he'd rubbed. He sighed.

"Maybe a hot shower and some rest. Do you have class today?" she asked.

"Yes, but I might be dealing with the authorities, so I'll have to see."

"What time? Can you get in a nap after you shower?"

"Afternoon classes, intern stuff in the morning and evening, studying around all of that when I can." He heaved a sigh. "I'm sorry I haven't been able to help you as much as I said."

"It's okay," Tig said. "Things happen. And now this. Why don't you shower and get some rest."

"Yes, I fixed up the office for you," Elizabeth said. "Are you hungry? I can make something."

"No. The coffee is fine."

"Here take this toast. Coffee on an empty stomach with all that stress can't be good." Elizabeth shoved her plate his way.

Hey, Freya said. *I was going to eat that.*

He needs it more. I'll make more toast later.

"Thank you. I'd love to get this smell off me." He folded the entire slice into his mouth.

Tig led him to the office room and Elizabeth heard him pointing out towels and asking if he needed anything. She went back to their bedroom.

A few minutes later Tig joined her. The house was quiet again. Almost like nothing happened. The cats had gone out the pet door, so they were alone.

"What was it like?" she asked.

"Pretty bad. Limited to his unit but it almost got into the eukies at the back. That would have spread to the neighborhood. He was lucky. If he hadn't woken up . . . I don't know. It started behind the house, so none of the neighbors saw. Burned fast and he barely got out. Glad Stacy hadn't been there. Worse than he made it out to be. That old wiring. People think they don't have to keep up their old units because they're renting them out. What if he'd been more tired, or passed out, or sick? A few moments might have made a difference and he'd be gone."

Elizabeth put her arms around him and they lay together. Karl wasn't all that much younger than Tig, but Tig looked on him as a protégé. He'd been training and helping him. Just in the last year, Karl had really come into his own, getting clients, going back to school, becoming responsible and dependable. She looked on him maternally, making him meals or checking on him.

They awoke near ten, the signal being Teddy jumping on the bed; a substantial weight pulling a corner of the bed down, jouncing them to wakefulness. Edward sat on the floor looking up. Freya had already made herself at home on the pillow next to Elizabeth's head without her knowing.

Elizabeth lay for a moment listening. Quiet. Either Karl was still asleep or he had gone. She figured gone, since he was so responsible. He still had classes and now paperwork to do. She promised herself to get to the store and buy a few necessaries for him. Toothbrush, paste, shampoo, a few things. She'd go through Tig's closet and pull out some tee shirts and emergency clothes to get him through a few days. She couldn't imagine losing everything she had and starting over. The most important things were Tig and the cats, but all the family photos, her grandma's dishes. . . to lose it all? Incomprensible.

She rolled on her side. Tig was awake too. They shared a kiss. Teddy stomped up the middle.

Hey, let's go. You're late.

"Where to?" Elizabeth asked aloud for Tig's benefit.

Kibbles.

"Okay. Tig, kibbles, and what is on your schedule today?"

Tig sat up and lifted Edward into his lap. "I was going to do the paperwork on that pond, and I had a consult on another job, too. After last night, I feel like spending the day with my wife and appreciating what I have." He leaned back and she kissed him again.

"Sounds nice. Maybe a short walk on the bluffs?"

"Perfect. I can catch up on some things here around the house, too.

They spent the day doing just that. Karl did not appear towards dinner, so they figured he kept to his regular schedule. But where was he going to study?

Just as they were settling into bed for the night, they heard him return.

"I'll just see if he needs anything," Elizabeth said. She padded down the hall and was about to knock on his door when she heard him mumbling, she assumed on his phone. She waited to see if he'd hang up and ask if he was hungry. Freya was the only one who'd followed her out of the warm bed. She picked her up and draped her over her shoulder.

The voice rose. "I know. It was intentional. I must be close because why else would someone try to kill me? I'm doing the best I can but I didn't sign on for this. Just trying to make some money. I didn't agree to life . . ." The voice lowered again.

Elizabeth froze. Her heart pounded. 'Life' like a prison sentence? And murder? She figured he meant the fire was set intentionally. What was he doing, who was he helping that would put him in danger? It sounded like he hadn't thought whatever he was doing was dangerous. Was he breaking the law?

Elizabeth turned and went into the darkened kitchen. She didn't turn on any lights, but went to the window over the sink and stared at the lights in the bamboo garden. She felt the tiniest purr vibrating from Freya and soothing waves washing from the tiny, furry body.

"Thank you," she told the kitten.

The mouse-sized purr continued, but Freya didn't answer.

Elizabeth didn't want to confront Karl about what she'd overheard. Not yet. What had she really heard? Was he was mixed up in something that scared him? Something that might have made some people angry? The fire investigation wasn't complete yet, so maybe it was guess-work on his part. Hard for her to believe Karl was doing something illegal. They both knew him pretty well after three years. Or did they? He'd had a rough beginning, Tig had told her, and she knew he didn't have much family, which is why they'd 'adopted' him, but a criminal? "I suppose anything's possible," she mused as she rocked Freya by the window.

Baby says don't worry, Freya said.

What?

Baby says stay calm.

Are you talking about this baby? Elizabeth pointed to her stomach.

Yes. Don't fuss. Baby doesn't like it. Elizabeth got a quick vision of the baby, arms crossed with a frowny face and knew it wasn't the baby, just her or more likely Freya's imagination. But she got the point.

"Right." She suddenly felt exhausted. Standing in one place was harder these days, too. She sighed. If the first trimester was so taxing, how was she going to survive two more? The next question was what to tell Tig? She didn't want to say Karl was a criminal. Maybe. Or in with the wrong guys. What did she know? *Get some facts,* she scolded herself. *Why make trouble if there isn't any?*

When she got back to bed, Tig was sound asleep. She made a mental note to follow up on the fire report with Tig. He might know before Karl. He had friends in high places in the fire department.

Twelve

Elizabeth woke alone. She heard the distant rumble of men talking in the kitchen and figured the cats would be there too, in case anything fell on the floor.

The room was fairly dark despite the clock saying it was time to get up. A quick peek out the window showed the foggy gloom of a coastal summer day. It would burn off by noon, but some days it was so hard to drag herself out of bed. She got her robe and pushed into her slippers and joined the guys.

Tig had made a fireman's breakfast for Karl: bacon, eggs, a mountain of fried potatoes and a giant plate of toast they were working through while they talked. Tig was getting the coffee pot for refills when she came in.

"Hey," he said and kissed her hello.

"Morning," Karl greeted her around a mouthful of toast.

She put the kettle on for tea. Lately she, or the baby, hadn't wanted decaf in the morning. Just tea. The coffee smell was still delicious, but drinking it didn't appeal.

Teddy lay in the middle of the action as per usual, Edward kept Tig's seat warm, and Freya sauntered out of the laundry room where a kibble and water station occupied a corner.

Teddy and Edward did not say a word, which was suspicious. Neither of them looked at her. She saw telltale scrambled egg crumbles as evidence. Teddy's crumbles were down his striped chest, meaning he hadn't moved to eat. Spoiled. Edward was working on cleaning his whiskers. Freya at least pulled off virtuous and innocent, but Elizabeth was sure she'd had her share of breakfast, too.

"Toast," Elizabeth said.

"Sure, hon, help yourself," Tig pushed the plate toward her.

"Thanks, but that's not what I meant. Freya loves toast, so I'm sure she's wrangled some out of you guys this morning. Like the guys talked you out of some scrambled eggs, right?"

Karl looked startled, and Tig looked moderately chastised. "Just a little," Tig said.

"How can you tell?" Karl asked.

"Those guys look super guilty." Elizabeth pointed to the boys. "They know people food is bad for them. But I admit, they get it out of me, too, sometimes. And I'm the guilty one for discovering Freya's love of buttered toast. She is not the slightest bit guilty about it, so she's harder to read."

Elizabeth pulled Freya into her lap and sipped her tea. "So what's on for today?"

Tig doctored his coffee. "I'm going with Karl to see if anything can be salvaged from his house. I doubt it. I'm going to help him follow up on the report, too. Sometimes they drag their feet and don't let the homeowner or renter know what's going on. I'm not going to let that happen."

Karl looked uncomfortable. "I told him he didn't have to. I appreciate the assist with the search through my place, but I can wait until the official report comes out."

"You can't file with the insurance company without the report, so the longer they delay, the longer they don't have to pay you." Tig stroked Edward who had resumed his place in his lap.

"Yeah, but it's okay. I'm sure it's fine, you know, old wiring in an old house. I have a lot going on right now and I've got to start looking for a new apartment."

"Are you and Stacy going to look together?" Elizabeth asked.

"Uh, I don't know. We haven't talked about it for a while. She's due back day after tomorrow."

"You can stay here until you two decided if you're looking solo or together, okay?" Elizabeth said. Tig nodded in agreement.

"I don't know if that's a good idea," Karl said. "I'm kind of in the way, and uh, I have a lot to do," he repeated.

He is worried he's putting you in danger from whatever he's doing, Freya said.

How do you know? Elizabeth asked. *That's pretty advanced for a baby creature, much less an animal. What's going on?* She sounded sharper than she'd meant.

I know the way I know that you worried about the same thing.

But I'm your person, you're supposed to know that, or feel *that, about me. Not everyone.*

I can't help what I know. Would you rather I didn't tell you? As my person?

No. I guess not. We'll talk later. Elizabeth realized she'd been quiet much longer than she'd meant to while talking to Freya.

"She does this all the time," Tig told Karl. "She's talking to the cats."

"What are you talking to them about?" Karl was curious, not shocked.

"You know, important cat stuff," Tig smiled and ruffled Edward's fur. "Like why Teddy only eats the heads off the mice and leaves the bodies in the yard."

Elizabeth was slightly insulted but mostly relieved she didn't have to come up with an answer. "Teddy does not have an answer for that," she added.

The topic reverted to everyone's plans and she was off the hook until the fire report was finished.

Tig and Karl cleared their dishes and went to dress for the day. Elizabeth sat a bit longer, enjoying Freya and the boys. She noticed the sun trying to burn through and thought it would be a beautiful day. Something bothered her, and she wasn't sure what. A lot was bothering her, but something specific she couldn't put her finger on. She would try not to think about it, and it would come to her. Or not. Pregnancy brain was having its way with her. She forgot the silliest things. Where her phone was, for example. Probably still charging. She'd been groggy when she woke, and the men hadn't had theirs out, so she had no visual cue.

She groaned as she stood and cleared her own dishes, putting leftovers and the coffee things away. Her feet hurt already. Was that possible? She could still see her ankles, so they weren't swollen. Yet. She started the dishwasher and waddled back to the bedroom for her phone.

Wait. Waddled? She tried to calculate in her head the weeks. Finishing the first trimester, she shouldn't be waddling. Should she? Glancing down, the bump looked bigger. Noticeably bigger. *Sheesh.* Maybe she should work on the nursery today. She'd take to her bed by next week at this rate.

She made it to the bedroom and slowly dressed. It was harder than yesterday. She'd just picked up her phone when Tig came to say good-bye.

"Do I seem bigger to you?" she asked him.

He was wary. "You look amazing," he said.

"No, it's not a trick question. I feel significantly bigger and wondered if it was in my head." She moved back and forth, shifting her profile. "Well?"

"Maybe? But that's good, right? I mean, you're supposed to get bigger."

"I don't know. I'm feeling so tired suddenly and I seem bigger than . . . just big."

"When's your next checkup?"

"Good question. Things have moved pretty fast around here." She picked up her phone and checked the calendar. "Oh. Today. How could I forget? 2 PM. Can you come? I think we planned it so you were off."

"Of course I can come. Karl and I will be done at the house pretty quickly, I think. I have to do a few pond business things, but I can do the invoicing from here, rather than on the fly, uh, in the truck. I should probably change that."

She put her hands on her hips. "You think? Now that your office is Karl's room, maybe you could get in the habit of inputting the costs in your laptop. We can print the invoices at home and I can mail them out. Rather than scribbling them on notepaper in the cab of the truck."

"I don't do that." He caught her smile. "But you're right, I need to organize a bit."

"You *do* do that, sometimes," she said. He smiled back.

"Busted," he said.

"If I keep going like I am, I'll be staying home more and more. If I help with the organizing of billing, ordering parts and things, you don't have to worry about that." She caught his look. "I'm not going to take over anything like client consultations or scheduling of jobs. You still need to do that. If I know you have a big job coming up a certain week, I can tell them you might do a consult, but won't be available for the job for several more weeks. Then at the consult, you can schedule them once you see the scope of the job. If I take care of the billing, it might make it easier at tax time." Tax time was not fun. Tig was more of an artist than an accountant, and Elizabeth spent hours with him organizing his receipts into the proper categories. One of their luxuries was a professional tax accountant. Last year Elizabeth had finally said she couldn't do the whole thing anymore. She thought they might be missing deductions or filing incorrectly. With her own business picking up as an 'animal consultant'—pet psychic not only didn't cut it, the IRS didn't have a category for that—and his pond business expanding, along with a baby arriving this year, it was time. The accountant still needed them to organize their receipts into the worksheet she provided. Still not fun, but much easier and more organized.

"Good idea," Tig agreed. "We can talk about the details later. I'll be back here by 1:30, okay? We'll drive in together?" The OB-GYN was in the city of Tolosa, ten miles away.

She kissed him good-bye and listened until they were gone. The house was always so quiet when he left. Suddenly overwhelmed, she sat on the corner of the bed, nearly squashing Freya who had silently appeared next to her.

She pulled the kitten into her lap. *Hi there, little one.*

Hi, Mom. They sat together for a few moments. Elizabeth heard the tiny mouse-purr as she called it, but only when she lifted the kitten and put her against her ear. Sometimes she could feel the slight vibration with her hand, but only if she concentrated. So quiet for such a fierce little thing.

The sun broke through and the back yard and pond looked brilliant through the slider.

Don't worry, Mom. Baby is fine.

What makes you think I'm worried about the baby? Freya did a slow blink, which Elizabeth knew to be like a smile. *Okay, I am worried. A little. I've never been pregnant, so I have no idea what's going on. I feel so uncomfortable. And big. I shouldn't be this big for a couple more months. I'm sure not overeating.*

Baby is progressing. Baby needs to be here, so baby is growing. Baby says not to worry. All is fine.

So the baby talks to you. Is this a regular thing?

Baby is kind of boring, so I don't do it much. But I check in every day.

Whoa. *Why can't I sense it? Talk to it?*

I am not sure. It's easy for me. Edward can do it, but he stopped since I came. No need for both of us. Maybe your job is to talk to us, and we talk to Baby?

True. I don't do people. They are more complex and not as fun, frankly.

Of course not.

"Enough of this for now," Elizabeth said. "Let's go look at the nursery and see what I can do in a few hours." She carried Freya with her to the other bedroom. She opened the window and a fresh, crisp breeze passed through. She and Tig had already decided to keep the pale yellow walls, thinking it would be good for either a boy or girl. They had some furniture in the room, a rocking

113

chair and a dresser with a changing table built in. Some newborn clothes they hadn't been able to resist, but the elephant in the room was the unconstructed crib. Did she want to tackle that by herself? In her prime, she could build pre-fabricated furniture with the best of them, but now? She felt insecure and inept. She decided to ask Tig to put it together sooner, rather than later.

Let's assume for one second a kitten has obstetric knowledge and is right that the baby will come early and is developing more rapidly, she thought. Things might move faster and not the way they'd planned at all. On a simple level, what if she just continued to feel unwell and couldn't do as much? They should be as prepared as possible.

Whatever. Elizabeth felt silly with this line of thinking. Animals were often prescient, so that in itself wasn't huge. They also paid attention and were privy to more intense senses than humans. At any rate, the doctor would clear up any development timeline questions today.

She dusted the dresser, moved the rocker to a corner and set a fluffy baby quilt along its back. The box with the crib judged her from the corner so she moved it into the tiny closet, realizing as she did so, that box was at the top of her weightlifting ability. When they'd bought it, she'd moved it with ease.

She sighed and sat in the rocker. Pretty comfortable. She imagined sitting here with her newborn, looking out the window at the lovely bamboo along the fence. If she scooched the chair a bit she could see the pond, the tall black taro plant sticking up six feet from the water. Gorgeous. With the window open, she heard the koi sucking at the surface. They sounded like kisses and made her smile. Freya jumped in her lap and they sat and rocked.

She must have dozed because she woke with a start, a little disoriented. "Man, I just fall asleep at the drop of a hat," she grumbled. Freya was gone from her lap but out the window, the two boys sunbathed on the hot tub deck, the occasional desultory slap suggesting a boy-fight might occur. One of those rare times when Teddy agreed to play with Edward, with the two of them standing-off too far away to actually hit each other. Paws raised, swinging at air, then a mad romp through the yard, just one, as Teddy was not athletic. Unless it suited him.

Then back to sunbathing, or eating kibble, or doing absolutely nothing. Her boys' antics made her smile. She must remember to fuss over them, too. The new kitten had taken all her time and focus, and it wasn't fair to Teddy, her 'cat boyfriend,' as she and Tig joked. Teddy loved the name and the attention.

Lunch was late. She had dozed right through the noon hour. She made a quick tuna salad sandwich, then several more in case Tig and Karl needed to eat, too. This baby really liked tuna, so maybe they should stop at the store on the way home from the doctor. Since she had Tig to do the carrying for her, it made sense. Teddy and Edward charged through the pet door; they needed tuna salad, too. Apparently.

"Okay, guys. A little, and NO mayo." Whiskers sagged in disappointment. "Where's your sister? She gets tuna, too."

Muffled replies as they scarfed their tuna, but in the negative. Elizabeth moved to the back door and called her. No answer. She sent out her cat-sense, which was practically automatically attuned to Freya. She was in the house, but not answering. Elizabeth checked the baby's room, then moved to the master bedroom.

Freya lay on her side on the bed, twitching slightly, completely limp. Not sleeping, but definitely not awake. Panic rose in Elizabeth and she forced herself to calm down. She lay next to her on the bed, not touching. She grounded herself and closed her eyes, allowing herself to move closer to Freya, to be with her consciousness, much as she would any animal she was communicating with from a long distance. Freya was not in the little body that lay on the bed. The body was healthy, and at rest, but did not house the Freya consciousness as Elizabeth knew her.

Elizabeth had never experienced this before. Something similar had happened with a giant prized koi, where a human spirit also resided within or with the fish. It was weird but it was a real person. Granted, one who had been dead for centuries, but this was different.

She might be dreaming. If so, it was a dream she was unfamiliar with in real life. She had touched a part of this Freya dream before, so she let it play out.

The same desolate beach with the cove surrounded by snow-topped mountains; a village, the dock reaching into the water. Huts set back from the beach and fires lit, skins hanging, fish drying. Glimpses of a life she was unfamiliar with. The smell. The ice cold air carried smoke, cooking meat, a slight brine from the sea, and as she moved past the huts, a tang of human sweat and curing furs.

She felt safe and invisible but very far from home. Her Elizabeth self was not in Freya. She was visiting her. She saw no cats, nor people for that matter. This village was inhabited, but where was everyone?

She followed a slight hum to a long house that looked like a meeting room for the village. The hum grew and she knew she'd found the people. Did she feel invisible enough to test it by going in? Not really. But she wanted to make sure Freya was safe.

She dithered outside a door of hanging skins, turning away just as the skins moved aside, and a woman about her age exited.   Elizabeth jumped out of the way to keep from being hit. The woman was dressed in layers of furs, and wore a short dagger and a longer sword. Her tawny hair was teased and braided into an intricate style. Their eyes met and Elizabeth's gray ones met green one with the familiar kaleidoscope she'd come to know outlined in black.

"Freya?" she asked.

"Yes. Why are you here?" Freya recognized her, too.

"I was worried. You, you're not in your body."

"I had business to attend to. That body is my home for now. I am borrowing it."

Elizabeth stood shocked. Perhaps she *was* dreaming.

"You are not dreaming. However, I am not sure this dream*walking* is good for the baby. You are here and there at the same time, and I cannot answer for its safety."

"Uh. Uh, why are you borrowing a cat body?" She had a million questions.

"Come." Freya dragged her around the side of the longhouse and out of view. "For lack of a better response, I am hiding."

"Hiding? In a cat body and in my time? I assume this is the past somehow?"

"Not really, but it is easier if you think so. No one will look for me in a cat body, and I needed to be with you and your baby, as well as the cat. All three of you have something I need, and I have something you need. It is mutually beneficial and keeps me safe."

"Who are you hiding from?"

"As I have heard in your time, 'it is complicated' and I don't have time to discuss it. This place is dangerous and *in* danger, and I have to come back to reinforce it, for lack of a better phrase. I am making plans both here and there." *There* indicated Elizabeth's time she thought. Or place. Elizabeth was having trouble following the conversation. She kept seeing a kitten overlaid by this human form. The eyes were the same, and the stripes and braids in the hair, although not the gray of the kitten, suggested the same pattern.

Elizabeth was growing tired, and human Freya grew impatient. "The longer I am explaining to you, the longer I am not doing what I need. Go back. I will return soon."

"Yes, I will." Elizabeth had no idea what else to do. She felt weak and unable to stand any longer.

"Go!" Human Freya pushed back toward the long house and Elizabeth began to fall. She awoke on her own bed, next to the kitten, exactly as she had been.

Tig came into the bedroom. "Sorry I'm late. We've got to go."

"Did you get your sandwich?" was all Elizabeth managed.

"I'll eat it in the car. Let's go. Are you okay?"

"Yes, I was asleep." She glanced down and Freya's eyes were open. The kaleidoscopes were vague, and if she didn't know better, empty. "Freya?" She stroked the kitten. Slowly the eyes focused, and Freya came back to the little body. Her wit and intelligence returned.

Yes. I am here.

Elizabeth had gotten a glimpse of what life might be like when or if the Freya consciousness left the kitten for good. Sad. She loved Freya. But if Freya was a person, she could not remain forever. Too much to consider. She kissed the kitten on the head, and Freya squinched her eyes in pleasure.

It's okay. Go. I'll be here.

Elizabeth and Tig jumped in the car and waved to Karl as they passed. What was Karl doing home in the middle of the day? she wondered. Her next thought: They were going to be late.

Thirteen

Tig and Elizabeth were indeed late to her checkup. Only by a few minutes and as usual, the doctor was running late too. Tig had managed to eat his tuna sandwich in three bites and had brought a toothbrush in his pocket. Once they'd checked in, he went to the restrooms to brush his teeth. Elizabeth was flabbergasted by his foresight. Hmm. She might not have remembered something like that given the same circumstances.

As Tig returned, the nurse called for them. Dr. Phillips, an attractive blonde, always managed to act as if she had all the time in the world for her patients, while at the same time, efficiently whisking them in and out. She asked general questions about health and energy, and then got down to the business of the ultrasound. Despite being in the warmer, the gel felt startlingly cold to Elizabeth's middle. The technology allowed unimagined details of the baby to be seen. Almost like a photo. Eerie, and even more so given what Freya had said. How much weight should she give a cat's word? Elizabeth decided not to think about it right now, but just enjoy the moment.

"Wow," Tig said.

"It's beautiful," Elizabeth said. The little face drifted toward the 'camera' and grimaced. They watched it in awe as it floated around for a moment.

"You still don't want to know the sex?" Dr. Phillips asked.

"No," they both answered.

"Okay, we'll keep it a surprise but eventually, with the resolution, you're probably going to see." Dr. Phillips turned the monitor away from them.

"About what I was asking. Am I bigger than I should be? Or is it? I feel huge, but according to the weeks, I'm at twelve?" Elizabeth asked.

"Closer to fourteen. That is interesting," Dr. Phillips said. "It's possible we got the conception date wrong, but not by a lot. This baby does seem to be developing faster than usual."

"Than normal?" Tig clarified.

"There is a range of normal, and your baby still falls within it, particularly if the date is wrong. Nothing to worry about. Everything looks very good." She closed out Elizabeth's screens.

"I'm so tired all the time, and it still feels like between yesterday and today, it grew a lot."

"It's possible. Growth isn't always an evenly paced thing. Like anything, plants, animals, people, growth is regulated by a number of factors. The main thing is baby looks great and is responding to stimuli, and you need to take your cues from it. Maybe baby is having a growth spurt, and your energy is going to that, not you.

Remember, eat well, rest often. That's my bumper sticker. The baby takes your nutrition first, your everything first, so be sure you have enough left over for you. If you're tired, rest. If you're hungry, eat. At this point, if you're eating like we talked about, you really can't eat too much. No junk, very little sugar. If it's all nutrient dense, you can pretty much eat what you want." She wiped off the remaining gel and helped Elizabeth sit up.

"Any other questions?" They both shook their heads. "Okay, we'll see you in four weeks unless you have any changes, okay?"

"Thank you." Elizabeth felt relieved as they headed out to reception to make the next appointment. And utterly exhausted. The worry had taken its toll, not to mention her 'visit' to the icy north somewhere. Or somewhen. *Don't think about it,* she told herself. Just make it home to lie down.

Tig drove and she was too tired to think about stopping at the store. Tig said he would pop in and she could stay in the car, so they did. She reclined her seat back and in only moments it felt, he was back with beer, makings for dinner and tuna for baby and cats, along with a few staples. With Karl there, they were going through food faster, and the bills were higher, but they'd agreed not to let him pay for anything until he was back on his feet.

At home, Tig shooed her back to the bedroom. She was too wiped out to argue.

She fell instantly asleep and dreamed of holding her baby. It spoke lengthy and perfect English and had a great sense of humor. She awoke a couple hours later much refreshed and surrounded by cats. Tig must have come in and closed the blinds because the room was darker than it should have been. She turned on the bedside light, and three sets of eyes blinked groggily at her. Freya was in her spot on the pillow next to Elizabeth, curled into a tiny circle. The boys stretched luxuriously, easily taking up half the bed.

Hi, Mom. How are you feeling? All the voices. She felt a strange sensation like a feather passing over her and realized Freya, she assumed, since the boys had never done it before this, was doing her version of Elizabeth's cat-sense check.

I feel pretty good. Elizabeth heard muted voices. Karl and Tig. Probably working on insurance papers or fire damage. She stretched.

"Shall we start some dinner?"

Absolutely. Edward.

Carry me. Freya.

I could eat. Teddy.

Elizabeth felt like her pants were strangling her, so she changed into her PJ bottoms and the elastic felt a little tight. Maybe time to get out some maternity wear! A flutter of excitement at that thought. Slippers on, she headed to the kitchen. The men weren't there, and voices came from the baby's room.

She stopped in the doorway. A sea of crib parts coated the carpet. Karl had the instructions and was attempting to match cartoonish parts' sketches to the parts themselves, Tig tried to lay them out in order, along with finding the correct tools that the 'toolless construction' neglected to mention. Good thing she had not attempted this herself.

"How did you know?" she asked Tig. "And thank you so much," she added.

"I figured time was flying by anyway, so why put it off. Now I'm sorry," he joked.

"I can't believe you're supposed to put this together without an engineering degree," Karl said.

"I was going to start dinner. Any requests?" Elizabeth asked.

"I started a pot of crack chili," Tig said and pounced on an Allen wrench.

"It's amazing. Thank you." Elizabeth was overwhelmed. Tig cooked for her today, too. Crack chili was their joke name for his tofu chili which was delicious and addicting, hence the name. In poor taste perhaps, but accurate as far as it went. She wondered when they would have to stop calling it that as a bad influence on the baby. Two years old? Hard to envision. Maybe she needed a visit with Janie and Garrett across the street. Going on two years old now, he had been impossible since the age of eighteen months when he decided just walking was not good enough, and began climbing everything and speaking in full sentences. Janie looked exhausted most of the time. Garrett was an excellent sleeper, his mother admitted. However, he did not need naps according to him, even if Janie did, and when he was awake, kept her absolutely hopping with his energy and curiosity. Garrett's dad, Terry, was a fire fighter like Tig and they worked out of the same station but on different shifts. However, although they too were best friends, they hadn't spent much time together lately given Tig's extra work and Garrett's arrival. A quick beer over yard work perhaps, but that was about it.

Elizabeth hadn't spent any real time with Janie for several months when she had last gone to the see the lunch show, which starred Garrett in his high chair, a large painting tarp and their old black pug Buster on clean up. It saddened her to realize how fast that time had gone.

With dinner on the way and the crib construction in hand, she made a cup of tea and took it out to the girls—as she called the koi who were not all girls—along with a handful of diced tofu, their favorite food.

She stood at the edge of the pond and dropped a few cubes in. The fish rushed over, including senior citizen Goldie, a huge golden metallic butterfly koi who usually just floated along. Princess Keiko, the leader of the group, a large black, white and red beauty, floated to the surface and made kissing sounds. Elizabeth knelt down and patted her gently on the head, as she knew the Princess enjoyed the contact.

How are you, Princess? she asked. The fish were harder for her to talk to than the cats, although there were similarities, oddly enough. Most of the fish didn't bother to talk to her, so Keiko was their spokesfish.

Well. We are well.

Sometimes Keiko used the royal 'we', so Elizabeth wanted to clarify. *How is everyone else? Anything I should know about?*

A monster came, she said and sent a picture of a raccoon, a large one, hands in the pond to the armpits, fishing around.

What happened? Tig had made the pond four feet deep so predators couldn't get in. Most of the fish were so big they were safe from removal, but an injury was always possible.

A wound. Keiko showed her Goldie with a long scratch.

Thank you. No wonder Goldie was following the pack. *Can you ask her to come to the surface for me, please?*

Keiko waited for more tofu and then slowly made her way to Goldie. They really were magnificent, Elizabeth thought. So beautiful. With her long fins, Goldie flapped her way to where Elizabeth sat at the edge of the pond.

Hi, Goldie. No response. She didn't really expect one. Most of the fish weren't talkers. *Can you show me where you're hurt?*

Goldie slowly rolled away and her light golden stomach had a long scratch with several scales missing. The scratch was not deep, looked clean and was healing.

Hurt? Elizabeth asked and gently mentally probed, feeling for pain.

The response was negative. It had hurt when it happened, but that was two nights ago. She felt guilty for not knowing about it. The scratch was on her stomach, so it was reasonable to assume neither she nor Tig would have seen it on their daily inspections. She dropped in a few more tofu cubes just for Goldie, figuring she'd need the calories at her age to help heal. She threw more cubes farther out and the herd went for them, circling and hoovering up the sinking blobs. When they stopped cleaning up, she decided they were full. The rest of the fish looked fine and ignored her, swimming in small circles, grinding every root off the taro and water hyacinth floating salad bar Tig had built. It was a world of its own with birds and frogs landing, making homes, and having snacks.

Elizabeth went inside to wash her hands and decided to make garlic bread. She set the table and got the chili condiments out: shredded cheese, chopped onion, sour cream and diced avocado. The chili smelled divine baking in the crock. She prepped the bread and stepped to the nursery doorway.

A nearly completed crib greeted her. "Wow! You guys are incredible! So fast."

They beamed with pride. "It wasn't going to beat us," Tig said.

"Once we deciphered that stupid set of instructions, it made sense, but man, it was like the *Da Vinci Code* for a while," Karl added.

"I came to see what time the chili would be done. I want to put some garlic bread in."

Tig glanced at his watch. "Now would be good. It's beer o'clock."

"You got it." She got them each a beer and returned to put the bread in the oven with the crock. She was suddenly so hungry she didn't know if she'd make the extra few minutes it took for it to warm. She set the timer for fifteen minutes, all she could manage. She refreshed kibbles and water, gave each cat a 'butt-combing' as they liked to call it with a fine-toothed comb that tickled their skin and cleaned their fur to shiny silk. The timer dinged. She washed her hands again and took out the bread.

At the nursery doorway she had an interesting sight. The crib was complete and reigned in the corner; a little Winnie-the-Pooh mobile drifted lazily overhead. That was new. Pooh was Tig's and her favorite cartoon as kids. His nickname was a derivative of Tigger, and they had planned to do the nursery that way, but they hadn't bought anything yet. He must have gotten it to surprise her. When on earth did he have the time?

Even more fun was seeing Tig rocking in the chair, Edward cradled in his arms. Karl lay on the floor, head resting on a folded baby blanket, both chatting away like this was the most natural thing. She smiled. She was so lucky.

"Dinner's ready." She returned to the kitchen and got glasses of water for the table and listened to them get up and move around like old men. Not that she was criticizing. She wouldn't have been able to get down on the floor, or back up again, she was sure. She looked down and her protruding belly now covered her feet. Great.

Fourteen

Crack chili dinner was a rousing success. But not for cats, who did not like chili. Freya scored on the toast-like garlic bread but she was not a fan of the garlic flavor and quit after one snippet, giving Elizabeth a look of disgust and disappointment.

After everyone finally slowed down enough to chat, Elizabeth asked about the salvage project at Karl's house fire.

"Pretty good," Tig said.

"Better than I thought," added Karl.

"A bunch of my clothes and some stuff in a closet only have smoke damage. I was going to take them to the laundromat and see if I can get the smell out."

"Nonsense. We have a great washer and I put Tig's stuff in there all the time. Give it a try, at least. Easier than sitting at the laundromat for hours or driving back and forth." Elizabeth had given up after one bowl of delicious chili, but still picked at the garlic bread. She was stuffed, but it was so enticing, she kept at it.

"Thanks." Karl scraped the bottom of his bowl and finally sat back. "So good."

Tig got them second beers. "We also found some of his paperwork and stuff in a box. I'm pretty sure the smell won't ever come out, but he can at least request new copies of records and order new versions of things. Keeping all his receipts, of course." He smiled at Elizabeth since they'd shared the 'tax receipts' conversation.

"That's great." Elizabeth drank her water. "You'll probably have to buy new shoes, too." He had only the one pair he'd thrown on in the middle of the night, and they didn't look in very good shape. "I don't think you can clean the smoke out of those. Hardly worth the time and expense."

"We didn't find his laptop," Tig said. "It wasn't in his car, and we didn't find it in the rubble. There's no place else it could be since Stacy's out of town."

"Yeah," Karl said slowly. "It was a little odd. We couldn't find anything from my computer station."

Tig's phone rang. While he took the call in another room, Elizabeth and Karl began to clear up. With her relatively easy end to the day, she felt pretty good. Still couldn't see her feet, however. She noted she had to stand farther back from the counter now. She ladled leftover chili into a container while Karl loaded the dishwasher.

"Interesting." Tig came back into the kitchen. "Initial fire report says arson."

Elizabeth and Karl stopped their tasks. "*Arson?* Do they think it's like an insurance fraud thing?" Elizabeth asked.

"They haven't gotten that far into the investigation. It was a pretty good set up, though. The electrical panel on the back of the unit was fiddled with and it was set to burn so it wouldn't be noticed from the street. We have a new investigation member, a youngish guy who just came back from a conference on alternate ignition sources and caught it. It was a good fix."

Elizabeth caught a look between Tig and Karl she couldn't interpret. "What?" she asked. They didn't say anything. "What?" she asked again.

"The location of the outside panel is on the other side of Karl's bed. The panel had a sophisticated timer set to go off in the wee hours when everyone would be asleep. If it was just for insurance, it could have been set for anytime, and probably from several places around the unit. Appliances are great for rigging, besides causing a lot of accidental fires. Kitchens are the best. But this was by his bed. It seems intentional; someone wanted to harm Karl."

"But why?" Elizabeth asked. "I mean, maybe they didn't know his bed was behind that wall. You'd have to know the layout of the unit, right? And if someone just wanted to set the place to burn, an exterior panel would be the easiest to rig." She continued putting items in the refrigerator.

Tig sat back down at the table. "Another point, if it was an insurance burn, that little unit wouldn't bring in much. They'd be better off burning the main house. The two structures were really too far apart for the fire to jump from one to the other in a neighborhood without being seen. I think someone was targeting Karl."

Karl had joined him at the table and ran a hand through his hair. He'd been quiet while Tig and Elizabeth discussed the issue. Elizabeth started the dishwasher. As she came to the table, she saw his pinched, white face. He looked very young right now.

"Karl?" she asked. "What do you think?"

"I, I don't know."

She thought he was holding something back. "Why would someone want to hurt you?"

He blew out a breath. "It could be Stacy's ex," he said at last.

That was a surprise.

"I don't know, but he's one reason she went back to see her folks. He'd been coming around, making threats. They'd broken up way before she and I got together, but apparently he thought they would get back together. She told me about him. He was pretty unstable and angry. He decided she was flirting with some guy one night at the Corner Bar, you know the place by the bay? Kind of run down and seedy?" They both nodded. "I think maybe she said thank you or something when he picked up her coat when it fell off the back of her chair. Her ex flipped and put the guy in the hospital. She broke up with him after that."

"So, he's been coming around again?" Elizabeth clarified.

"Yeah, he's been texting and emailing her. She left to be with her folks and decide what to do. She didn't want to try and get a restraining order or anything, but she may have to. I saw him waiting for me on campus one day. I headed the other direction, but I've seen him around too often for it to be a coincidence."

"Would he know how to rig a panel? Elizabeth asked.

"From You Tube," Tig said. "He may not be super smart, but you can Google anything. Or he may have friends in low places who'd help him out."

"Look, you guys, I appreciate everything you're doing, but this may be all for nothing," Karl said. "If it is him, maybe I shouldn't be here in case he follows me. I don't want you two in danger."

Tig and Elizabeth shook their heads. "You don't have anyone else right now," she said. "You're staying put for the time being."

Karl smiled. "The flip side is the initial report is mistaken and the fire was an accident. There are so many little units and garage apartments in this town that are not up to any code, it's a wonder more things don't burn down more often." Tig nodded his agreement. He would know.

"I'm ready to crash," Tig said. "Let's not jump to conclusions. Either it's an accident and the report is wrong, however unlikely, or it's intentional and we don't know why." At Elizabeth's questioning look he added, "We don't. We're speculating it's the ex. It could still be a poorly executed insurance scam or another as yet unknown motive."

Karl stood. "I'm ready to crash, too. Is it okay if I start some laundry now? Will it bother you guys back there? I'm running out of clothes."

"No, you're fine. I think everything's cleaned up here. Help yourself. Also, feel free to grab food anytime you want, okay?" Elizabeth reminded him.

"Thanks." Karl shuffled tiredly to the front porch where a rustling sound indicated he was sorting clothes from a plastic bag. Elizabeth was grateful the smoky garments had stayed outside until they could be laundered.

Tig carried Edward back, and Elizabeth had Freya. Teddy swayed to the bedroom, his tummy gently swinging to and fro, his tail in a question mark. Elizabeth watched him enter the room from her perch on the bed and thought again what a sweet cat he was. She patted the bed although he needed no encouragement to jump up.

Elizabeth brushed her teeth and returned to bed seeing it was later than she thought. They'd spent more time at dinner, talking and then cleaning up than she'd realized. Tig was already tucked in, Edward by his side, Teddy in the middle at the bottom and Freya on her pillow. Elizabeth walked around the bed to kiss Tig goodnight because meeting in the middle for a goodnight kiss was out of the question.

It wasn't 'til she was lying on her own side, warm and cozy and drifting off that she realized the neat distraction job Karl had introduced when Tig suggested the fire might have been set with another motive entirely. He hadn't acknowledged that as a possibility. She had no idea what that could be, but her curiosity was piqued, and she remembered again how his schedule did not align with what he said. Her last thought before sleep: sometimes she thought too much.

fifteen

Morning was drizzly. A heavy mist blanketed the trees and made it look like an English moor—in her mind and in the movies, because she'd never seen an English moor in her life. The house was silent. Everyone was still in bed. Normally they'd all be up by now, but with the weather clamping a lid on the town, with warm bedclothes and covered in cats, both she and Tig had stayed abed.

The clock said get up, but she let herself drift back to sleep for a bit. *Mom. Mom. Mom!* Teddy's soft voice was insistent. She awoke to find him staring an inch from her face. *Open the door.*

Oh! Of course. Poor kitties. With Karl staying there they'd been sleeping with their door closed, and the cats couldn't get out to the night litter box. Teddy must be bursting for him to wake her. She was surprised to see it was going on 9 AM. Tig still slept on beside her. He'd been working so hard and now he was taking care of Karl, too.

Karl. She got up and opened the door. The kitties sauntered out, and she followed, tying her robe closed. The house was still quiet, but she needed some tea and think time.

Water on to boil, she began a pot of coffee. Karl's door was still closed so she assumed he was in there. She checked the street in front of the house. No Karl car. Maybe he was gone. She went to the laundry room and his clothes had been removed from the dryer. She refilled kibbles and water and opened the back door. The cats had made a beeline for the pet door, since they much preferred the great outdoors to the litter box. That was only for emergencies. And babies, if you asked Teddy.

With the back door open it was chilly, but everyone wanted back in, and she shut it after they'd taken their sweet time about it. Teddy even had the nerve to sniff the door jamb. She was getting a little frustrated before he looked up at her with his lovely yellow-green eyes and smiled. Her heart melted and she picked him up, which he mostly hated. "That's what you get." She hugged him close and he didn't resist.

Tig wandered in as the coffee finished brewing. She got out cream and sugar as he poured his first cup and sat looking semi-stunned at the table. Usually he was an up and at 'em morning guy, and she was the slug.

She kissed him hello. "Morning." She brought her tea to the table. "Want toast or anything?" she asked.

"Not yet. This is good." He sipped and sighed. "I have training today." Some days he had to put in extra hours for special training. He got paid for it, so it was all good, but it threw the schedule out of whack.

"What are you learning today?"

"Not learning. Teaching." He sighed again. He had been getting more training gigs and those were helpful financially, although stressful for him. He had been sent to several specialty trainings, wildfire fighting, urban special training and some others. He was then expected to train the rest of the crew. Today, it didn't seem as though he'd prepared for it, so she hoped he was ready.

"Anything I can do to help?" was her roundabout way of asking if he'd copied handouts.

He focused on her. "I know what you're doing." He smiled. "Yes, I prepped. I just haven't thought about it for a week. I don't have to start until noon, so I have some time to review the materials. He took another life-giving sip.

"It's almost ten already. How about some breakfast? Is lunch part of the training, or are you expected to eat before?"

"Before. We go until three and then take a break and then go to six." His shift was 7PM to 7AM so he'd stay at the station tonight. She resisted her own sigh. They'd had a pretty nice couple of days together, considering.

She bustled about making a large brunch. He used a lot of calories, and today promised to be busy for him. In no time he was changing and gathering his gear, racing out the door. The house was too quiet after he left. Where was Karl?

The cats had wandered back out and then in again. They found her once more in the nursery.

Maybe she'd buy some baby bedding today. Since Tig had gotten the mobile, the Winnie-the-Pooh theme was set. She felt she could buy more. And maybe some official maternity clothes. She had one secret outfit she'd bought long before she was pregnant. When they were just talking 'someday.' She'd not told Tig, just hidden it in her closet. She felt silly and unable rationally to explain her need to have such garments. Now she was happy she'd let herself do it. It looked like she'd need them to get to the store to buy more with her quickly expanding middle.

Elizabeth was not a fan of clothes shopping. Tools, toys, odd items, yes, but clothes, not so much. She was a jeans and tees person mostly, so she didn't see a need to buy a ton of exactly the same. She did have a fondness for interesting logos on her tees. That was totally different. However, she was excited about maternity wear, so she dragged out her 'secret' outfit, a black and white patterned short sleeved top with a flair where the bump was. She paired it with black maternity leggings, although she didn't need the elastic panel to stretch as far as it could. Yet. She found some black flats in the back of her closet with all three cats' help. She usually wore sports shoes, and grubby ones at that, but she felt like dressing up a bit. It also helped that the flats did not need her to bend over, or see, to slip her feet into them, since now she could not see over her bump without some effort. She tested how far she'd have to bend to view her shiny shoes and felt a distinct kick to the kidney. She envisioned a tiny foot rebelling against the floating house shifting and smiled.

She kissed each cat on the head and checked to make sure they would not expire due to hunger or thirst in the couple hours she would be gone. She grabbed a light sweater, her phone and purse and waved good-bye to three sad faces whose expressions would fit in a Dickensian workhouse.

Twenty minutes later she was happily rummaging in Target's maternity section. Until her recent pregnancy, she hadn't realized the department was there.

One reason she disliked clothes shopping so much was trying everything on. At times she just bought things and took them home, returning what didn't work. She had become pretty adept at style and size guesstimation. Today, she figured since most items would be rather large on her until the third trimester, she delighted in throwing tops and pants in her cart based on color and their seemingly random size chart.

Where she lost enthusiasm was the nursing and maternity bras. She knew she'd have to try some on, but that did not appeal in the slightest. She bribed herself to try one on by promising herself an in-store Starbuck's treat. She laughed to think how close to 'son' Teddy she was in terms of food.

Mission accomplished, she checked out and headed to the cafe. She was more tired than she'd thought. A cup of herbal tea and a chocolate treat would help get her home. She still had her clothing in the giant red cart and pushed it to one of two open tables near the window. She chose the corner and made a little den with the cart.

It had also been overcast in Tolosa when she'd arrived, but now the sun was shining and she people-watched as she sipped her tea. Her brownie tasted delicious, and she tried not to inhale it in two bites, all the while hearing her doctor's words in her head about nutrition. She sighed. Really, though, when had she done this last? Not forever, she rationalized. Her feet ached. She hadn't been on them this much for several weeks. Ever since the bump got so unwieldy so fast.

Her inner musing was cut off by a conversation at the next table. She'd been admiring her swollen ankles, head down and hadn't seen who sat there. She knew the voice. Karl sat with his back to her, and she bet he wouldn't recognize her, head down behind a giant shopping cart and far from her natural environment.

He had packages in his own giant red cart, so perhaps he'd been replacing his smoke damaged items. She didn't know the man who sat opposite him. Forties, silver hair, looked tall, thin, with a strong face. She used Karl's head to block so she could eavesdrop.

They spoke quietly, but the tables were close together. Other than this twist of fate, it would have been a relatively anonymous and private place to meet.

"I'm worried," Karl said. "I'm doing my assignment, but it didn't go as planned. Someone burned down my house!" His voice rose at the end.

What assignment? School? Maybe this was his advisor? Weird not to meet on campus.

"Just stick to it. We're watching. We're not sure how they twigged you, but we think they followed the IP address. Did you ever work from home?"

Karl lowered his head. "Maybe. Once. I don't know."

"You were warned about that. All work was to be done on site or from the lab."

Elizabeth tried to get a glimpse of the man, but saw only his profile looking out over the cafe. It sounded like they were talking about school assignments. She didn't really know what Karl was studying.

"What do I do?" Karl sipped from what was clearly a cold coffee by now. "I told my girlfriend to stay at her parents for a few more days, but I'm staying with this couple. They're super nice, my boss, actually, but are they in danger?"

Were they in danger? Elizabeth willed the man to say something encouraging.

"The safe house is not available. We'd have to move you out of town and it's not feasible with the project at this stage."

"What do I do?" Karl repeated. His voice shook, and he sounded so young.

"We'll put a watch on the house," the man said. "Have you noticed anything there?" Karl shook his head, no. "The fire failed if they were after you. Have you been followed?" Another head shake. "Anything at the rescue center?"

"I don't think so," Karl said. "I haven't been back in a few days. I did what I was supposed to with their computers, and everything else was remote. I haven't needed to go back."

What the heck was Karl up to? What rescue center? The Wildlife Rescue Center where he'd been 'interning'? He claimed to be doing data entry. Clearly more was going on.

"Did you move the money or not?" the man asked impatiently.

"Yes. It was easy. It's in the account, just like you said."

"And you tweaked the data so the difference disappeared?"

"Yes." Karl sounded impatient now, too.

Elizabeth's heart sank. Karl was doing something that sounded illegal. No wonder someone was after him. What kind of money were they talking about?

"I need you to move another chunk tomorrow. It needs to go sideways and disappear."

Karl sighed. "How much?"

"A grant is coming through and it needs to get diverted. A hundred."

"How much longer do I have to do this?"

"Until you've paid back our investment. It's too late to get out of it. Not if you want our help."

"Fine. But leave the Murphys out of it."

"I said we'd help. You do your job and everything will be fine."

"Except for the arson."

"That was unfortunate. We'll handle it."

"Where am I supposed to go?"

"We'll work on it. In the meantime, stay put. We can watch you all if you're in one spot."

Somehow that sounded more sinister than reassuring to Elizabeth. She was getting stiff sitting there, but she was trapped at the far table until they left.

"Fine." Karl grumbled. "I can't wait 'til this is over. I didn't know what I was getting into."

"You knew. Do what you're told and it'll be over soon. Now wait five minutes." The man got up and strode out the automatic doors.

Elizabeth's heart sank for Karl. Five minutes felt like an eternity because now she had to get rid of the huge cup of tea, and the anxiety of the meeting only made it worse. Karl finally left the store too, head down, dejectedly pushing his cart of replacement items. He pushed his wares outside right past her seat at the window.

She would never make it home so she stopped in the ladies' room. What was happening? She had to tell Tig, but would he confront Karl and maybe make it worse? If someone was after them, and someone at this guy's end was 'protecting' them, whatever that meant . . . she didn't feel safe.

She loaded her car and started home. Her ever-growing stomach made her feel vulnerable. Was this a mob thing? Was there a mob in Tolosa? There was the incident with the Yakuza, but surely, that was a one-time thing. What were the odds of another mob?

Suddenly she wanted to be home with the cats, washing maternity clothes and putting linens on the crib. Linens! She forgot to get Winnie-the-

Pooh sheets. She sure wasn't going back since she was half way home.

She pulled into the drive. Great. Karl was here. Why? She still cared for him, but right now she wanted to be alone in her own house.

She grabbed her parcels and dragged herself inside. So tired. Karl was on his way out. He had a laptop with him. Was it *the* laptop with secret files or whatever? She thought he said he hadn't found it. Either that had changed, or he'd lied about it, too. She was hungry and tired.

Karl flew out with a, "See you later!" Irrationally cheery, given the conversation she'd overheard.

"See ya." Hers was less cheery. She made sure the doors were locked.

She fixed herself a tuna sandwich and didn't argue with the cats about their share. Back it the bedroom, she flopped down, kicking off her shiny flats. *Naptime.*

Sixteen

Elizabeth awoke feeling much better. A little sorry she'd been so short with Karl, but really! What had he gotten them into? Freya napped on her pillow. Edward stretched out in Tig's spot, and Teddy lay upside down on the carpet, arms stretched, eyes closed wearing a happy smile. Occasional paw twitches and chewing motions made her think he was eating mice heads in his dreams. *Ew.*

She remembered Tig was training all day and then had his regular shift. She really wanted to talk to him about the conversation she'd heard, but didn't feel right about dumping it on him over the phone when he couldn't get home for a whole day. Maybe Karl would be home tonight? She didn't know if that made her feel better or not. If he was a target, not. But if 'security' came with Karl, even undercover, maybe that was good.

Edward's tummy needed a rub. It soothed her to feel his soft black fur with just a few white hairs. Freya moved from the pillow to snuggle close to Elizabeth. Elizabeth pulled her under her chin so she could give her kisses. She heard the tiny mouse purr and was soothed.

All this pondering wasn't helping, so she got up and dragged her purchases to the laundry room. She put on a kettle and began removing the tags so she could wash her things. What to do about dinner? She still wasn't very hungry, but at least she wasn't nauseated anymore. She didn't know if it was due to time passing or to Freya's constant curing of her nausea. Either way she was grateful.

She decided to make a pot of marinara sauce. Easy enough. She felt sorry for Karl, and made enough for him, too. She made about a gallon, figuring he could have it or she'd freeze it. Salad and garlic bread. Always comfort food. She sautéed onions and garlic and dumped in crushed tomatoes, fresh basil from the pot growing by the back door and a splash of red wine. The alcohol would cook off and it made it taste so rich.

While the sauce simmered and her clothes washed, she went into the baby's room. She opened the dresser drawers, thinking to put her spare maternity items there, and found packages of sheets, a few soft blankets and towels, along with many items needed for a baby diaper changing station. Tig must have been on Google. He probably would not have gotten a wipes-warmer without some help. Her eyes teared up at his thoughtfulness. And stealth. While she'd been whining about not feeling well, not only had he been working two jobs, but he'd taken the time to figure out a nursery set up and git 'er done, as they said.

After unpacking all the linens, she took them to the washer. Her clothes washing cycle was done and she threw that in the dryer and then started a new washer load. She couldn't wait to make up the tiny crib. She also washed a couple little plush animals she'd found. A Winnie of course, and a Tigger.

The sauce smelled divine. She found she was a bit hungry and set some water to boil for pasta. She ate a small bowl of salad to tide her over. Since she was on her own for dinner, she could eat in stages, standing up if she liked. The cats stationed themselves in the kitchen, the center of the universe.

"It's not a meat sauce," she explained.

Cats needed proof so she put a drop in front of each of them on the tile. Teddy was disgusted and disappointed as usual, with her thoughtlessness. Edward found a piece of spaghetti noodle with his sauce and batted it around. He was so cute she didn't mind the slight mess the trail of sauce made. Freya ignored the sauce, but Elizabeth knew what she waited for. She had made a piece of garlic bread without garlic for Freya. Just buttered toast. She broke off a piece and gave it to her.

"Sorry, Teddy," she told him.

You are not.

I'm a little sorry. I can't make a special meal for you right now.

Maybe tuna juice?

Maybe. But later.

Humph.

She went down to the mailbox at the street to check for any security. Or the bad guys. She wasn't sure she'd know the difference. Half a block away, a black SUV parked in front of the neighbor's empty second lot. No one she knew on their street had a black SUV. Maybe someone had a guest. Or they *were* being watched. By good guys or bad guys? Or maybe she watched too much NetFilms. The mail was unexciting and she made sure she locked the front door when she came back. Usually they only locked the front door at night or when they left the house. Now that she was alone, she would make sure it was locked all the time.

The front door rattled and she froze. Someone was trying to get in. The pasta water began to boil over. She knew she locked the door, but she needed to check. The water spilled onto the stove. She turned the burner off and crept to the front window by the door. She couldn't see the SUV from here, but what if someone were trying to break in? The door rattled again and swung open. She about had a heart attack and her pulse raced.

Frozen, she couldn't move and couldn't defend herself. Karl stepped in and she was relieved she hadn't thought to get a weapon. That could have ended badly.

"Oh, hey Elizabeth." He got a good look at her. "Are you okay?"

She nodded and began to breathe again. The baby gave her a good kick for that. She gasped. It wasn't very big but it packed a punch.

"Here, sit down." Karl guided her to a kitchen chair. "What happened?"

She shook with released adrenaline. "Water, please."

"Sure. Of course." He brought her a glass. "Want me to drain this?" He indicated the pasta. She nodded.

She felt weak and helpless. Not a good or familiar feeling. Freya had long finished her toast and now climbed up Elizabeth's pant leg. The tiny claws were sharp and grounded her. Elizabeth thought that was the point. The dryer buzzed, loud and long and startled her. She gasped again. *I'm a mess.* Freya settled in her lap.

"What's going on? Are you hurt?" Karl pressed. She must look as bad as she felt.

"I made dinner." Her thoughts were disjointed, but she tried to make sense. Maybe she needed some food. The tuna sandwich had been a long time ago.

"Okay. Do you want to eat something?" She nodded. "Can I help?" She nodded again. The adrenaline drained. She felt it pass through the baby and sensed its discomfort. Freya began her work, soothing and comforting. Elizabeth knew she was doing something for the baby, but wasn't sure what. Freya also did something for her. She felt calmer and safer, and she felt the baby settle from its earlier erratic movements.

What are you doing? she asked Freya.

Helping baby. You scared it, and I am removing the fear.

Elizabeth could tell the hunger-weakness feeling was lessening for both of them and was grateful.

*Baby sleep now. All better when it wakes.
You eat. You better.*

Why are you talking like that?

Like what?

Like a bad western? Only a questioning
sensation. *Skipping words. I don't know. It sounds
funny.*

*It's how I talk to baby. I forget sometimes to
use all the words. You know what I mean, so what's
the difference?*

*You didn't talk like that in your world. You
talked like a person.*

I am *a person. Here, I am in a tiny, furry
body, incapable of many things I used to do. It is
necessary but annoying.*

Why are *you here? You said to help me or
the baby. From what? With what?*

*There are things in the world older than you
know.*

*I'm sure there are. What does that have to
do with me?*

My home is in danger.

*You said that. From what? What are you
doing about it?*

*My land endures. But perhaps not the way it
was meant to. The way it should. The way it needs
to.*

"Hey, what's going on?" Karl held a plate of
pasta and sauce and looked from her to the various
cats. "Are you doing it again? Talking to them?"

Elizabeth nodded.

"You look really serious. Are you okay?
Are the cats okay? Is one of them sick?"

152

"No. They're fine. I just need to eat."

"Uh huh." He put the plate down in front of her. "What else do I need to get?"

"Make a plate for yourself. I made enough for you, too."

"That was nice of you." He looked genuinely pleased.

Freya still lounged in her lap, even thought there was considerably less lap for her. Either she was growing or Elizabeth was.

"Salad's in the refrigerator and garlic bread is warming in the oven. Can you pull them out, please?" She gulped her water. "And more water, too?"

He complied and joined her at the table. He started to eat and she got a few bites before she decided she couldn't wait. Mob or not, she had to know what was going on.

Seventeen

Elizabeth felt better after a few bites of homemade food. She dropped the occasional noodle for Edward, and Freya received bits of buttered toast while lounging in her lap. The roles were reversed now that she had stopped shaking. Freya had done her job of soothing her and the baby, and now Elizabeth was feeding and cuddling her while feeding herself. Not the best table manners, but sometimes feeling good won out over etiquette. Karl also looked better with a meal in him.

"Grab a beer," Elizabeth said. She was not above bribery herself and maybe a beer would help him relax. And tell her what she wanted to know. How to begin? Just jump in with her nosiness and spying? Might as well. If he thought she knew more than she did, maybe he'd be more forthcoming.

"I wanted to talk to you about something," she began. Smooth.

Karl uncapped the top on his beer and took a swig. "Okay. What's up?"

"I'm not sure where to start, so I'll just jump in. I need help making sense of some things that happened." She watched the muscles on his face tense, although he took another bite and kept up a good front. He nodded.

"It started small, you know, not a big deal, but I saw you a couple times at the Wildlife Rescue Center when you said you were in class, or couldn't help Tig." She saw his expression harden the tiniest bit. "I know, you said you were interning there for a business class, but why didn't you just tell Tig that instead of ly—misleading him?" He put his fork down. "Then the fire happened. The report says arson, and I agree. I overheard you talking a couple times and I think there's more going on. You told Stacy not to come home for a while. You feel you're in danger. Why?"

He ducked his head, but she thought it was a delaying tactic, not that he was ashamed. Something in his face shifted, and she wasn't looking at the same Karl she'd known for three years. She wanted him to make sense of this for her, but she also wanted him to commit to either another lie, or come clean. She was afraid which one it would be.

"It's true. I've been working at the Rescue Center for a class. I did some data entry for them, but it was only a couple days. I'm back on campus for the most part. The fire was probably Stacy's ex. That's still under investigation. It could have been the homeowner or an unclarified accident."

He was very smooth. Although she'd heard this before, he sounded as if he were testing her as he spoke, waiting to see if she accepted what he said.

She didn't. "That's all great, but I have new information. You're in some kind of trouble. Are you working for the mob?"

He froze. Then he burst out laughing. "You're kidding, right?" He kept chuckling so she didn't answer.

Finally she said, "I'm worried about you. I know something's going on. What is it?"

"I'm fine. Really. There's no mob here." He took another swig from his beer.

"Okay then. What was the meeting you had with that guy?"

"What guy?"

"In Target! You were scared, I could tell. Okay, at least worried."

A series of minute expressions shifted across his face so fast she didn't have time to process them. "My advisor? Tall guy, silver hair?" She nodded. "He's my degree advisor. I've been trying to take more credits than he recommends, and get in those intern hours, but he's worried I'm overdoing it. Now with the fire, he's concerned I won't be able to finish the semester properly."

"He wanted you to move something. A hundred something. You didn't want to do it. What's really going on?"

Karl couldn't hide his surprise. "It's for the class. I have to do bookkeeping, and they set up a false audit on a fictional account. Each of us in the class has a company we do fake bookkeeping for, and each week they give us a problem to solve, like a real world problem. It's a huge part of our grade. I wasn't able to do the earlier assignment because of the fire. I haven't been able to find the flash drive with the project info on it, and he was giving me a bit of a hard time about responsibility. But he knew the fire wasn't my fault so he's cutting me some slack and giving me another chance to turn in the work. He's a good guy."

Elizabeth pondered this. It sounded right. She wasn't a student a top university like Karl. He'd been at the community college up 'til this year and he'd had an opportunity, a grant she thought, to change schools. Now he was at Tolosa Poly Tech, one of the top schools in the country. No wonder he was worried. Poor guy. She felt a little bad about grilling him.

"We okay?" he asked.

She nodded. "Eat as much as you want. I'm pretty full. Not as much room in here as there used to be." She struggled to her feet and cleared her plate.

"I'll clean up. You can lie down or whatever." He rose and began to rinse plates and cutlery and put them in the dishwasher.

"Let the sauce cool. I'll put it away later," she told him.

"Sure. I have to study at the campus library, okay Mom?" he said good naturedly.

Oh, boy. She deserved that. "Stop it. I'm sorry. I was just worried."

"I know and I appreciate it. Thank you for letting me stay here. It should only be a few more days."

"When Stacy comes home?" she asked sharply. She just remembered the part of the conversation where he said he'd told his girlfriend to stay at her parents to keep her safe. Now she didn't feel so silly.

"Yeah, next week maybe. She's been enjoying her time with her mom especially. She doesn't get home much so this has been nice."

He sounded so sincere! She'd had no idea what a great liar he was.

She waited until he left to come out of her room again. She turned on the porch light and began to shut the front blinds. His car started and he drove past the house to the corner. As she closed the second blind, a black SUV slowly followed in his wake, far behind him. She'd forgotten that, too. A tail or his security detail? What a great detective she was. Couldn't break a college kid and forgot half the questions.

She needed Tig. Tomorrow they would tackle Karl together. If they were in danger, he really couldn't stay here. Could she throw him out? Maybe they should call the police. Whatever he was into, it seemed he couldn't handle it alone. *Advisor, my Aunt Fanny.* She wondered who the man really was. A criminal getting Karl to do criminal things for him? Or his mob? She didn't believe for a second there was no mob.

Sleep was a long time in coming. She and the cats all watched NetFilms. The baby and kitties slept through it all, but she couldn't concentrate on the plots as her own drama swirled in her head.

Eighteen

Since she had fallen asleep late, she slept past Tig's arrival home. He let her sleep in, but opened the bedroom door at some point and let the kitties out. She felt groggy and crabby and unrested. Washing her face revealed a blotchy, creased face that resembled a pumpkin. She turned sideways in the mirror and gasped. She was huge. Maybe the baby was twins. What else could explain her rapid growth? She was afraid to step on the scale, but did anyway. Sure enough, she weighed significantly more than her allowance dictated. Maybe she should go to the doctor again. It hadn't even been a week. She was overreacting. She was upset and hadn't had enough sleep. That was it.

She wrapped her fuzzy robe around her and went to find Tig. He sat at the table with a cup of coffee and Edward draped across his lap. He had the *Tolosa Herald* spread in front of him.

"Morning." She kissed him and put on the kettle.

"Morning. You okay?"

"Didn't sleep. Don't feel so hot. We have to talk."

"Uh oh. That doesn't sound good."

"It's not." She was too cranky to sugar-coat it. "It's about Karl."

"Better than about me." He tried to lighten the mood, but she wasn't having any.

She put a couple pieces of bread in the toaster and magically, Freya appeared like a little shadow. Teddy strolled out of the laundry room, licking his lips.

"What's happened? He's only here a few more days. Did he do something?"

"You could say that." Her toast popped and she buttered it, bringing it to the table. She sat and lifted Freya into her lap. She tried to figure out where to start. The Rescue Center, she decided. "This may not seem like anything, but I've been thinking something's going on, and Karl might be in trouble," she began. She repeated the bits he already knew about Karl's supposed internship and took Tig all the way through the Target cafe and the black SUV the previous night.

Fortunately he didn't stop her to ask questions. She might have bitten his head off. She was not usually this cranky. Perhaps a call to the doctor's office might be in order. She could talk to the physician's assistant and maybe get some advice. Later.

"Are you sure you heard what you think you did at Target?"

"Yes."

160

"And are you sure your interpretation is the correct one? Karl's explanation isn't true?"

She thought carefully. "No, I guess I'm not sure. I know it sounds far-fetched, but there are a lot of loose ends. What about the SUV? The advisor-guy said he'd put a security detail on him. On us! Why would he do that if there was no danger or nothing to worry about? If it was a fictional business for a class? It's not a fictional SUV."

Tig spoke carefully. "Is it possible, the SUV had nothing to do with Karl, and it was on the street for another reason?"

She scrubbed her face with her hands. "I guess. Now with you, during the day, I'm confused. I thought I'd tell you and we'd confront him together."

"When he gets up, we'll ask him, okay? And if he seems credible, we'll let it go. All right?"

"Yes." Tig kissed her. "Are you going to sleep now?" she asked.

"No. We only had two medical calls last night and they were early, so we all had a pretty good rest."

"That makes one of us," she grumbled.

He laughed. "I'll do some watering until Karl gets up. After we talk to him I have a consult and a parts run for a new job."

"Okay." She didn't want him to worry about her, so she kept the phone call to the doctor quiet. How could he not see she was huge?

She had left a message at the doctor's office. The PA would get back to her. It wasn't an emergency so she had to be satisfied with that.

She caved in to her exhaustion and went back to lie down. Freya was already on her pillow so she must have known. The boys were out supervising Tig.

She lay on her left side, the way the doctor told her to start sleeping, and put her hand next to Freya, touching, but not on her body. Immediately there was a connection and she was propelled to the same icy barren village. Only this time, people teemed from the huts to the beach, getting ready for something. From the energy, it didn't seem good.

The woman she knew as Freya raced from a hut toward the beach, but veered toward her when Elizabeth appeared. Elizabeth was relieved no one else could see her.

"What are you doing here?" Freya panted. The implied *again*, was attached.

"I don't know. I didn't uh, bring myself here. We're asleep at home." Elizabeth didn't know how or why she'd been transported here. It felt real. It felt cold. She shivered.

Freya pulled a skin robe off a drying rack near a hut and threw it over Elizabeth's shoulders. Better.

"What's going on here, Freya? Is everything all right?"

"Everything is not all right. I told you my land was in danger, and it is. We are preparing for war."

"Why do you think I'm here? I didn't come here until I touched you, uh, the cat-you, and I— just" Elizabeth noticed she was not super pregnant. "What happened to the baby?" She started to panic. "Where's my baby?"

"It's fine. Only his soul is within you. You are not really here, the way I am not really with you in your world. Only my soul is. He resides fully within you as is proper."

"Oh. Okay. Am I safe here?"

Freya grabbed a long spear. "I have to go. It is not safe for you, I think. You should not stay."

"What? If I'm not really here, how am I in danger?"

Freya began backing toward the beach. Elizabeth noted many ships sailing, moving toward the shore through the narrow inlet.

"If my cat-body is eaten by a coyote, it is possible my soul would not be safe, as its house would be destroyed. I might not be able to jump home or into another house fast enough. The same for you. If you are damaged here, you might not be able to get home in time to survive."

"But, I'm me, here, too!" she yelled. "I'm not a cat!"

Freya began directing more men with spears. They spread out along the shore and headed up toward the low hills. Elizabeth's breath came in short bursts. She should go back to her body. Weird to think that. If what Freya said was true, she didn't want to die here. But she didn't want to leave yet. Everything about this place was strange, yet real. She felt the grainy beach under her feet.

The icy water lapped against the shore and smelled slightly of brine, making her think this little inlet led to the sea and was not part of a lake. Fjord! That was the word. So, where did these other warriors come from? She had not done the research she told herself she would, so why did she think it was a fjord? Perhaps the people and place fit with her long-ago studies on Vikings. It made more sense than Tig's guess about Egypt. Despite Freya's presence as a cat, she saw nothing resembling a desert or the Nile or anything that spoke of pyramids or mummies.

She hurried back up the beach to the long house and hid behind it. She would leave if things got too heated. *No one seems to be able to see me, so I should be safe for a while*, she thought.

What she hadn't planned on happened a few minutes later when the horde of screaming men leapt off their ships. Faster than she would have thought, they raced up the beach toward the houses. One threw a spear which came very close to her head as she was trying to figure out where else to hide until she could magic herself back home. She threw herself on the dirt, and stomping feet roared by. Now she knew what Freya meant. Even though they couldn't see her, and weren't aiming for her, she still might die here.

The smell and sound of a roaring fire stirred her to action. She was terrified to move and terrified not to. The long house she hid behind was on fire. What was with fire? she wondered. Karl's house, now this. . .

How far to the start of the spindly trees? The near trees had been cut to build homes, she guessed, making the tree line farther away. Could she get there unstomped on before another spear or rush of crazy warriors swept past? Her refuge was burning, and the heat would drive her away before the flames did.

Before she ran, she tried to see how Freya's forces were doing. Everyone looked the same, yelling fighting men and women dressed in similar furs, wielding similar spears, wooden shields, many with swords or battle axes. She couldn't tell who was who and many were splashed with blood. The smoke from the fire drifted lazily among the fighters and buildings, making it harder to see. She didn't see Freya, but occasionally heard the higher pitched yells of female fighters. Rather than run, she crept and dodged uphill, away from the water. Out of the smoke she saw a man strike down another and turn in her direction. She felt comfortable in her invisibility and looked for a way around him and up to the trees. Then she realized he was looking right at her. In her new pink maternity top with the word BABY and a downward arrow, polyester stretch pants and bedroom slippers, topped by the fur cape. His mouth gaped.

She had no idea how she was suddenly visible but took his frozen fear as a sign to get the heck out. She passed him far out of sword range, but heard him mutter something like, "volvo," as she passed. *That can't be right,* but she didn't have time to think. If one man could see her, perhaps many could.

Judging by the noises, the fight was moving away from the beach and up to where she wanted to go. She pushed further into the trees and felt safer. The smoke was less here, too. From the beach she had seen the tree line thinned the higher she went, so she tried to move laterally along the ridge.

The sound of many running feet was just behind her and she ducked behind a tree she wished were not quite so spindly. Her camo outfit of a hot pink tee stood out in this world of mostly grays. She hoped the fur cover was enough.

A group of bloody, armed fighters, both men and women, staggered by and she was relieved to see Freya bringing up the rear.

"Freya," she whisper-yelled.

Startled, Freya whirled, sword at the ready. She lowered her weapon in relief. "What are you still doing here? This is dangerous. You should be gone."

"I know. I got caught in the battle and tried to get away. Something weird happened. A guy could see me."

"Where?"

"I was hiding behind your meeting house trying to figure out the safest place when the other guys set it on fire. The smoke was so heavy I could barely see. I was trying to get to the trees and this guy, I don't know if he was theirs or yours, killed someone else and turned and saw me."

"Are you sure?"

"Oh yes. He acted like he saw a ghost."

"Dressed like that, I'm sure he did," Freya said.

"Can everyone see me now? Is it a time thing?"

"Time thing?"

"That I've been here so long that my invisibility is wearing off?"

"Where again was this?"

"Near the big hut. It was on fire and smoke filled the clearing. I couldn't stay there."

"Hmmm. Walk with me." Freya began walking up the steep hill which was quickly becoming a mountain to Elizabeth. The sounds of battle came both in front and behind them. Elizabeth did not like the thought of being trapped in the middle.

Bedroom slippers were not the best footwear for battle or a hike so Elizabeth had a rough time slithering uphill following Freya's sure stride.

"Oh. I know." Freya turned to face her and Elizabeth gratefully gasped huge breaths. What was the altitude here? A million? Where was here? A real place or just in Freya's head, however real it felt. A terrible smell drifted toward them. Blood. Lots of it.

"I have to get home," Elizabeth said.

"Yes. The warrior could see you because of the smoke."

"The smoke?"

"Yes. It allows spirits to be seen. We use smoke from night fires to see invading spirits, or sometimes our shamans use smoke to call forth a spirit or ancestor. We can see it if the smoke is dense enough. Here you are a spirit, and the smoke revealed your presence." She chuckled. "I don't know who saw you, but I would give a lot to hear his story later. If he lives." She turned and continued uphill.

"Hey, wait. I've got to get home. How do I do that?" Elizabeth scrambled after her, slippers sliding off at the steep incline.

They entered a small clearing devoid of smoke. The smell emanated from here. Many wounded lay dying, or moaning in pain, limbs deeply gashed or severed. The dead had been pushed to the side to make room for the newly injured. Elizabeth had never seen anything like this, not even in dreams. The noise of the wounded combined with the smell of offal and blood was overwhelming. She slid onto her bottom on the steep hill, as Freya strode to check the men and women. Other than the shrieks of pain and groans of suffering, there was only quiet conversation as people tried to help each other. She did not understand the words she heard but was filled with grief for Freya's people. Was this a victory? She supposed she'd find out later. She was so tired. She lay back on the hill and watched others hustle bringing water and what comfort they could to the dying. She closed her eyes and drifted away.

Elizabeth woke in her own bed, still touching Freya. Freya had curled into a natural cat sleeping position, and she stroked her soft side until she heard the mouse-purr that signified her wakefulness.

As they often did upon waking, the green kaleidoscope eyes showed no other presence for a few moments. "Hi, baby," Elizabeth cooed. She supposed she'd have to adjust to having a mere cat. It was still difficult to comprehend a human presence in her kitten, no matter how humanized she made Teddy and Edward. Freya was a different creature.

Freya came into the body, and Elizabeth knew immediately. "Do you always go there when you sleep?" she asked the kitten.

Not always, but often. It is how I check on my people. I have to return here since I can't be followed. Not many know of this place.

You mean the future?

This place is beyond their imagination.

Do you remember when I was there with you during the battle?

Of course.

Remember I said someone could see me? Freya tilted her head in acknowledgement, the white fur patches along her nose and between her eyes glowing in the dim light.

He called me a car.

What?

Something like that. When I tried to scoot past him without getting my head cut off, he let me pass but he called me a Volvo.

Freya turned her mouth up and her eyes squinched shut. She was laughing. *No, whatever that thing is, it is not a car for him.*

"Well?" Elizabeth waited for Freya to get herself under control.

He called you a volva. A witch. Possibly the best explanation for him. And you.

A witch? That's rude.

169

No. For us it is not. Witches are not as you understand them. They are healers or others of magical abilities. It would not be unusual to see one during a battle. Perhaps not dressed as you were. Freya smiled again, that eerie but completely readable facial expression.

Elizabeth looked down at her own clothing and smiled, noting the furs had stayed in Freya's world. *I guess. They can't read, right?* She indicated the pink BABY and arrow.

Not your language they can't.

"Okay, time to get up. Dinner. Tig should be home soon. And then he has to go again." She was getting tired of all this alone time.

Freya read her mind. Again. *I am here. I can protect you.*

Elizabeth smiled at the tiny creature. "I appreciate it. I don't know how you would do that, but I bet you would try."

Freya did not look pleased at Elizabeth's doubt of her abilities.

Elizabeth stood and noticed something odd. Her slippers were not by her side of the bed. She thought she had fallen asleep with them on, fully clothed, but now they were nowhere to be found. She had another pair somewhere in her closet, but where would the others be? Sometimes she left them by one of the doors, but wouldn't she remember that? Maybe not with the pregnancy brain. And her giant stomach was back. She remembered in the dream she was much slimmer and was able to run up the hill. Sort of run. In the slippers. They kept making her slide. That was it.

She knelt down in her closet, a small walk-in, and dug out her other pair under her hiking boots and several pairs of pants that had fallen off the hangers and covered the shoes on the floor. She hadn't worn those pants in a while, nor would she, but she hung them up anyway.

She pulled the replacement slippers out and sat on her bed. This pair had backs, which is why she didn't wear them. She liked to slide her feet in and go. However, she lifted one foot with great effort onto the other knee to fit the back of the slipper on and stopped.

The bottom of her sock was coated in dirt and leaves. She brushed it off slowly. A twig stuck in the weave and she pulled it out, then used a finger to put the heel of the slipper over her foot. She felt as if she were going into shock again. She lifted the other foot and found the same mess. This sock also had a splash of blood on it. She felt dizzy and set her foot back down, crushing the heel of the slipper flat. A sharp set of tiny claws in her thigh brought her back.

"It wasn't a dream?" she asked Freya.

No. Of course not. All this time you thought you were dreaming?

"Maybe. I guess I hoped so." She swallowed. "If I had died there, what would have happened to the baby?"

His soul would have gone to another host. Freya was matter of fact.

Elizabeth felt sweat form on her forehead and dizziness swept over her. She lay back on the

171

bed, and Freya crept up on her chest, a light but solid presence.

What would have happened to my body here?

What do you think?

Dead?

Yes. But I would never let that happen. I told you, you are needed in both worlds, so my job is to keep you safe, but also make sure fate is met.

"Are you serious?"

Freya's green eyes were inches from her own as she sat on Elizabeth's chest. *I have a limited amount of time to do what needs to be done.*

"Time limit? How long?"

The baby decides.

"And the baby is speeding up." Elizabeth made it a statement because she felt it to be true. She didn't need the doctor to confirm it. She also remembered something else. "You said 'he.' As in the baby is a he. Did you mean it? Is it a secret?"

No. You didn't want to know, but it is no secret. He is coming.

"He's healthy right? This early development is not an indication something's going on?"

He is healthy.

"I don't think I can take any more of this. I'm probably hungry. Perhaps insane." She lifted Freya off her chest so she could roll over and sit up. "Oh my gosh. It's late." She'd slept through any meeting she should have had with Tig and Karl. Tig was probably gone to the consult or the parts run. She needed to figure out dinner and what she was going to do about Karl. Too many things. Too many weird things.

She carried Freya out with her and opened the back door so the boys could come and go. Sure enough, Tig was gone, and a note on the counter indicated Karl had not arisen, so Tig had not been able to talk to him.

"It's mid-afternoon! Pregnant people get naps, but not young healthy ones." She knocked on Karl's door. No answer. She knocked again.

She still held Freya who said, *He's not in there.*

Elizabeth opened the door. She wasn't absolutely sure, but she didn't think he'd been back at all from his study session last night. His bed was not made, but that was not unusual. However, the pile of laundry and school notebooks on the desk looked untouched. If he had a study session, would he have taken the books? He might have changed clothes to sleep, or to leave again today.

No, Freya said. *He has not been here at all.*

Elizabeth didn't know how she knew, but she believed her. Smell, maybe? Even she could smell dirty socks and sweaty tees, but that didn't indicate a time frame.

She closed the door again. She had maybe an hour before Tig came back to share a meal and swap stories. She decided she would not tell him about Freya's world and her visit there, or that she learned she could die back in time and be dead here, too.

Finally she put Freya down. The kitten was fast becoming a security blanket, and Elizabeth

173

wondered if that was a good thing. Freya trotted out the back door and up the steps to the back gate. She let herself out the little door and Elizabeth checked in with the boys. They were lounging on the fallen log, keeping an eye on a pocket gopher hole. At one point, the gopher had poked his head up, probably a week ago, and ever since, the boys kept a vigil to see if it would again. The odd lizard provided entertainment, and mostly Edward liked to bring them in unharmed as presents for her. Lately it was too hard for her to get on the floor and catch the lizard herself. She'd begged Edward to stop, citing her size and inability to get up and down. So far, he'd respected her wishes, although he didn't understand. *Who wouldn't want to catch a lizard? It's hard to imagine more fun than that,* according to him.

Everything seemed so normal. This couldn't be some in-depth dream, could it? She knew the fire at Karl's place was real, and she knew she was rather bigger than she thought she should be at this stage. But all the Freya stuff, she had no outside validation. Perhaps some elaborate hormone pregnancy construct? It was very like a dream. Her socks. Maybe she had sleep-walked. She hadn't done that since she was a child, but it was possible. No one else had been home. She only had a kitten for verification. Was she losing it? She had never doubted her abilities before, even when the fish started going all Samurai in late Spring. She'd thought that was weird, but this paled in comparison.

She drew in a shaky breath. How to get some kind of reassurance? She had no idea. *Treat it on the line between dream and reality for now, but try not to freak out,* she told herself. Maybe focus on the Karl issue, which was plenty big. She had no way to prove or disprove Freya was a human warrior in a kitten's body. Perhaps she'd fabricated it as an escape? In her saner moments, she was terrified of giving birth. Of surviving the birth. Sure, millions of women did it, but she was scared. She hadn't admitted that to Tig. There was nothing he or anyone could do about it. Her doctor had assured her she would always be available, and the hospital was fifteen minutes away, ten by ambulance or a fast-driving Tig. The fire station was three minutes away, and he'd already told her if he thought for a second there was a problem, he'd drive her right onto the apparatus floor of the station for help. She smiled imagining that. They all knew her there so she'd get the best care, however embarrassing it might be.

She felt a little better. She found herself staring out the laundry room window at the pond and the back gate. She saw a little gray tabby face at the Plexiglas cat door and smiled. Freya used a paw to push through, not wanting to smash her face. Teddy didn't mind just shoving through the door with his head. Edward used his delicate hands, too. He had a unique way of feeling around the edges of the door to break the suction and then oozing through in his boneless fashion. Freya, however picky she was about preserving her face, was all business. Once the coast was clear, she came in and trotted right for Elizabeth.

Elizabeth checked the big freezer in front of her and decided Tig could barbeque for dinner. She did not want the steaks she saw, but knew both Tig and Karl would. She would make a big salad and she spied some sourdough rolls, too. Good. Dinner was as good as done.

She pulled out the steaks and rolls to defrost and then gathered salad things. Almost 4 PM. *Time flew when you stood around and did nothing after a long nap,* she thought. She pre-heated the oven for the rolls, not knowing when Tig would get home. She chopped lettuce and tomatoes, grated carrots and sliced onions. She mixed her special dressing separately so she could just toss the salad when the steaks were done.

Suddenly her dirty socks bothered her. She also didn't want Tig to see them and ask her difficult questions. Best case scenario she was sleep-walking, but it would bring up a whole host of issues she didn't want to face, starting with, what if she fell in the pond? She was sure she'd wake up, but would she really? The sides were super slippery and if no one was home, would she be able to get out by herself? In her normal days, of course. She could stand in the middle and still breathe, but if she was knocked out or otherwise disabled? As for the socks, better to change them and avoid Tig's questions. Deep down, she knew she had not sleep-walked. She had actually been someplace and that scared her.

Nineteen

She gathered up a load of laundry and put on clean socks. She'd just started the washer when she heard Tig's truck back in. The cats did too because Teddy and Edward trotted in from the back. Freya was already there, having "helped" her pull food from the freezer and change her socks. For once, Freya was silent throughout, not commenting on her ponderings.

Tig blew in and gave her a big hug. "I missed you guys today."

"I missed you, too. How did the consult go? New client?"

"I think I've got the job. I have to write up an estimate, but based on our discussion, it's a go. I talked them out of a waterfall, but I might branch into small water features. People love the sound of running water."

Elizabeth nodded. She loved their own waterfall and water features around their property. The cats did too since they attracted birds. Tig had set up a water alarm that went off when the cats tried to hunt some poor bird bathing in the waterfall. Many a day someone got squirted and stomped around mad until he dried. She had told them to knock it off, but they were cats. They couldn't seem to break the habit. Innate nature. The best Tig could do is cat-proof the more attractive-to-birds areas. It had worked so far. Although the boys knew about the water jet, they couldn't stop themselves.

"Good idea. Can you barbeque? I've got steaks defrosting. One for each of you. I'm not having steak. The baby says no." She smiled. "I might have tuna with my salad."

"I might buy stock in canned tuna if this keeps up." Tig peeled off the steak packaging and began to layer herbs and spices. "Did Karl ever get up?"

"Actually, I don't think he was ever here."

"Are you sure? You fell asleep and I left. He could have awakened and left for school again."

"I suppose, but I checked his room and it doesn't seem like he's been there. I've been keeping an eye on it in case he leaves food in there. I don't want a bunch of dirty dishes piling up and attracting bugs."

"If it's true, he hasn't been here since last night when you guys talked at dinner?"

"He said he was going to study at the school library. He's an adult, but should I worry? He doesn't have anywhere else to stay with Stacy gone."

"Yeah. I have to go to work tonight, but tomorrow, if we haven't heard from him, we'll do some checking. Can you call the Rescue Center and see if he's been there? Maybe someone there let him crash with them."

"Good idea. I'll do it now." Elizabeth dialed and recognized the voice of the receptionist. No, Karl had not been there. As far as she knew, his task was over. He had been sent by the university to work on their computers in conjunction with a class. That's all she knew and since it was almost 5, she clearly wanted to go home. No, she didn't know anyone who might have let him stay with them. She didn't know his last name; she had nothing to do with interns. They came and went all the time. Elizabeth thanked her.

Tig was out warming the barbeque and adding water to the pond. Edward followed Tig around waiting to be picked up. Teddy lounged near the pond, apparently chatting with Princess Keiko who had risen to the surface. She was bigger than he was.

She came right to the edge and Teddy draped a paw over the water. She rose and put her head under his paw. He patted her and she blew bubbles and made kissing sounds of pleasure. Elizabeth had never seen this interaction before. Maybe it was something they did when no one was around. She knew if she asked Teddy, he'd go all fuzzy and she'd get no answer. Keiko never told her anything unless she wanted to. *She'd be a great spy,* Elizabeth thought. Keiko only had to go sit on the bottom of the pond and ignore Elizabeth, and she'd never get an interrogation. Cats were much easier. At least Teddy could be bribed, but even then, he had moments where he'd hold out.

Tig looked relaxed and happy. She was glad for him, he worked hard, but she wanted some help with this Karl thing. He wasn't home enough to know how scary it was, how she felt Karl was truly missing, and how much this pregnancy worried her.

She tossed the salad and set the rolls in the oven to warm as Tig put the steaks on to grill. Her phone rang, a restricted call. To her relief, it was the physician's assistant returning her call after hours.

She explained her concern over her weight gain. She'd been taking her blood pressure with a home monitor and it was normal. The upshot was babies grew at different rates but a little more weight gain was no cause for alarm. The PA saw in the notes that perhaps the date of conception was off, and told her not to worry as she had no other symptoms of concern. If it continued into next week, they would see her. Elizabeth thanked her and hung up, a bit reassured. If she thought about it, she didn't feel anything was wrong, except the speed at which the baby was growing. Maybe it would just be a huge baby. Freya said it was fine. Maybe she should tell the doctor. "My cat says the baby's doing great!"

Still, a she felt relieved, at least for now. Tig brought in the steaks and she set the table, bringing out the rolls and salad. Since Tig was going to work, no beer. She got big glasses of ice water for her and iced tea for him. No caffeine for her.

180

The boys took up their usual positions, and Elizabeth lifted Freya onto her lap. A bad habit, but based on available real estate, one that would not last.

"I was thinking," she began. "We could go to the Poly Tech campus tomorrow and see if anyone's seen Karl."

"Honey, it's a huge campus. Where would we start?"

"The library for one. I have a picture of him on my phone from when you guys worked on that pond last year. He was covered in sweat and had a big streak of dirt across his forehead. He looked about five years old. He was so happy."

"He's not dead, you know. Just AWOL."

"I know, but I'm worried. I want to do something and I don't want to do it alone.

"Of course I'll go with you. Are you up for that much walking?"

"I think so. I know where the library is, and there's metered parking nearby, but we'll have to figure out where the Business Administration building is. If that guy is really an advisor, he should have an office there, right? Maybe he can answer some questions."

"You have been thinking about this." Tig had inhaled his steak and was working on his salad and roll number three.

Elizabeth got up to get more tea and water. She opened a can of tuna and six ears swiveled toward the sound. She scooped it onto her salad and put tiny bites near the boys. She put Freya's on a tea saucer on the next chair. Spoiled.

"I've got to write up that job estimate if I want to get it. If we're going to be *investigating* tomorrow, I can't do it then."

"It's not funny."

"I know. But I feel like a detective."

"You don't think something's happened to Karl?"

"Not really, but I'm willing to help put your mind at ease, Nancy Drew."

"If I'm Nancy Drew then you're the Pink Panther."

"He was the criminal. You mean Inspector Clouseau."

"Yes, I do." She smiled.

"You got me." He laughed. "You might be glad for all the training Cato provided if we get ourselves in trouble." He kissed her and began to put away the dinner things. "I'll save Karl's steak for him."

Envisioning her husband as Clouseau with the ever vigilant Cato made her smile as she finished cleaning up. Tig went to Karl's room, normally his office, and began to write up the estimate on his computer.

He returned with a printout and something he held between his thumb and forefinger. "What's this?"

"A micro SD card?" she said. "I don't use them so it's not mine."

"It's Karl's I think. His room was sort of a mine field so I moved some stuff and this fell out of a shoe. It was between the tongue and the brand label on top of the tongue. I tripped over the shoe and it slid out."

"What do we do with it?" Tig asked.

"It's probably homework. Remember he said he couldn't find the flash drive his project was on?"

"No, I don't."

"Maybe only I heard that." Elizabeth couldn't remember.

"It is extremely unlikely this fell into the little space between the tongue and the label of an athletic shoe. It was hidden intentionally. I don't know anyone who hides homework in a shoe."

"Do we look at it?"

"I don't know. What if there's more to this than we know?" Tig asked.

"If we don't look at it, we won't know what to do with it. If it *is* homework, we'll feel really silly calling the FBI."

"What do you mean the FBI?"

"I was just kidding. I'm sure it's nothing. We'll check at school tomorrow and then go from there."

"What do we do with it until then?" Tig was rolling and unrolling the estimate.

"Back in the shoe?"

"I guess. For now."

Tig was distracted as he readied for work. Elizabeth could tell this new development had changed his view of Karl's absence and perhaps of even the fire. He left for the station and although she'd had a nap, she was exhausted from her adventures in Freya's world. She barely remembered to throw the clothes into the dryer before she decided to go to bed.

Out of habit she turned on NetFilms for the cats; they did love routine. She dozed through a comedy and gave up.

She awoke to Tig arriving home about 7:30 in the morning, finally feeling pretty rested. She hoped Karl had come home in the night, but as she passed his closed door, Freya said, *no*.

Twenty

Tig had made blueberry pancakes and she felt hungry. She was ready to eat and get serious about her plan to look for Karl and his advisor. She remembered no dreams, which she was grateful for since she'd had a full dream regimen the day before. Or dreamwalking as Freya called it.

The boys were waiting for bacon, but Freya wondered if blueberry pancakes were like toast.

Elizabeth kissed Tig good morning and got her tea steeping. Tig looked tired.

"Busy night?" she asked.

"A bit. A few medical calls and we had a small industrial fire in those units behind the grocery store." He waved the spatula in that general direction.

"Bad?"

"No. Classic. Oily rags, combustibles, you know." She did. It was like she had taken the courses with him. "It was still small when we got there."

"It helped that it was three minutes from the station," she said.

"Everything in this town is," he joked. It wasn't far from the truth. A few of the ranches were a bit out of the way, and the rich section toward the coast from their own home stretched far up into the clouds and took some navigating on narrow, winding streets to reach. Lots of medical calls up there, but for the most part, the fire department was able to service the community quickly. In the middle of the night, literally no one was on the street except perhaps the one lonely sheriff's deputy. He or she spent some time hanging out at the fire station with anyone who might be up with a pot of coffee brewed.

"I'm glad it was controllable. You look tired, though."

"You know some nights, you get woken up a bunch of times and your body just says, forget it, I'm not going back to sleep if you're going to keep waking me up."

"I'm sorry." She sat at the table and sipped her tea. Tig placed a platter of pancakes and the jug of syrup down.

"About half of us gave up so we played poker and gambled away the deeds to our homes." He set down his coffee and scooped his bacon onto a plate. Elizabeth wasn't eating anything greasy anymore. She eyed it and wondered if she'd ever want to eat it again.

"Did we lose the house?" she asked, cutting her pancake into precise squares, a blueberry in each section.

"Nope, we got Mahan's plus Robert George's cottage at Dragon Lake." He referred to one of the reservoirs an hour north that revealed its dragon shape from the air.

"I wonder if Joanne will like that," Elizabeth joked. She knew Robert George's wife slightly from work gatherings. "Well done." She ate her pancake slowly, savoring it since she got very full very fast.

Tig ate quickly, like he did most things. In his business, if you didn't eat, you might not get to if the bell rang mid-meal.

"Seriously, he said we could use it anytime. They only use it a few times a year. He's having a party later in the summer."

"It will be so hot up there and the lake level is low. I'm not sure I want to go."

"We'll see."

She rose and put her dishes in the sink. "If it has air conditioning, I'll consider it. This baby is in charge, not me, so it depends when the barbeque is." She had not told Tig about her worry over her burgeoning size. Or the call to the PA. A twinge of concern about how much she was keeping from Tig. Today would fix one of those issues, so she felt a little better.

"I'm going to get dressed. Can you leave in half an hour?"

She saw from his face he had no idea where they were going. "Sure," he said.

"Tolosa Poly Tech to see if anyone's seen Karl?"

"Right. No problem. I'm a little tired. If I can get back by the afternoon for a nap, I'll be good to go for tonight. Cross fingers no fires."

"Absolutely." Fires were a rarity in this tiny community, but medical calls within the aging population a constant. "I'm sure I, we, can use a nap, too by then." She rubbed her active belly. Now sometimes, she could feel a foot, she thought it might be a foot, from the outside, not just within. Kind of exciting.

Right on time they pulled out of the drive. She told the cats they'd be back in a couple hours, but as usual, her excuses fell on deaf ears.

Tolosa Tech sat snugged on the other side of town against beautiful, climbable hills. The giant T of the school rested proudly on the hillside above the dorms and could be seen for miles. Neither of them had been on campus for a while, and they discovered many roads blocked for construction of new dorms that looked like an entire village was being built. After driving a circuitous route they found a metered lot not far from the library. Elizabeth figured she could walk the distance, but wondered how far the Bus Admin building would be, and if she could make it before her energy gave out.

She sighed and dug out quarters from the glove box stash.

"Do you know what you're going to say?" asked Tig as they headed toward the large glass doors.

"I thought I'd just show his picture around and ask if anyone's seen him. Why?"

"Maybe start by asking people if they were here, or worked here night before last. It might narrow it down."

"Good idea. Now that we're on campus, I feel this might be a waste of time. I'm sorry, Tig." They passed through metal detectors, then RFID readers designed to keep people from stealing the books. It felt like she was going into the courthouse with all the security. She noted cameras just about everywhere.

"I see them, too," Tig said. "I don't know what good they'll do since we have no authority for them to show us any footage."

Wide stairs went up the whole seven floors. She knew because the center of the building was cut out and the stairs and halls edged an open courtyard on the ground floor where the circulation desk was. Huge rooms branched off on both sides, with study carrels and corners filled with comfy chairs and long tables also with chairs.

It was daunting. She felt her ankles swell just looking at all the stairs. If she used an elevator, she might miss something.

"This isn't going to work," she told Tig. "Maybe I'll just show his picture to the people working the desks?" Her spirits sagged. Karl could be there now, dozing in some nook, studying in a comfy cranny and she'd never find him.

"Send me the picture and we'll split up. I'll start asking at the top and you start down here and we'll meet in the middle. If we only ask the workers and some students, it's still better than nothing." He smiled encouragingly.

"Great idea." Impulsively, she kissed him. He didn't even say *I told you so.*

She texted him the image, and he rode the elevator to the top. She began with the main circulation desk and after half an hour, she was only on the second floor. She'd discovered, manned information kiosks on every level, plus, each floor had an 'employees' area. There books were stashed before being returned to circulation or pulled for damage. She found each of those private doorways and after finishing floor 2, she texted Tig her progress.

He was having the same problem, but since he was more mobile he'd made it down to floor 5. She was about to head up to 3. The figured they'd meet on 4 somewhere. On 4 her legs gave out. She found a soft chair with a foot rest and waited where she could see Tig coming down the stairs.

"Any luck?" she asked when he plopped down beside her.

"I'm getting the feeling he may have lied about coming to the library that night."

"Maybe not a lie if something happened to him," she said.

"You were all about espionage and now you're defending him?"

"It's still espionage if someone did something to him."

"It's a long leap. He's probably somewhere else, working or figuring out the insurance stuff, or replacing his damaged things," Tig said.

"He already did that, remember? I told you what I heard at Target? He had packages with him so he did some shopping."

"Maybe he needed more than what Target offered." Tig rose and held out his hand. "Let's go."

"I guess." She needed both his hand and a shove off the arm of the chair to get up. Her legs ached. How much more walking was wise? The doctor did say to exercise. Rationalizing this excursion, she waddled to the elevator and pushed the down arrow.

At the circulation desk she asked where the Business Administration building was. The nice twelve-year-old volunteer gave them a paper map of the campus and circled the library and the Bus Ad building. Fortunately, their parking lot was between the two.

She sighed in relief. "I think we need to put more money in the meter," she said. "And I need a cold drink."

Tig agreed. After depositing more quarters in the meter, they saw the flashing beacon of a drink machine next to the glass doors. She felt like a dying man seeing Las Vegas. She had enough flat dollar bills to satisfy the persnickety machine to spit out a cold water and an orange juice. They drank half of each, then traded, in about five seconds flat.

The Bus Ad building was a long, one-story building in a capital tee shape. An arm of the tee connected to another building and she heard music down the hall. She didn't have time or inclination to explore, but it sounded nice and the cool hall was relaxing after the strain and size of the library adventure.

They wandered the hall reading bulletin boards and checking room numbers. Toward the far end she found restrooms and bolted in with a quick, "Be right back," to Tig. He was used to that by now. Even before her pregnancy she had excellent restroom radar and rarely passed a bathroom she didn't use. Just good policy. Now, however, she had to go all the time, with less ability to prepare.

She came out and found him staring at a bulletin board display of clubs and activities, and one interesting photo. Staff and Administration of the department. "Look at this," he said. "Recognize anybody?" He hadn't seen Karl's 'advisor,' but she had described him.

"That's him!" She poked a finger at the glass covered photo. Tom Abramson, Deputy Department Chair. "He's a real advisor? I was so sure he wasn't."

"It seems so. Let's see if he's in his office." Tig checked the building map; it wasn't a one story building after all. The stairs at the end of the hall went down to level B, and his office was located in B27. It looked like all the professors' offices were on the lower level, classrooms were on the main floor. They could either go down another set of stairs right here, or walk all the way back to the tee and take the elevator.

Elizabeth was excited and opted to stagger down the stairs. She had been worried when she'd seen a basement. Again, probably due to too many NetFilms, but there had been some strange things going on. However, the stairs were well-lit and the long corridor led to more more bulletin boards; the industrial gray-brown tile and yellowed walls indicating one of the older structures on campus. She had noticed along with the dorms, the Engineering Department was getting a new home. An odd-looking one, very modern glass and chrome, but she figured it was Engineering so it had to make a statement.

A few doors were open indicating someone was inside. B27 was back at the tee, so they could have taken the elevator after all. They turned the corner to the tee.

"24, 25, 26, here," Tig counted. The door was closed, but he boldly tried the knob. It turned. He let go and they looked at one another.

"Knock," Elizabeth whispered. He did.

"Come in," a voice said.

Tig turned the knob and pushed open the door, not entering. Elizabeth peered around him.

"Yes? Can I help you?" The man from the photo. And the cafe. Elizabeth regretted their bold adventure.

"I hope so," said Tig.

"Are you lost?"

"Are you Tom Abramson?" Tig countered.

"Yes. What can I do for you?" He was obviously puzzled. She knew they did not look, or certainly act, like students.

"We'd like to talk to you about Karl Durst."

Elizabeth saw the slightest change in his eyes. Because of her work with animals, and pets in particular, she was very attuned to facial expressions, including minute ones. In her line of work, it could mean the difference between being bitten and moving out of range in time.

"I don't believe I know him?" A slight question, so if he was caught, he could claim, uncertainty? He was good, Elizabeth thought. She knew that though, from the cafe.

"You are his advisor, I believe?" Tig said.

"Possibly. I have several hundred students on my roster, and I don't always meet them all; not right away anyway. Especially if they are new to the program. I can't give you any academic information, even if you are his parents."

Elizabeth snorted. Karl was only a few years younger than she, so obviously, they were not a college-age kid's parents.

"We're not his parents," Tig said.

"How can I help?" He was wary, but Elizabeth saw he felt safe now.

"He is our employee and friend and has disappeared. He said he was coming to study at the library two nights ago and hasn't been seen since," Tig explained.

"Are you sure? Maybe he's at home."

"His home was burned to the ground, arson, and he's been staying with us. So, no, he's not at home. He might be in danger. We're worried about him."

From Tig's tone, Elizabeth knew he was getting mad, though he still sounded civilized.

"Why have you come to me? Isn't this a matter for the police? And doesn't he have to be missing, if he is in fact missing, for twenty-four hours?"

194

Elizabeth jumped in. "We're coming to you, not the police because you know him. I saw you talking to him, and now you pretending not to know which student he is doesn't help. Have you gotten him involved in something criminal?"

"What? That's outrageous!" His reaction was perfect and studied. Elizabeth was sure now, he *was* involved, in something, and perhaps other students had been cajoled into participating too.

"I was in Target the day you met with Karl. I asked him about it and he said you were his academic advisor and he was doing an internship for a business class. I find it all very suspicious."

"What is suspicious? That I am his advisor? His internship? You are not his parents, so what is your involvement in his education? I am not obligated to tell you anything about his work here. A student's education and academic record are private until his grades are posted and degree conferred. I know the student to whom you refer. He was a late returnee."

"What's that?" asked Tig.

Abramson sighed. "A student who did not go straight to college from high school. I will tell you he's having a little trouble adjusting to the rigors of university work. It's part of my job to meet with such students and guide them. He's not alone in his struggle. We met at the cafe because it was more convenient for us both."

It all sounded good. It matched what Karl had said, but something didn't feel right to Elizabeth.

"I was unaware Karl had a mother figure who was stalking him." He thought this was funny.

Tig had accepted the man's story. But he hadn't seen and heard the conversation, he hadn't seen Karl at the Wildlife Rescue Center, hadn't talked to Karl and sensed his underlying fear, despite his bravado.

"We appreciate your time." Tig stood and stuck out his hand. "We care a lot about him. Yes, it's been a challenge for him to go back to school, and we're supporting him however we can."

"That's admirable. I have a class, so I really must go." The men shook hands, but Abramson did not offer his hand to Elizabeth. Fine with her, she didn't want to touch him anyway.

He shooed them out of his office and locked the door, grabbing a leather briefcase as he did. He took off down the hall, to avoid further conversation, Elizabeth thought. A frisson of fear rose in her belly. He was a dangerous man, no matter how cloaked in academia he behaved.

"Hey, look." She pointed to the class schedule pinned to the board next to his door along with his office hours and notices from the department. "He doesn't have a class now. He just wanted to get away." She took a quick photo with her phone.

"I get it." Tig tried to make a joke.

She glared at him. "He's lying about something. Maybe everything."

"Hon, it doesn't have to be a big conspiracy. College students are weird by nature. Maybe Karl stayed with a friend from school to study and didn't want to call us too late. Maybe it just didn't occur to him."

"After all he's been through. After all we've helped him through, he wouldn't just disappear." They headed to the elevator. "He could have texted us," she mumbled.

"He's an adult. It's been just over 24 hours. We have no reason to suspect foul play, as they say."

"What about the SD card?" Elizabeth asked.

"What about it? We don't know what's on it."

"That's right, we don't."

"Let's not jump to conclusions. I'm wiped. I need to sleep a little before I go in, okay?"

Elizabeth was filled with remorse. Her phone showed it was almost noon and she was hungry. Tig was probably starved. "I saw a little walk-up food window at the edge of the parking lot. Let's see if they have a snack to tide us over 'til we get home, okay?" she said.

Tig brightened considerably. The window was actually the side of one of the cafeterias so choices were vast. Tig got two huge slices of pizza, and she ordered hummus and pita and some stuffed grape leaves. They sat at one of the many little picnic tables in the shade and enjoyed their meal. The day was warm but breezy and at this noon hour, filled with energetic young people eating and talking.

The ride home was mercifully short and they fell into bed immediately. Her last thought was not of the 'case,' but what's for dinner?

Twenty-One

The afternoon raced by. After Tig and Elizabeth returned from Tolosa Poly Tech and lunch, then had their nap, they both awoke groggy and sluggish. Cats loved naptime, and it was rare that Tig slept during the day, so they were ecstatic at this anomaly.

"I am still so tired," complained Elizabeth. She had begun to sleep on her left side, not only because of the doctor's recommendation, but because the baby was so big it was uncomfortable on her back for very long. Traditionally she was a back-sleeper, but she or the baby adjusted quickly. Her left meant she faced Tig. He tried to sleep on his side to tone down the snoring, but inevitably he ended up on his back.

As soon as she woke, she saw he was awake too, but hadn't moved because Edward slept on his chest. "I don't know how you do it," she said. "As tiny as Freya is, if she's on my chest very long, she feels like a twenty pound weight."

Tig smiled and stroked Edward who stretched under his hand. "He's so cute. I can't move until I have to go to work. Besides, he doesn't usually do it at night."

I'm a good boy, Teddy said smugly from his spot at the bottom of the bed. A wise choice since he had the most room.

Yes, you are, said Elizabeth. *I can't reach you down there, though.*

I know.

You're not being that *good if you don't want to be petted anyway,* Edward said.

I like petting, just not all the time. I'm not needy like some. Teddy rolled on his back exposing miles of creamy speckled downy fur, 'Bucky down,' Elizabeth and Tig called it, for no remembered reason.

Tig was able to roll over onto his side and still cradle Edward who hadn't moved. Now he lay boneless in Tig's arms like a baby on the bed. "She's hilarious," Tig said. "What a pretty princess." He reached a hand out and was just able to stroke one tiny jawbone with a finger.

That reminded Elizabeth of Freya's other life, as what? a warrior princess? some kind of warrior and some kind of leader and she sobered, remembering her time with *this* Freya was limited.

Freya heard her. *Don't worry. I will visit. I also think you will like this fur sack I chose.*

Elizabeth was surprised at her terminology. She couldn't tell if it was derogatory or a joke. *Fur sack?*

Freya laughed, her tiny, crackly sound, almost no sound, where the sides of her open mouth turned way up and her eyes squinched shut. *Yes. I*

199

chose it for a reason. The being I share this body with will be more than compatible with you. Try not to worry. All will be well.

Easy for you to say.

Yes, it is. But it will be, and I am working very hard, as you may recall, to right things. She sent Elizabeth pictures of the battle, pictures Elizabeth had not seen while there because they happened to Freya, away from Elizabeth's hiding place.

What did you say during the fight? Elizabeth asked her. She heard Freya shout, *or.* Or something like that. In her language? Elizabeth couldn't tell.

I did not mean for you to hear that.

It's not like I can understand your language. I thought that man called me a car, so what is it? Another car? she joked.

No. I called to Oor. My husband.

Elizabeth was so shocked she gasped.

"What is it? The baby? Are you okay?" Tig asked, leaning in.

"No. I'm fine. Just a kick." Elizabeth realized she hadn't lied; the baby had given her a swift one. She lifted her top and saw her stomach rolling like the surf.

"Whoa!" Tig's eyes were huge. "Can I touch it? Does it hurt?"

"Yes, and sometimes. Right now, given his size, it's mostly a surprise. A good kidney kick can be pretty uncomfortable."

Tig lay his hand on her belly and she felt a shove, like when a swimmer kicks off from a pool side. She imagined him doing laps in there, and it made her smile.

"Did you say, he?" Tig asked, hand still resting on her stomach. She nodded. "Is it a real 'he' or did you just use that word?"

"It's a real he."

"When did you find out? And you didn't tell me?"

"It's not official, but it's probably true. I may go in to check next week and get it verified."

"Oh. A feeling, or did one of the cats tell you?" He sounded only slightly sarcastic.

"Um. Freya. Apparently, she can talk to him, whatever that means. She let it slip. I think it's true, but if she's wrong, it doesn't really matter."

Tig processed this.

She's not wrong. Edward. He was a surprise.

Do you talk to the baby, too? And you haven't told me? Elizabeth asked, a little peeved.

I can, but I don't. That's her job. But she's right.

Teddy, do you know anything about this?

Nope. Not me. I don't hear them, and I don't hear your baby. It might have to be on the other side for me to talk to it.

Why? What other side?

I don't know. I don't ask and I don't care. Maybe not other side. Outside? Yes, I think that's what I meant.

You mean after it's born? He's born?

Yes. Like a real person.

That sounded like Teddy.

"I have to go to work in a couple hours. Let's make some food." Tig had recovered at least to a degree. He carefully got up, leaving Edward still on his back, eyes closed, paws in the air.

Food sounds good to me. Teddy gracefully rolled off the bed and sauntered out the door after Tig.

Elizabeth wasn't sure if Tig was mad. She had known "it" was a he for a couple days now. She'd meant to tell him, but a lot had been going on both here and in Freya's battle. What a concept. She hoped the battle was some sort of metaphor, but the more she thought about it, the less likely it seemed. She remembered the smells: smoke, brine, pine, blood and worse. She didn't think metaphors had smells. Wrong.

Elizabeth made her way to the kitchen. Her back ached. Dinner. Why did it always come down to dinner? Fortunately, Tig was on it. He'd found a motley collection of vegetables, some of the koi's tofu and had put some rice in the cooker. Stir fry.

She put the kettle on and got out a peppermint tea bag. After the baby's water show, she felt a little queasy. She knew she needed to eat so mint tea was the go-to. A cup of tea and she'd probably feel fine. Where was Freya? And a little cat cure.

She scooped Freya into her ever shrinking lap and put her feet up on the next dining chair to give a bit more space. Freya curled herself, sat on her brisket—an unusual position for her—and closed her eyes. Elizabeth watched her while delicious smells of sautéing onions and garlic

202

wafted over. Tig brought her tea since she couldn't move.

She sensed the weight of the kitten on her lap and felt it grow more substantial. Not heavier, per se, just more. It was solid, and her nausea flowed down her body and was gone. A strange sensation. Then she realized what Freya was doing. She had grounded herself, much like Elizabeth did, to meditate. Elizabeth had not been able to make herself feel better, but it's what she did for animals all the time! And Freya was doing it for *her*. Maybe she could learn to do it herself.

Freya's eyes opened. Elizabeth sipped her tea.

"Feeling any better?" Tig asked.

"Yes, thanks. That smells amazing."

"It'll work for first dinner," Tig said. Tig's appetite was enormous, and his job required many calories. She knew they'd have a big dinner at the station as soon as the designated chef for the shift figured out what to make. And she thought she had it rough. Dinner for two. What about dinner for twelve, or however many they had on any given day? She promised herself not to complain again, knowing full well she would. She sighed.

"We have to think of boy names if you're sure Freya's right," Tig said.

"I'll find out next week."

"I guess I should know by now to believe the cats."

"They're not fortune tellers, they just are intuitive and tell me what they see or hear."

"They don't lie, right?"

"I haven't met an animal who does, but I suppose it's possible. Teddy lies about food and how he's starving, but I don't think that's the same thing. They believe what they're saying to be true, so it's truth for them."

"I get it." The rice cooker shut off. It was pretty quick when making rice for the two of them. "Do you have any ideas yet?" Tig brought over the dishes and utensils.

"I've been thinking. Something Irish? Sean?"

"Maybe. Also, Aiden." Tig brought shoyu and hot and sour sauce.

"That's nice, too." They began to eat. Less conversation than usual. Elizabeth was thinking of names and assumed Tig was, too.

Thor, Freya said.

What?

I will name my son Thor. You should too. It's a great, strong name in my land.

Elizabeth remembered Freya had mentioned a husband. Still hard to wrap her mind around that.

"Uh, Freya suggests we name him Thor." Elizabeth said this mostly to relieve any residual tension between them.

Tig smiled. It worked. "Thor, like the god of what, thunder?"

"I have no idea. But she says it's a good strong name and she will name her son that."

"What son?"

Rats. Elizabeth had not mentioned to Tig AT ALL that Freya was anything more than the usual talking cat. She had kept all the 'alternate

204

world/life' stuff from Tig, and now she'd just gone and opened her big mouth.

"I guess, she means when she has kittens," Elizabeth said lamely. "I mentioned spaying to her when we first got her, but she's so small, I haven't thought of it since."

"Is she . . . active?"

"I don't think so." Elizabeth knew human Freya was, especially if she had a husband, but the kitten was too young, the kitten-body, she amended. What did she know? Less and less it she thought.

"Since she's the one who told you the baby was a boy, I suppose it's only fair to add Thor to the list." Tig smiled.

"You're kidding, right?" Elizabeth looked down at Freya in her lap.

No. My son will be a great warrior. Freya stalked down her legs onto the next dining chair.

"Sure. Add it to the list." *Sorry,* she said to Freya.

I should think so.

Tig finished all the remaining stir fry plus the rest of her serving. Her stomach filled so easily these days.

She sent him off to work and once again, the house felt empty without his exuberant presence.

However, now he was referring to the baby as Thor, much to Freya's delight, and Elizabeth realized she'd created a monster. She gathered everyone up and headed back to lie down. Again. Would this exhaustion ever leave?

She had just clicked on her 'List' on NetFilms when her cell rang.

205

Twenty-Two

Elizabeth was shocked to hear Karl's voice when she answered the 'unknown caller.' Fully expecting a sales pitch, she almost cried to hear him.

"Karl! We've been so worried! Where have you been?"

"I'm not sure I should say over the phone. Can you meet me?"

"Now? It's after 7." For Elizabeth, that might as well be midnight. But since it was summer, it would be light for a couple more hours.

"Yes. Remember where I dropped the roasted chicken dinner and made a huge mess?" he asked. He referred to the local market where he and Stacy had gone for takeout.

"Yes," she answered cautiously. He sure was being careful. Or paranoid.

"Can you meet me there in half an hour?"

"Okay. Should I bring anything? Are you all right?"

"I'm fine. Just make sure you're not followed."

They disconnected and now *she* felt paranoid. She dressed quickly, going from PJs to sweats and a tee with a hoodie; pretty much outdoor PJs. She slid her feet into sports shoes she kept loosely tied so she didn't have to bend over. The cats did not like her bustle and anxiety when it was clearly NetFilms time.

"I'm going to see Karl," she said aloud. "I'm a little concerned, so try to stay connected to me and I'll be back as soon as I can. I have to go. I have too many questions that need answers."

You should tell Dad. Edward. *I don't think he'd want you to go.*

"You're right, but he can't do anything right now so I would just worry him."

I will be with you, Freya said.

Teddy narrowed his eyes. *You'll be fine.* He went back to sleep.

"I'm glad one of us is so sure."

She gathered her phone and purse and grabbed a box of granola bars in case Karl hadn't eaten. They *were* meeting at the big grocery store. As circumspect as he'd been for any unwanted listeners, she knew exactly where he meant. He had told both of them about when he and Stacy had gone shopping for a romantic picnic, and he had chosen all these things from the deli and promptly dropped them, spilling chicken, potato salad and a huge bag of chips that hit a corner of a display on the way down and burst in a shower of potato chip confetti. The bottle of soda also dropped when he'd tried to save the rest and split, sending a foaming syrupy shower over the deli. The manager was not happy, and Karl was so mortified that he scrambled to clean it all up. It was one of the first dates for Karl and Stacy, and he was worried she'd never want to go out with a klutz like him again. The opposite was true. She thought he was sweet and thoughtful and they'd been inseparable since. Until now.

The sky had its 'just before it's beautiful' look. The overcast had blown away and the sun was dropping to a light blue-gray before another startling sunset. Elizabeth flipped on the porch light in case she got back late. She had no idea what to expect, but put a shred of paper in the door as she closed it. Not as easy as she thought, but after watching a lot of James Bond and other thriller movies, she decided to try seeing if someone entered the house.

A block away from home she remembered she'd only have ask the cats. They would most likely shriek if a stranger came in anyway, even a non-human. She remembered when Buster, Janie's ancient pug across the street, witnessed a roach invasion in the kitchen and hollered about invaders, terrifying them all until they figured it out.

She did not see a black SUV when she pulled out of the drive, but also thanks to many spy movies, she drove a meandering route toward the bay, back to the small business district and then through the residential area without seeing another vehicle behind her for more than a block. It was time for folks to be coming home from work, so there was traffic, but it all moved on and away. She finally felt comfortable turning into the back entrance of the parking lot. She assumed Karl didn't mean in the deli itself and parked near the second door toward the back.

A homeless man sat on the wide sidewalk near the shopping carts, back against the wall. The temperature dropped as the sun did, and he shivered as she approached. She dropped a dollar into a flat cardboard soda tray where a few people had already dropped money.

"Elizabeth," he said. "It's me."

"Karl?" His disguise was thorough. He looked as if he hadn't bathed in days. "What are you doing? Like this?"

"I haven't been out and I was afraid. I didn't want to come to the house."

"Where have you been?"

"Follow me. You're sure no one saw you?"

"Yes, I'm sure. I drove around for a while before I came here."

"Good." He gathered his change and took off across the parking lot. She had a hard time keeping up with him.

"Karl, slow down. I can't go so fast."

He didn't turn around, but slowed his pace a bit. She picked up on his anxiety, but her unwieldy frame did not allow her to speed up. He went down a set of stairs at the back of the parking lot she did not know existed. It led to a lower street filled with apartment buildings. He went to a dated green one-story structure and followed a central path to the end unit in the back. He glanced around before pulling a key and opening a creaky, unsubstantial door.

She caught up as he entered. A wave of mold hit her nostrils. "I need to sit down. Do you have any water?" She meant bottled, but he got a glass and filled it from the tap. She looked dubiously at it, but panting and thirsty, she took a cautious sip. Not bad.

"What is this place?" she asked when her breathing edged toward normal.

"This is Stacy's studio. I couldn't think of any place else to go. At least she's not here so she's probably safe." He sat on a saggy couch, finally seeming to relax a little. "I don't think anyone knows where this is. It's so small we didn't spend much time here. We were always at my place."

Baby Thor had not appreciated his ride down the stairs and her panicked state, and he made that quite clear. She rubbed her stomach and tried to send him calming waves. He wasn't fooled and did breakdancing head spins in there.

"Karl. You disappeared. We were so worried. What happened? What's going on?"

"I'm not supposed to talk about it, but it's getting out of hand. You guys are the closest thing to family I have besides Stacy, but I can't tell her anything. It was all I could do to get her out of town without making her suspicious." He sighed and pulled off his hoodie. He looked thin. Rats, she'd left the granola bars in the car.

"Are you eating? I know it's only been two days since you fell off the grid, but before that? When your house burned down and all this . . . whatever it is? It's not school, right? Are you really in school?"

Karl nodded. "That's how this whole thing started. I decided to start slow, with summer school. Take a few general ed classes to kick start my new dream." He laughed bitterly. "The dream has gotten out of hand, and I don't know what to do. I'm not supposed to talk about it except with my 'advisor,' and he hasn't been very helpful."

"Are you involved in something criminal?"

"Yes. It started out pretty simple, a way to make extra money. Maybe a career path of sorts. It changed so fast and now it seems like he doesn't know how to help me. The fire surprised him, too. I think—I don't know what to think. I'm sorry to get you involved."

"Whoa. Back up. It is something criminal? I thought I knew you better."

"It was supposed to be temporary, but it got heavy almost right away. It turns out I'm better at it than anybody thought."

"Great. Does Abramson know where you are?"

"No. Only you. I made a mistake and used a computer that wasn't safe. I knew I shouldn't, but I was in a time crunch, and honestly, I didn't think it was a big deal. Turns out I was wrong, and things went south almost immediately. Abramson is furious, his bosses are furious, and I was tracked."

"What did you do? What *are* you doing?"

"When I transferred to Tolosa Poly Tech I was given a set of placement tests because I had gone to community college first. It turns out they were more than placement tests. I was approached to do some computer work, moving money around.

I was assured I would be protected, that no one would know who I was or where I was in the cyber world. Because of my mistake, it all came crashing down."

"What's going on that this is such a big deal and your life might be in danger?"

"I didn't know at first. I was given the internship at the Rescue Center but I didn't know the accounts were for them and others like them. It *was* for my class, but I also had access to certain accounts from their terminals. Once I was in and modified my access, I could get into those accounts from anywhere."

"So, you're moving money, stealing it, really, and someone found out?"

"Basically."

"Was that part of the 'hundred' Abramson mentioned at the cafe?"

"Yes and more. I've been moving money for weeks, but I don't know who it belongs to. All I see are numbers and code and I don't have the access to match the numbers with names. This is getting too big, and I've been noticed. Abramson is waiting for instructions on what to do with me. I don't know what it means. I decided to hide. I have some insurance though."

"What kind of insurance?"

"I copied the account numbers and dollar amounts from those transactions and put it all on an SD card. If something happens, maybe I can use it to bargain. For all I know, the money's been moved again by someone else, and the card might be my only security."

"Oh, Karl. What a mess. Should we go to the police? I'll go with you."

"I think it's too late for the police. I don't think they can help me, or protect me."

"But they have a cybercrime unit now."

"I think this is way bigger than that. In fact I know it is. I think Abramson is the only one who can get me out of it."

"Isn't he also the one putting you in danger? By getting you into this 'job,' for lack of a better word?"

"Yes. If I'd followed his instructions to the letter, I wouldn't be in this mess. I just wasn't thinking."

"What are you going to do? Do you have food?"

"I don't know and I have some."

"It's not safe for you to go out. How can I help?"

"I'm pretty sure you're being watched. Maybe not all the time, but you have to be careful."

"Okay. You still have that cell phone you used, right?"

"I got a new one. I bought a bunch at their recommendation when I started this job. Some they gave me, and some I got on my own. I change phones every time I use one. I can't risk being traced. They probably know I'm still in the area, but I don't have any place to go and no money to go with. Anyway, you won't be able to call me, but I can call you. I'll try to let you know I'm okay every couple days. If you need to get a hold of me, put a note in the handrail at the bottom of the stairs. It's hollow, and I'll check it every day—every night. It will take me a day probably to get anything you leave, but it's all I can think of."

"I don't understand why they picked you?"

"Turns out, my misspent youth playing video games among other computer related adventures made me sort of a genius. With a little refinement and training, they made me a more advanced hacker than I already was."

"Hacker? Oh, no. Oh, Karl. I'm so sorry."

"It's okay. Really." Elizabeth teared up and she grabbed his hand. He let her for a moment. "You should probably go. Can you get up the stairs okay?" She nodded. "Be careful. I'm sure they know what your car looks like."

It was almost dark as she made her way back to the unlit stairway. She watched her footing carefully going up. The grocery store parking lot was comparatively bright so that helped as she ascended. At the top she had to pause to catch her breath.

Hey, are you guys there? she called to the cats.

I am. Freya. *Edward gave up. He said you were* my *person. Teddy hasn't woken up except to eat.*

Elizabeth smiled. *Figures. I'm okay and on my way home. Thanks for looking out for me.* She suddenly felt exposed under the sodium lights and hurried to her car. She had parked near the doors out of habit, but now wondered if that was such a great idea. She scanned the cars to see if anyone waited and watched, but the parking lot lights weren't very good. Not too many cars at this time of night, and she didn't feel like trotting around to check.

She sighed in relief once she sat in the driver's seat. She pulled slowly out of the back of the lot, trying to see if she was followed. She turned up the alley by the loading dock and waited. A green Prius coasted silently behind her, but didn't make the same turn into the alley. She felt isolated here and moved onto the street, turning toward home. More traffic here, but nothing stood out. Would she be able to tell?

Worry and adrenaline started to pull her down; she was exhausted. Too much information to process now. She'd talk to Tig in the morning, and maybe they'd figure it out together. She wasn't going to keep this to herself. She kept her head and drove a circuitous route. She wanted to be sure she wasn't followed or stuck in a cul-du-sac. Thank goodness for many weekends hunting at garage sales. She knew the odd dead-ends of this town.

It was full dark by the time she reached home. She was glad she'd left the porch light on, but again, she felt exposed. She'd taken the precaution of driving around the block before pulling into the drive, but any criminal worth his salt would have changed cars anyway. She promised herself to take note of the cars on her end of the block in the future.

Twenty-Three

After her adventure with Karl and all the skulking around, she was hungry.

Me, too. Teddy.

Yes. Edward and Freya.

"Why not? Tuna juice shooters all around. Belly up to the bar," she said.

What are you talking about? What bar? Edward asked.

You're weird, Mom. Teddy.

Freya just flicked her tail and waited for a tiny dish of tuna juice. Elizabeth made a sandwich and used her best soccer moves, keeping the boys, mostly Teddy, from stealing someone else's tuna juice.

Bedtime never felt so good. No energy for NetFilms, so she sent Tig a goodnight text and fell into dreamland.

Morning was gray and dreary. She awoke when she heard the front door close. Tig was home. Karl was unlikely. She remembered she needed to tell Tig about her clandestine meeting last night. That was not going to be well received.

The cats escorted her to the kitchen. Tig had coffee brewing, so he probably slept more than went on calls.

She kissed him hello. "How was it last night?"

"A few medical calls, but not too bad. One at four, but it was resolved quickly. Why are they always at four?" he joked.

She put on her kettle and sorted a tea bag and cup. "I had a little adventure last night myself."

The cats had gone outside, but were now returning complaining of the mist. It made them wet, and even the tiniest bit wet was cause for a protest to the tune of, *why don't you fix the weather?*

Tig sat and Edward immediately popped into his lap. "Yeah? What happened? Baby okay?" His tone was a bit reserved, and she knew he was thinking if it was baby-related or serious, he should have been notified immediately. Which was true, and she hadn't.

The kettle boiled, and she poured her water, stalling. "Karl called. From a disposable phone. He's fine," she interjected because she saw he was ready to jump in. She brought her tea to the table, letting him have time to process.

No more questions came so she continued. "You're not going to like this, but I didn't call you on purpose. There's nothing you could have done without messing up the whole shift." If a fire fighter leaves early for whatever reason, the whole station is on hold until he or she can be replaced.

217

They were a unit, and if a piece was missing, the station was removed from calls.

"So what happened to Karl?" Tig sipped his coffee.

"I agreed to meet him nearby. He was scared, and I was so worried. I felt safe enough. It was still light out so we met at the grocery store." Tig's eyebrows raised, *go on.* "Then we walked to Stacy's apartment down the hill from the store. I made sure I wasn't followed."

Elizabeth got up and retrieved two ice cubes to cool her tea faster. Freya joined her after she sat down. Elizabeth immediately felt calmer, grateful for the little cat's presence.

"Karl didn't think anyone knew where Stacy lived so he felt safe enough. Even we didn't know, did we?" Tig shook his head. "Apparently she sublets so her name isn't on the lease. Smart. Karl said they mostly stayed at his place so," she trailed off. "It's not important. I'll jump to the main parts. He's been hacking. Computer hacking," she clarified. "Apparently he has some amazing skills and was recruited when he transferred to Tolosa Tech."

Now Tig looked more interested than mad.

"It was a job of sorts. A way to earn money and Abramson was his, I don't know, recruiter and contact. It *was* part of his classwork, the internship, but it was also a cover. Karl's been hacking for money but he made a big mistake. He didn't follow their directions exactly, so he was discovered and has been in hiding since. He is sure the fire was intentional, probably to kill him, either as

218

punishment from higher ups, or maybe to cover up the hack from the big criminals he was stealing from."

"*Stealing?* Was he stealing money? This is huge!"

"I know. It's bigger than he understood, he says. He was 'hired' to move money out of certain accounts and into other accounts. He doesn't know who owns either set of accounts because he only works with numbers and code. However, it does have something to do with the Rescue Center since he said he had to be there once or twice to access the terminals directly. Maybe some of that was a cover for his real class work, but he doesn't know."

"Like bank accounts?"

"I assume so. Huge amounts of money, hundreds of thousands and multiple times. I think he's in real trouble. Neither of us knows what side Abramson's on, but he's in it up to his eyebrows. If he's using his position at the university to recruit kids he's still a criminal, but if he's trying to eliminate Karl, and maybe other kids, to cover up this hack, then it's even worse."

"I can't see a way out, either. Maybe after we have a chance to think about it we can try to help Karl. I'm just not sure how," Tig said.

"I suggested the police, but Karl thinks they can't help, that this is too big. I don't think going to the university would help, since I'm pretty sure this guy is not an idiot and has covered his tracks. He can probably plead ignorance, and I bet a cookie there is no trail that leads to him, except an inordinate number of students who are now hackers. Not proof though."

They sat silently for a moment, sipping and petting cats for comfort.

"Karl and I figured out a relatively safe way to communicate," Elizabeth continued. "It won't work in an emergency, but it's something."

"What?"

"At the bottom of the stair handrail that leads from the store parking lot to those apartments, Karl said we can leave a note in the hollow if we need to reach him. If he needs us, he'll call. He has a bunch of cell phones and dumps them after he uses them. So, he can get us, but we can't get him quickly."

"I didn't know there was a stairway in the store parking lot."

"Me neither."

"But there is another problem," Tig said.

"What?"

"If we're being listened to, to find him or any other reason, on our phones or us here in the house, he can be tracked."

"What do you mean if we're being listened to in the house? Is the house bugged?"

"I don't know. But maybe we should act as if it is. All someone needs to do is listen from his or her own car on the street. These listening devices can pick up anything. Our phones might be bugged, so calls and texts are out. We need to come up with a code or something."

"Are you serious? It's a real thing?"

"I am, and it is. If this is something so big the police can't help, and Karl is in hiding afraid for his life, it might be that big."

"You seem to have gone from chief skeptic to all-in suddenly."

"We talk about this stuff at work. Everything you've said has already happened somewhere to someone. It's not just in a spy novel. I mean, look at Edward Snowden. We're talking top government agencies."

Elizabeth's hand shook as it rested on Freya. Her eyes filled. She was as big as a house, the incubation unit for a whole person, and if her life depended on it, which she felt it might, she would not be able to run away or hide.

"Hey, hey, hey." Tig got up and came over. He knelt next to her and hugged her. "I can talk to someone at work and maybe get some advice."

"You can't tell anyone anything! Look what's happening to Karl right now."

"No, I won't mention specifics, but maybe just an idea of what we can do to be safe."

"Move to Montana?"

"Besides that. It seems we're being left alone for the moment. They know Karl isn't staying here, and maybe they don't know he's been in touch."

"Oh! I forgot to tell you. He said he got insurance. He put a bunch of information on the SD card you found. I forgot to tell him we found it. Shoot. I can leave a note for him. He might feel better knowing his insurance is safe."

"Maybe we should just give him back the SD card? Leave it at the drop? Then he can have it back and it's his problem," Tig said.

"If something happens to him, we might need to give it to someone. Should we look at it first?"

"Would you even know computer code if you saw it?" Tig asked. "If it's truly secret information, and Karl is as good a hacker as he says, it's going to be password protected, firewalled and maybe even with that thing where if the wrong person tries to access it, it self-destructs."

"I don't want to mess with it. I just want to get rid of it." Elizabeth felt tears rising.

"This is a mess. I'll call my guy and see if he can meet me today. I don't want to wait until shift tonight. We shouldn't talk on the phone and I definitely don't want to do it with a bunch of fire fighters around. They're a nosy crew."

"Should I come, too?" She got herself under control.

"I think no, for now. It would make sense for me to see him because we work together, but since you seem to be out of it for now, let's try to keep it that way," Tig said.

"I haven't seen anyone around the house since Karl left. I thought maybe they kidnaped him and that was why. Since they don't have him, they might be waiting for him to come out of hiding. I didn't see his car at Stacy's. Maybe he parked it someplace else so if they find it, they won't find him. Oh, poor Karl. We have to help him."

"We will. I'm going into the outback to call. Just in case." Tig referred to the area outside their back gate that butted onto a 25,000 acre state park. They often went on walks, though not lately. It was fairly rugged terrain and it made her smile to think of pushing a stroller around there. Her thoughts went to the baby sage rabbit and she sent out feelers, looking for him. She also remembered he was not the brightest of rabbits, so she sent out a general query to their sage village.

She still had her hand on Freya and after a moment, Freya acted like an antennae, amplifying her request. Elizabeth received a faint response. All was well. A distant wave of gratitude and it was gone. She knew she would get no further answers in the future since the rabbits would not remember her. It must be nice to forget trauma if enough time passed, she mused. But maybe not so nice to be a baby sage bunny, and everything wants to eat you.

"All right, everyone. We have things to do." She gently put Freya on the chair and set her tea mug on the counter for later use. Thor was hungry so she made some instant oatmeal with the last of the fresh blueberries.

"I should have gone into the store last night when I was on my 'mission,'" she said. Then she immediately regretted her joke. If they were being listened to, she had to be more careful. She wondered how they would go about finding one. From television, she thought they were small and difficult to find. She'd wait for Tig and his expert.

She went to check the mailbox. Really she wanted to check the street. Maybe she should start watering the front yard more so she could watch. It might be suspicious since they had finished a new landscaping, sort of a California-Japan fusion requiring almost no water.

The sun was out and burning off the morning mist. Junk mail. Fine with her. She carefully looked it over while scanning the street. Nothing new. The same old cars. She carried the fliers in and tossed them into recycling. She went through to the pond, grabbing a handful of diced tofu on the way. While she waited for Tig, she watched the koi snorfle up the tofu. The girls were fine. It was lovely and quiet this morning. She went up the few stairs to the 'viewing port' and brushed off a few cobwebs before sitting.

Elizabeth figured Teddy and Edward were both out with Tig since the only thing they loved more than being in the outback, was being in the outback with their people. She used to sit on the fallen log and watch them play, but since her whole body had changed and her center of gravity shifted, the log was supremely uncomfortable.

You could bring a pillow, Freya said as she settled herself near Elizabeth's knees, the only spot left after Thor expanded over her thighs. Maybe a little footstool was in order so she'd have a bit more lap.

Good idea.

The fish were so relaxing to watch. It tickled her to see them graze on the water hyacinth and circle endlessly looking for tiny bugs. A frog colony had set up in the huge black water taro plant and she hoped they knew to stay in the mesh. Koi would eat eggs, pollywogs, and at their size, even a small frog. *Nature,* she sighed.

Tig returned and sat next to her. "Okay, I'm meeting someone who can help us for coffee in an hour. We'll figure something out, okay?"

"I know. It's going to be fine." Elizabeth parroted Freya, but honestly, she had to think that or go crazy.

It is going to be fine, Freya said.

How can you possibly know?

I have learned there is a crossing where your world and mine meet. I don't know if it ever has before, or ever will again, but for now it is here. I have to think it will be fine, because for some reason, our worlds are connected. If my world is in jeopardy, so is yours. I am in battle much of the time.

So, your battle, the one I saw, is going on all the time? More or less?

It would seem so. Volksvang is in constant conflict, Freya said.

Volksvang? Is that the name of your village?

It is more than the name of the place and more than the physical place. It is in our hearts, too.

It's so small. Aren't you worried all your people will die? Elizabeth asked.

They are the strongest of the strong. As long as not all of them die, they will come back, which is one reason I have to keep coming back here. So long as I live, Volksvang will live.

"I'm going to start some laundry," Tig said. "Do you need anything?" Elizabeth shook her head. "I'm going to rest later before tonight's shift. I've decided to postpone my pond jobs until we figure this out, okay?" He kissed her and went inside.

She would be happy to have a nap when Tig slept later. She wanted to ask Freya more about her village, and how her dead warriors managed to 'come back,' but when Tig spoke, Freya had taken the opportunity to join the boys.

Twenty-Four

While Tig was gone to meet his friend about their options, she realized she did feel better. A little safer. And only one more night shift until he was off for two days. Normally he'd work on ponds more, but since he'd mentioned putting those off, she felt reassured. Maybe they could do something normal for a change.

She decided to do some grocery shopping, and while she was there, she could drop a note into the hollow of the handrail and let Karl know they'd found the SD card and were keeping it safe. Part of her felt she was in some sort of TV drama, that this couldn't be real.

She gathered up her purse and keys and headed to the store. She'd made a list of sorts, but with her 'pregnancy brain' she knew she'd forgotten a number of key items. She wandered each aisle, hoping for the best. She planned several meals, and gathered some staples.

After check-out she loaded her car and sat in the driver's seat, wondering what to write in her note to Karl in case someone else found it. She finally settled on:

We found your gym equipment. If you need it, let me know and I'll bring it by.

"This will probably fool nobody," she mumbled and carefully went down the stairs. They were cracked and uneven, the handrail wobbly in its footing, and she was glad she hadn't known when going down the first time in the dusky evening. At the bottom she looked around to see if she was being watched. With a hundred apartment windows within a block, she had no way of knowing. She had already folded the note, so when she felt safe-ish, she sat on the bottom step as if tired, which she was. Her feet felt like flippers with her swollen ankles. After a moment, she grabbed the rail with two hands as if standing again was a Herculean effort—not a lot of acting required—and quickly stuffed the note in the hollow. To any watchers, she had just turned and walked back up the stairs after coming down for no apparent reason. She'd have to work on her covert ops.

Mom! Mom! Help. Someone's in the house. Teddy's panicked cry clenched at her heart.

Freya? Is it true? Sometimes Teddy exaggerated.

Yes. A stranger. Looking for something. He is in your room and going through the house.

Where are you guys? Are you safe?

Yes, we went out our door. She meant the pet door.

Where are you now? she repeated. By the time Elizabeth was back at her car, she felt like she'd run a marathon. She tried to talk to the cats

228

and start the car at the same time. She wanted to throw up. Call Tig. This was a big one.

We're hidden in the outback.

Good. Stay there. I'm coming. I'm telling daddy, too. Don't come to the house until I tell you.

She called Tig but it went to voicemail. He must have his phone turned down if they were in a restaurant or coffee shop. She left a message and a text then drove as fast as she could without getting a ticket. She didn't know what she would do when she got home. Certainly not confront anyone. Maybe she could get a description or license plate. The grocery store was only five minutes from home going the back way, avoiding two of the tiny town's four traffic lights.

She sent a constant message for the cats to remain hidden. She got nothing from Freya and had a feeling she wasn't listening. For all that she was a warrior in her time, she was still a six pound kitten in this one, Elizabeth thought grimly. However, Freya failed to realize it sometimes.

Elizabeth drove past the house. Everything looked normal. She didn't see any unusual cars nearby. No black SUVs.

Are you guys still safe?

Yes. He's gone, though, Freya said. *I don't know if he found what he wanted, but he was very fast. He went through your room, Karl's room and the baby room.*

Freya, don't come in the house yet. I'm waiting for Tig. Her phone rang. Tig.

"What's going on?"

"The cats told me someone was in the house searching so I called you. I was at the grocery store and I came home."

"What? You're home?"

"I'm in the car on the street. I haven't gone in. The cats say the person is gone. Can you come home now?"

"I'm on my way. Two minutes." She looked in her rearview and saw his truck barreling down the street a block away.

He pulled up behind her and leaped out. "Are you okay?"

"Yes, I'm fine. Should we call the police?"

"No. I'm going to check it out. They might not have been there to take something out. They might have put something in."

"Like what?"

Tig pulled out a small cell phone-sized device. "I explained to my guy, who's the brother-in-law of my friend, what's been going on, and he brought me this to see if the house is bugged. It won't detect a long-distance listening device, only something in the house."

He crossed the street and entered the house. She saw he needed his key, so it was still locked. An eternity later, three minutes on her cell phone, he came back and beckoned to her. She pulled into the drive and parked in her usual spot. She told the cats they were home, but to wait until she told them it was safe. She remembered her melting groceries and brought in a couple bags. Tig hurried to help.

"I did a quick sweep and didn't find anything, but I'll check again," he whispered as he grabbed the last two bags from the car. She nodded.

She called the cats and put away the food as Tig made his way through the house again, this time searching slowly. She was dying to see what, if any, damage the burglar had done, but decided to wait until Tig had finished.

"Seems okay," he whispered. "I think we still have to assume an enhanced listening device, like a parabolic microphone, might be used, so we need to be cautious." At her blank look he continued, "It's a microphone but it hears long distances and through walls. Not magically, it's really sensitive, but the farther from the source, the more other noises it's going to pick up too. Our street is so quiet it could probably hear us. We might want to start turning on the radio or TV if we're going to have Karl-related conversations."

The cats hustled through the little door in the back gate. She opened the laundry room door, and they streamed in. She picked them up each in turn and Teddy allowed a snuggle for a moment. They must have been terrified. They didn't like it when the neighbor used his leaf blower or the UPS lady brought packages to the door. They did like people, but only when properly introduced.

"Are you guys okay?" All affirmative. She decided tuna juice would take the edge off, and in fact, she was hungry herself after all her efforts with the stairs. She made tuna sandwiches for herself and Tig.

"I don't see a big mess," Tig said after another pass of the house. "Whoever searched did it carefully and didn't want us to know they were here. They didn't count on watch-cats." He smiled and petted each of them as they placidly lapped tuna juice.

"Did they find anything?" she asked.

Tig had taken a big bite of sandwich. "I don't think so, and all our money is still there."

She nodded, assuming he meant the SD card because they didn't keep any extra money in the house.

She finished her sandwich and got a big glass of water, then sat at the table. Her ankles thanked her.

"I'm going to move my truck." Tig had left it on the street while checking the house.

"Are you guys really okay?" Elizabeth asked the cats again.

Sure, from Edward.

Why? from Teddy, probably already forgotten.

Of course. Freya. She clambered into Elizabeth's lap, and the boys went out to lie on the warm patio stones near the pond.

Did you see who came in?

Yes.

Tell me everything.

He came from the back. Whoa. That was unexpected. But smart. No one would have seen him at all from the outback. *He did something to the back door and came in.* She sent Elizabeth a picture, like a video, of a male shape in a hoodie,

232

jeans, and sports shoes with a ball cap pulled low. He carried a small case, she presumed had tools or bugs in it. Unless it was to hold whatever he wanted to steal. He knelt and Elizabeth assumed he picked the lock. *The boys were eating kibbles, and I was waiting for you on your chair.*

She sent another picture-video of the boys scurrying for the pet door in the living room as the person opened the door. It was from Freya's point of view, and the boys looked terrified as they scrambled to get out before he came in. From the chair tucked under the table, Freya was invisible, but she froze, waiting for the man to pass her. Elizabeth felt Freya's heart speed up, her senses sharpening as she worked out her best escape plan.

Elizabeth became angry that this person had frightened her cats so much, but was grateful they had gotten out of the house. Who knew what a frustrated criminal would do to an innocent house pet?

Then what?

I went outside when he went down the hall. I didn't see after that. We all hid and called to you.

You did exactly the right thing. She picked Freya up and lay her gently over her shoulder. Freya relaxed into her and Elizabeth put her ear against the fragile-feeling ribcage and felt the mouse-purr. "I love you, Freya."

I know. I love you, too. Now put me down. A tiny but strong little hind foot pushed out, and Elizabeth laughed and set her on the next chair.

Tig came back in and sat opposite. "I'm still hungry. I feel like burgers. I'll barbeque and tell you what I learned?"

It was only half a question because he was already moving, pulling out the ground beef she'd just bought and spices. She nodded, and he went out to pre-heat the grill. The boys returned with him, circling like sharks knowing there would be bits that somehow fell to the floor in their vicinity. It almost felt normal, but her heart fluttered when she thought of what could have happened. A paw settled on her leg. Freya.

"I know, I know. It's fine," Elizabeth said.

"What's fine?" Tig asked.

"Freya knows I'm anxious. She's calming me." Elizabeth pointed to the paw.

Tig raised his eyebrows. "Wow. On purpose?"

"Yes. She is more attuned than the others. Maybe not attuned," she amended, "but she responds to it more the way humans need."

Tig nodded. He knew both the boys could be quite indifferent or dense to their humans' needs for comfort when they didn't feel like providing it.

"Why don't you come out with me while I cook. We'll set you up at the picnic table with a cushion and you can put your feet up. Then we'll chat." She knew he meant about his conversation with his friend.

Once she was settled, he put the burgers on the grill and joined her. "First let me say, I don't know this guy. He's the brother-in-law of someone

234

I do know, so I trust what he told me. It's not too good."

"Okay."

"He works for the FBI, and after I gave him the info I had, the first thing he said is he doesn't think this is FBI jurisdiction, so he couldn't help me directly. From everything I told him, he said it sounds like big-time money laundering and the biggest customers are the cartels. It usually involves foreign countries." Tig let that sink in while he rose to flip the burgers.

"Cartels? You mean, like South American drug cartels? Like DEA stuff?"

Tig nodded. "Be right back." He went into the kitchen and brought out condiments and buns. "You want your bun grilled?"

"I guess." Elizabeth was dazed and not very hungry. "What are we supposed to do?" Pieces of news stories where severed heads lined the streets of Mexico flashed through her mind. "I mean, Karl didn't have anything to do with that, right?"

"If he's moving money for cartels, he's in trouble if he gets caught or tries to quit. You don't quit a cartel according to, uh, Bob, let's call him."

"But that's in Mexico or Colombia, right? Not here."

"Bob said the cartels have moved north and are trying to establish a foothold here. The big Mexican gangs have moved into California and so have the cartels."

"Oh, my gosh. I had no idea."

"Most people don't. Bob has nothing to do with this because the FBI doesn't work outside of

235

the US. Or so I'm told. However, the CIA, NSA, DEA do. I can't see calling up these agencies and trying to get help. I feel like someone would find out and we'd be in more trouble than we are. Right now I think we're just being watched, but they haven't moved forward until today. I don't know what would have happened if you'd been home. Or we both had been. If they wanted information, or felt we had something of value, we'd have been, uh, asked." She read that as *interrogated*.

Tig pulled the burgers off the grill and brought them to the table, and busily dressed his bun. Elizabeth felt a little queasy so she pulled pieces off her patty and dropped them for the cats who obliged and cleaned them up. She ate her lettuce and tomato slice, then followed it up with a pickle. "I don't know what to say or do," she said.

"Me neither. Bob is going to do some checking for us, unofficially, but for now we sit tight. He offered to watch our house at night, you know surveillance, but I said I'd check with you. I didn't know if you'd feel better or worse. Maybe if someone is watching our house and a second, unknown entity, Bob, is watching the house, that could make it worse."

"Worse how?"

"They, the bad guys, would know we know."

"But we don't know!"

"We know something; we just don't know what we know."

They stared at each other for a moment and Elizabeth burst into giddy laughter. "Oh, my gosh.

I can't believe this." She almost said, "Freya's war is easier to deal with than this," but remembered just in time she'd told Tig nothing of that.

She picked up the remains of her mangled burger and splashed ketchup and mustard on her bun. She should eat, keep up her strength. She missed Freya from her lap and glanced down, seeing she had no lap at all. Not good. Perhaps moving up her check-up was in order. She'd call later and see if they could squeeze her in sooner. She smiled thinking of being tailed to the gynecologist's office and how awkward that would be for the criminals.

"What?" Tig asked, seeing her smile.

"I'm thinking of the baby and maybe I should get a check-up earlier than my regular appointment. I seem to be growing at an inordinate rate."

"You mean Thor?" His smile was rascally and almost normal. She knew he was worried but trying to ease some of the tension.

"Sure. Thor. Freya will be thrilled." A huge kidney punch and she groaned. "I can't tell if Thor is as thrilled, however," she added.

"I want to come."

"I'll call and see when I can get in." She picked up her plate and glass and waddled inside. Tig followed with his own dishes plus the condiments. It was quite a juggling act.

"I know I should make two trips. But *you* know I can't." He was still trying to cheer her up.

She kissed him. "I'm going to lie down. Are you going to join me? You said you needed to sleep before your shift."

"Yup. I'm going to water a bit and then I'll be in."

While they had made the front yard xeriscopic, the back was a lush tropical jungle and did require a bit of watering. Tig liked the task because it gave him time to think; it relaxed him. The cats liked watering, because it was another time their people were with them and lots of bugs came out. Edward especially liked leaping for sky-raisins as they called flies and other flying insects. Teddy did not leap for anything anymore. In his youth Elizabeth had seen him jump and catch a hummingbird in midair. It startled them both and he let it go, no harm done, but he got a big scolding from Elizabeth.

She lay on her side and picked up her phone to call the doctor. It rang in her hand, unknown caller.

"Hello?"

"It's me." Karl. "I got your message. I don't want my gym stuff, you keep it, okay?"

"Sure. Are you all right?"

"I've been doing some thinking and I'm going to talk to, uh, my advisor. I have to do something about this. It's getting out of hand."

"Oh no. That's not safe!" Elizabeth protested.

"I want to know if you guys will go with me. I want out and you know just about all I do." He sounded young and afraid.

"I'll talk to Tig but I'm sure he will. I'll leave you a note tonight."

"Hurry. I don't think I can wait much longer. Stacy's coming home. I can't stall her anymore. I don't want you or her in any more danger." His breathing was heavy. "I want to go tomorrow, okay?"

"Okay. I'll leave you information. Don't go by yourself."

"I'll try not to." He disconnected.

Tig came into the bedroom while the phone was still in her hand. "Get the doctor's office? When can you go in?"

"No. That was Karl. He wants to meet Abramson and have it out."

"That's crazy."

"It gets crazier. He wants to go tomorrow and wants us to go with him. For security, I guess."

"Just because we're there doesn't mean Abramson isn't going to do something. Maybe not at this second, but at some point." Tig sighed. "Okay. But I want to tell my guy what we're doing."

"Are you sure that's a good idea? We don't really know what's going on ourselves. Maybe you should wait until after this meeting."

"I want to tell someone where we're going and why. We need a little insurance," Tig said.

"What about Janie and Terry?" Their across the street neighbors and best friends.

"I didn't want them involved, but I guess it's the best we can do for now. I'll let them know."

239

"Let's rest for a bit and rethink. We can tell them after our nap if you still think we should."

Elizabeth had a hard time falling asleep, but as usual, Tig zonked. Didn't he have thoughts? He must be really tired from working all night. She didn't ask him how his shift had gone.

Twenty-Five

After their nap, Elizabeth and Tig decided not to involve their neighbors after all. They split the difference. Tig would leave a note at the station tonight for his friend, who would give it to his brother-in-law if they did not return. It sounded so dark. So ominous.

Elizabeth would also leave a note in the handrail so Karl didn't have to throw out another burner phone. She was spending more time at the store than ever. Just as well since half the time she didn't remember what she was supposed to buy. A few weeks ago she'd come home with toilet paper and a package of blueberries. Her lengthy list still lay on the counter where she'd left it. And she wasn't nearly as dimwitted then as she was now.

"At least I'm getting my exercise." Nothing suspicious about a hugely pregnant woman going down the stairs and back up again without visiting anyone or doing anything. She didn't think anyone would believe she was out for the fun of it. "Maybe it'll be the last time." She hoped. The meet was for tomorrow, and since Karl wasn't using his car, she said they'd pick him up in the store parking lot at 10 AM and head to the university. She checked the picture of the advising schedule she'd taken on her phone. According to that, Abramson had office hours then.

She was too tired to fake a grocery run, so she drove home. She and Tig had eaten some homemade sundried tomato and corn chowder she'd found in the freezer. Soup and warm rolls and a salad made a quick dinner before he'd gone to work. Quick was all she could manage these days. She locked up and took everybody back to the bedroom with her.

She'd promised the cats NetFilms, so they all watched a British crime drama, which everyone had grown fond of. When she awoke and the crime was being solved, she decided she'd have to see it again with Tig which assuaged some of her guilt for watching it without him. After all, it wasn't like she knew what was going on. Lights out, and she slept straight through until Tig's truck revved backing up their short but steep drive.

She remembered he was off for two days and had said he'd be with her. She also remembered they were chasing down Abramson for some answers and was less excited about that.

By the time she made it out to the kitchen, Tig was dicing veggies for omelets and the smell of toasting bread brought Freya racing back from her morning outside routine.

Elizabeth put the kettle on and kissed him good morning.

"Want an omelet?" he asked.

"It smells great, so yes I do. But a small one please, not pillow-size." Tig made gigantic omelets for the shift at work where they had an enormous cast iron skillet. Elizabeth couldn't lift it, much less cook with it. Tig enjoyed making huge things. The fire fighters didn't mind, either.

Tig nodded. "Lightweight."

"Yup." Elizabeth buttered the toast and put more bread in. "I feel like jelly. Want any? Mom sent some of her homemade pomegranate before they left on their anniversary trip."

"Absolutely. I love that stuff." Elizabeth's parents were celebrating thirty years and had gone on a month-long sojourn to Europe. Her dad owned a business which made small parts for airplanes, and it had ballooned when he had diversified for drones. Apparently the parts were critical.

Thinking of her parents reminded her that although their trip had been planned months ago, with plenty of time before the baby was due, that was before Thor took charge of his own development and showed every intention of arriving early. Really early.

Great. One more thing to worry about. After she had this latest check-up, she'd send her mom a text and see what was what. Her parents were nearing the end of their adventure, but would it be soon enough?

"Here you go." Tig set down a laden plate and her cup of tea, which she'd completely forgotten about. Freya poked her nose above the table from her vantage point on Elizabeth's stomach.

"Thank you. All right, here you go." She tore off a piece of buttery toast and set it on the next chair. Freya leapt lightly over, and Elizabeth could now access her food. "This is a small omelet?"

"For me, sure." Tig set down his own giant omelet along with home fries, ketchup and hot sauce. "Need anything else?"

Elizabeth had already taken a bite and shook her head. The eggs were light and perfectly cooked while the cheese melted around the diced onions and peppers. Tig had laid a row of sliced avocado across hers, knowing how much she loved it. She spread some of her mother's home made pomegranate jelly on her toast and sighed with pleasure. She missed her mom and looked forward to grilling her on all things baby.

Her parents had only the most skeletal of itineraries, so she didn't know where they were at the moment. They wanted to be 'spontaneous' they said. Elizabeth could understand, she supposed. They were very detail oriented and organized in their daily lives. They had to be to keep a small business afloat these days and fulfill contracts along with getting new ones. Traveling off the grid was a way to combat structure. They had cell phones so the business could reach them.

Breakfast complete, they got ready to pick up Karl. Elizabeth was a little anxious about how the meeting with Abramson would go, but she didn't think he'd try anything right now. But his basement office was kind of dark and creepy, she recalled.

Tig drove Elizabeth's little car because the back seat was more comfortable than the tiny back bench in the truck. Karl waited for them in his 'homeless man' guise once again at the rear entrance to the store.

"Everything okay?" Tig asked Karl once he was settled and they were on their way to the campus.

"All good so far."

"Are you eating?" Elizabeth asked. She felt a little guilty about the huge breakfast they had just consumed.

"Yes, but it's getting kind of scant at Stacy's. I know I'm right near a store, but I'm afraid to go out much."

"Here. This is what I forgot to give you the other night." She handed him the box of granola bars that was still in her car.

"This is great, thanks." He immediately opened one and took a big bite. Now Elizabeth felt worse.

The ride was short and metered parking was available, so they made it to the basement level of the Business Administration building in no time.

"How do you know where Abramson's office is?" Karl asked.

"We visited him here," Elizabeth explained.

"We wanted some information when you were missing. He wasn't very forthcoming," Tig added.

"He wouldn't be. It's his job to keep secrets. Mine, too, I suppose, but I blew that big time."

245

Tig and Elizabeth exchanged a look. They reached his closed office door, but could hear a muted conversation inside. Elizabeth saw a new flier on the board advertising a campus club called the White Foxes. Apparently it was a hacking club which didn't sound wholesome to her. Encouraging an illegal act? She was about to enquire when Karl spoke.

"We can wait here for them to finish," Karl said.

"So he is a real academic advisor?" Tig asked.

"Yes, in the Business department. It's his cover, you could say. He does have a doctorate degree and is a professor here, but his main job is recruiting, as you probably figured out."

"It seems strange to, I don't know, stalk kids to get them to break the law. For money, right?" Elizabeth was already tired of standing and glanced around for someplace to sit. The floor was out of the question because she'd never get up again.

"It's a job for a lot of us. Some students go on to become operations officers. That's not for me. I don't have the guts for it."

"What's that?" Tig and Elizabeth had both picked up on the term "operations officers."

"Like an agent, I guess you'd say," Karl said.

"What are you talking about?" Elizabeth asked.

"What did you think I meant?" Karl asked.

"You said you were involved in criminal things? You were moving money illegally for uh,

246

bad people!" Elizabeth's mind went blank at this new angle.

"Yeah. But for the good guys." Karl looked a bit outraged.

"You haven't been very clear about this from the start," Tig said.

"I couldn't! I had to keep it all a secret. I screwed it up almost right away." His voice rose.

"Who is doing all of this? You're just a kid!" Tig said.

"The CIA."

"CIA!" Tig and Elizabeth both said just as the door opened. Abramson looked angry.

"You two again. Why am I not surprised? I am conducting a meeting with a student. Do you mind keeping your voices down?" A pale freckled face peeked around Abramson from where the student sat in front of his desk. Abramson turned to her. "I think we're done here, Bethany. If you need further help with the assignment, I can see you at next week's office hours. And no, you can't have another extension."

Bethany rose and left the office, looking sideways at the unusual group entering.

"Is she one of the hacker kids, too?" Elizabeth whispered.

"God, no. She doesn't know how many beans make two. If she'd apply herself, she'd do better, but a long time ago someone told her she wasn't smart enough, and undoing that now is a challenge." He moved around his desk and sat. "I see we have to clear some things up. Sit."

Elizabeth gratefully sank into a rock hard office chair. Karl pulled out a folding chair, and Tig took the remaining seat, a footstool.

"I'll start," Karl began. "I need help. You know I've been hiding, but these people, my friends," he indicated Elizabeth and Tig, "have been helping me and now they're in trouble, too."

"How much trouble?" Abramson asked.

"We're being followed, we think, and someone broke into our house yesterday," Tig began. "They didn't find what they were looking for, but that doesn't mean they won't be back."

"What were they looking for?"

"I backed up the files before I ran," Karl said.

"Where is the back-up?"

"Somewhere safe."

"Okay. Your back-up was noticed. Much of the activity we were monitoring has ceased but if you have a copy, we can still get them, maybe."

"Is this a cartel? Drug money?" Elizabeth asked. "What's going on?"

"I can't tell you most of it. It's not cartel money, as far as we know, but it is money laundering on a big scale. It also involves the federal government. That's all I can say at the moment. We're close to rounding up the top guys, but Karl made a huge mistake, despite his training. Not only was his hack discovered, but the back-up was noticed."

"So the fire was an attempt on his life," Tig said.

"Yes. He used an unsafe computer and he was traced." Abramson glared at Karl. "Amateur mistake, one you'd been warned about, and trained against. It almost cost you your life."

"Why would they try to kill him if they knew about the back-up but didn't know where it was?" Tig asked.

"We're not sure. Maybe they thought it would be destroyed in the house fire, and now he's reasonably safe because they still want to find it. They don't know where it is, which is why your house was searched, but you were not contacted. Which is good."

"Good?" Elizabeth squawked.

"If they thought you had it, they'd have been far more aggressive. They don't know where Karl is, or this would be a different conversation. Let's keep it that way."

Karl nodded. "What do I do now?"

"I have a safe house for you. I'll move you today."

"What can you tell us about this case?" Elizabeth asked.

"Not much until it's closed. We are near, as I said."

"What's going to happen next?" Tig asked. "Are we safe from whoever is after Karl?"

"Yes," Elizabeth chimed in. "Once Karl is at the safe house and they can't reach him, will they come after us?"

"Unlikely," Abramson said. "Karl has been 'gone' for several days now as far as they're concerned. Unless they were watching you carefully, which it doesn't appear they were, Karl is 'still gone.' They have no reason to come after you unless you have new information. Do you?"

"No. I don't think so," Elizabeth said. She looked at Tig who shook his head.

"I'm off for a couple days, so I'll be around, but should we go out of town?" Tig asked. "I can't imagine going against someone armed."

"At this point I would caution you against doing anything outside of your normal routine. Our people are very near gathering enough intelligence to make arrests. With Karl's information, we're likely to be successful."

"Why don't you just arrest them if you know who they are?" Elizabeth asked.

"When I said "money laundering," and Karl told you he was hacking, it failed to fully express the scope of this operation. Computers can be accessed from anywhere. These accounts are all over the world. We are putting personnel in place to make arrests, but we need what Karl has to finish this piece. To make sure we have the evidence to make charges stick."

"Okay," Tig said slowly. "So, these are international hackers? With the guys at the top also scattered around the world?"

"Yes. The guys at the top, as you say, are highly insulated. They keep several steps removed from the process. They have shell companies and live in countries that are not eager to work with us. It can be delicate and difficult. We need some of the higher level people as well as the hackers to flip in order to do this."

"Flip?" Elizabeth asked.

"Yes. Inform on their bosses. They need to be assured of our protection before they'll help us. All of this needs to be in place before we can move."

"Wait a sec. These hackers, these criminals, will be protected as a reward for their crimes? Like witness protection or something?"

"Exactly. Otherwise there's no reason for them to help. They either keep going or they're dead."

"And Karl's in danger from these same people?" Tig asked.

"Very much so. However, he's in a better position because he was already working for us."

"Let me see if I follow," Elizabeth began. "Karl is a hacker. Pretending to be a bad guy, but really working for the CIA as a good guy?"

"Yes," Karl said. "Sometimes the bad guys are called Black Hat hackers, and so the good ones are White Hats. Like in the cowboy movie days. Ours are based out of here, the university hacking club, so we're White Foxes." Elizabeth remembered the club flier.

"You're not good at keeping information to yourself, are you Karl?" Abramson said.

"They're my friends! And they figured out most of it anyway."

"Perhaps espionage is not going to be your strong suit. You are an excellent hacker, so maybe an analyst or technician is a better option."

"Really? I could maybe still work for you guys?"

"Certainly not until you graduate and go through full training." Abramson smiled. "But let's all live through this, first, all right?"

Karl looked a little brighter.

"So Karl will be with you," Tig said. "We stay put for now. What do we do if someone comes back or breaks in again?"

"I will put an officer on you. You won't know he or she is there. Keep to your normal routine. It shouldn't be more than a few more days." He turned to Karl. "How soon can you get me the back-up?"

Karl did not look at Tig and Elizabeth. Elizabeth sensed he did not want Abramson to know the SD card was with them. Perhaps he didn't fully trust Abramson or he wanted to protect Tig and Elizabeth.

"Today. When will you take me to the safe house?"

"Also today. Can you go now?"

"No. I need to do a few things first. I'll go back with them," he pointed to Tig and Elizabeth, "and then finish what I need. Should I come back here this afternoon?"

"I have to teach a class, but I can pass it on to my teaching assistant so I can meet you. 3 PM?"

They all agreed. Karl opened the office door. "Oh, hey," he said.

"Hi." Elizabeth recognized the squeaky voice of the student, Bethany.

Elizabeth had gotten stiff sitting on the metal chair. Tig helped her up and they moved into the hall.

"Bethany, did you need something else?" Abramson asked.

"I left my text book in your office and I need it to study. I'm sorry." Her voice went higher. "I didn't want to interrupt you. I'll just get it now." She darted in and retrieved a book from the top of a stack. "I'm sorry Dr. Abramson. Thanks!" She bolted down the hall.

Abramson looked displeased. "Amateur mistake. I've been chastising you and I do the same thing," he said to Karl.

"What just happened? She forgot her book. You're right, she's not very with-it," Tig said.

"I've been so consumed with Karl I overlooked the obvious. I think Bethany set me up. Her book may have been bugged, and I was too distracted to check. Idiot!"

"She isn't—she can't be, what? Another officer?" Elizabeth asked.

"She might be, and if so, she's a pro." Abramson paced in the hall. "We need to move up the time table. Can you do that?"

"What? Why?" Karl asked.

"She didn't just forget her book. It was probably a bug, and although I sweep my office daily, and did this morning upon my arrival, I didn't between your visit and hers. If she's as clever as I think, she brought it with her and planned to leave it. I might not have caught it until my next sweep tomorrow."

"How would that have helped her? Them? Whoever," Tig asked, frustrated. "If you were going to find the bug anyway, how does that help them?"

"They can access the information remotely. It was just a fluke she retrieved the physical bug now, although she didn't have to. She waited outside, I think, with some kind of enhanced listening device. When she realized she'd gotten gold, it was in her best interests to get the bug. We can tell a lot by the bug itself."

"Wouldn't you know who planted it? Wouldn't she be exposed?"

"Not necessarily. Today I have my busiest office hours, so if I were to have a meeting that could benefit them, it is reasonable to assume it might be today. With so many people coming and going, it might be hard to pinpoint who brought the bug. Also, she is very good. She's been in my office many times, asking for help, requesting assignment extensions, asking exhausting questions."

"Are you sure she's not a real student? She attends classes?"

"Oh, she's a real student all right. They are very detailed in the placement of their assets. She attends classes, but doesn't do her homework often, which allows her access to me or other professors for information, depending on what she's after."

"She's so young-looking. And I see she's an amazing actress. I would never have guessed," Elizabeth said.

"I should have guessed. It's my job. At any rate, we need to move this along. They think I'll have the back-up by 3PM. Let's go." He picked up his office phone and called his TA to cover his classes. He grabbed his briefcase and locked the door. "As much good as that does," he mumbled.

As they left the building, Abramson said, "I'm going to expedite the process. Here is my burner number. Don't use names if you call it." He scribbled the number on two pieces of paper he gave to Tig and Karl. "Go. Be fast, but be careful. We might only have today to get this in place. I won't feel good until you're in the safe house, Karl, and we have the information."

He turned to Tig and Elizabeth. "If Bethany is what I think she is, you might need to go some place else for a couple days. Can you do that?"

"No, I don't think so." Elizabeth thought of the cats. She was not willing to leave them unprotected, but couldn't think of a place they could all go. "What about the operative you promised? If the secret is out, can we have more protection?"

"I don't have more people, but maybe I can put the officer in the house with you, instead of on the street."

Tig and Elizabeth eyed each other. Both were clearly not comfortable with that either. "On the street is fine," Tig said, cutting off Elizabeth. "Let's go. We'll be in touch."

Twenty-Six

After Elizabeth and Tig left the Bus Ad building, she whispered, "What was that about?" referring to Tig's quick acceptance of an operative watching on the street rather than with them in the house. "I think someone inside with us would be safer. After all, the last criminal came in the back door."

"I know. That's why I'm calling Bob for help. It's only for a couple days and we'll have two operatives."

"Why didn't you just tell Abramson that?"

"Because from what Bob told me, things move pretty slowly in government, and he would never get approval in time. If he's just 'a friend' visiting, they won't do anything. They may not know. The street operative will, but I'll tell him or her a friend is visiting. I don't *think* they'll do anything."

They made it back to the car. "So Bob is just hanging around ready to help us out?" Elizabeth asked.

"I don't know," Tig said. "All I can do is ask."

Karl had been quiet the whole time. "Who's Bob?"

Tig guided the vehicle toward home as he explained. "Bob is a friend of a friend, so to speak, who works for the FBI. I went to him for help when you disappeared, and things were looking pretty bad. He told us how things were likely to work, hypothetically, since he can't discuss anything about anything. It was literally pulling teeth to get that much information."

"How much information?" Karl asked.

"What danger we might be in and what it sounded like was happening here. I wanted to protect Elizabeth, and you of course. With the attempt on your life and then your disappearance, we were getting a little freaked out."

"A little?" Elizabeth added.

"I'll call Bob and set it up. I assume you're getting your, uh, gym equipment? Going to work out?" Tig pulled the car into the drive.

"Yes. Then going back to . . ." Karl got out.

"At least you'll be safe and it won't be for long. A couple days?" Elizabeth awkwardly maneuvered out of the passenger seat. It was harder without the steering wheel to use for leverage.

Karl helped Elizabeth to the door while Tig fumbled his key in the lock. Elizabeth felt like an ocean liner edging her way through the door way.

A dark blue sedan passed their drive and coasted to a stop. Bethany got out and raced to the front door before they realized she was there. She followed them inside.

"I'll take your back-up, Karl." She pointed a small caliber gun at the group who froze in the entry.

"It's not here."

"Oh, really? So all this cloak and dagger is for entertainment?"

"It's in a locker at the gym here in town."

Elizabeth felt the baby kick at her distress. She told the cats to stay outside, danger was near. They were attuned to the sounds of the cars returning and always came in to greet them. She prayed they'd been late and would stay away. In answer, she heard the cat flap.

"What was that?" Bethany asked.

"Nothing," Elizabeth said and repeated her silent demand they go outside. Freya sauntered into the larger dining room where they all stood.

What are you doing? Elizabeth asked Freya.

I'm going to help.

No. It's dangerous. Where are the boys?

Outside. They listened to you.

"That doesn't look like nothing," Bethany said.

"Just a cat door," Tig clarified.

"When I ask a question, I expect a full answer," Bethany managed through gritted teeth.

"Okay, okay. I'll take you to the gym," Karl said. "You don't need them." He pointed to Tig and Elizabeth. "I'll give it to you, and nobody needs to get hurt."

"Right. I'm just going to let them waltz in to the authorities with my description and a little story of what's going on. I don't think so."

Bethany still stood with her back to the screen door which was not latched. Freya began rubbing against Bethany's leg and looking up at her dewy-eyed.

"Get that thing away from me or I'll shoot it," Bethany said.

"I'm sorry. I'll get her." Elizabeth didn't think. She stepped forward to retrieve Freya as the kitten leaped and latched all her claws into Bethany's thigh. Bethany screamed and the gun wavered. Tig and Karl surged forward, pushing Bethany out the door as Tig grabbed the gun. Freya had released her claws as fast as she'd launched. Elizabeth was knocked to the floor out of immediate range, but managed to grab Freya. Karl slammed and locked the heavy wooden front door.

Bethany shrieked in frustration and ran down the drive to her car. In the few moments they all took to recover, they heard her rev her engine and race away.

"We might not have much time," Karl said. "I'm taking the SD card to Abramson now. If she follows me, so be it. If she believed me, she'll wait for me at the gym, but I'm not going there. Are my shoes still in my room?"

Elizabeth nodded from the floor where she still clung to Freya. Freya was in full consolation mode, which Elizabeth needed. Thor was mad and kept booting her in the kidneys. He was head down now and since he was so big, didn't do full spins anymore, just kicked her where he could.

Tig recovered next and gently helped Elizabeth up and into a dining room chair. She didn't let go of Freya. Elizabeth realized how close she had been to getting shot, and what could have happened to her, Thor, Freya—all of them.

I told you I would help.

Yes, you did, Elizabeth told her shakily. She was just getting her breath back.

It's fine. It's all fine, Freya said, not realizing it had become a sort of a joke. Elizabeth laughed and kissed her, pressing her ear against the tiny ribs to hear her mouse-purr.

Karl came out of his room wearing the other sports shoes with the SD card under the tongue label. "Can I take your truck?" Tig nodded. "If I can get there ahead of her, I think we'll be good. I haven't gone through all this for her or her criminal syndicate to win." Karl's jaw was set. He had packed a small gym bag, for going into hiding, Elizabeth presumed.

"Be careful," she admonished.

"You too." He was out the door before she could say anything else.

Tig was already on the phone to Bob. Elizabeth faded out of listening as the shock of the event slowly stole her energy.

Tig disconnected. "Bob's on his way. We have a while before dark. I'm going to call Abramson and tell him what happened. We need his operative ASAP. Are you all right?" He looked carefully at her for the first time.

"I'm not sure. I think I should lie down."

He nodded at Freya. "Your little girl sure helped save the day. Was it on purpose or did she just want up?" He helped Elizabeth to stand.

"Oh, it was on purpose all right. She knew exactly what she was doing." Elizabeth tucked Freya under one arm and put the other around Tig. She really didn't feel good now. She tried to remember if anyone kicked the baby or if she landed on him. She didn't think so, but she felt queasy and disconnected.

Freya, can you tell what's happening to Thor?

I will check.

Tig helped put her feet up on the bed. "I'll make you some mint tea, okay?"

She lay on her left side and Freya snugged up against the baby bump which had become a mountain. They both closed their eyes. Thor also settled, the strange heaviness lessening. Elizabeth drifted off to sleep while Freya worked her magic. She prayed Bethany didn't come back before Abramson's officer, or Bob, or someone, rode to the rescue.

The dreamwalk began as usual, with the war. She had arrived again with the village meeting in the long house, the same as the first time. Now she understood more of Freya's village or land or Volksvang. This was just before the battle began. Now she knew she was invisible, unless there was too much smoke. She glanced around the scattered huts and up into the trees where she saw the small face of the white fox peering out. It quickly vanished and she entered the meeting room through the long skin door coverings.

Freya entered too and saw her standing in the back of the room. Elizabeth could not understand the language, but again, since she knew this was moments before the attack, she grasped what was happening.

Freya came to her. Her long hair was braided, shells and beads intertwined. Was that a bone in there, too? Ew. Elizabeth noticed she also had on war make-up, of a sort. Strange symbols in black looked like charcoal, and her eyes were outlined with wings that stretched almost to her hairline.

"Do you understand now?" Freya asked.

"I understand better," Elizabeth said. "I don't understand *why* you are at war, but I know there *is* a war."

"I am hot." Freya pulled back her cloak of heavy pelts and revealed a pregnant abdomen as large as Elizabeth's. After a quick confirmation, she saw her own had disappeared, just like the last visit.

"You never said you were pregnant, too!" Elizabeth said, her eyes roaming the warrior's body. "Are we at the same point in our pregnancies?"

"Yes. We are joined. The babies are joined. That is why I told you the baby decides."

"Decides when to be born?"

"Yes."

"Wait. We each have a baby, right? We're not, uh, sharing one, are we?"

"Of course not." Freya smiled briefly. "You are a strange one, Elizabeth."

"*I'm* a strange one?" Flashes of Freya running and fighting up the mountain on her last visit made her wonder at her own weakness. Freya was pregnant and a warrior, but she, Elizabeth, could barely get her slippers on and make it to a grocery store in a car.

"How long is a goddess' pregnancy? Is it like a human's?" Elizabeth asked.

"It depends."

"It *depends*? Depends on what?" Elizabeth didn't understand.

"It depends on several factors. The goddess involved." Freya smiled. "The need for the offspring. The father of the new god. You see? It depends."

"In our case, our pregnancies are linked, you said?" Freya nodded. "But the babies determine the birth." Freya nodded again. "So my baby's birth, based on how fast he's growing, will be earlier than a regular human pregnancy?" Freya nodded for a third time. "And he's healthy?"

"Of course."

Elizabeth sighed.

"What is it?" Freya asked.

"I'm just figuring this all out. You seem to be aware of things before I am, so I'll ask. When you said, 'the baby decides,' you didn't mean my baby. You meant *your* baby, right?"

"Correct. My Thor is in control. He is a god even now, before birth, but he is not free to fulfill his destiny until then. After his birth, he will control thunder, weather, many things."

"So you are naming your baby, Thor?"

"I said as much. Yours, too, you said?"

"Uh, we haven't decided."

"I have heard you call him that. He hears you, too. He believes he is called Thor."

Great. Time to change the subject from gods. "This war. Why is it happening? And why is it happening every time I come? Does it not end?"

"I will be brief because it is about to begin. My land is tied to your land, as I have said. My warriors die and return, as long as I return. Do you understand this?"

Sure. Right. Elizabeth nodded. Made perfect sense.

"Our people have begun to fail us. In the Earth world, our subjects have gone to other lands and found other gods to worship. As more of them worship outside of here, our world begins to crumble. We must fight to keep ourselves alive. Even if we die doing it." Freya pulled open the skin door and went outside. Elizabeth followed.

"Do you see the forest?" She pointed up the hill, away from the little beach to where Elizabeth had taken refuge before. Elizabeth nodded. "Look carefully. What do you see?"

Elizabeth studied the tree line. Did it look closer? The trees looked a little thinner. Hard to say for sure, since she had been running uphill in the middle of a battle in bedroom slippers, the screams of the wounded and dying enveloping her. What she could say for sure was the upper edge of the trees, where it should have turned to mountain and sky, was faded. No other word for it. It had lost color and substance. Crumbly, maybe? But it did disappear into nothing. And it wasn't a nothing, like she just couldn't see it, as if it were too far away, but it faded into actual *nothing*. That scared her beyond any fear she'd felt in her life. What if she'd run up the hill like last time? Into the nothing? Would she disappear? Would her body at home die?

She began to tremble. Freya shook her arm. "Battle commences. I must go."

"Do I have to do exactly what I did last time?" Elizabeth asked.

"No, the battle does not depend on you. You could make it more difficult, perhaps, but you can't truly change the outcome."

"That's a relief."

"Only our children can do that." Freya took off running. How did she manage being so pregnant?

Behind Elizabeth, men and women again streamed out of the long house. Warriors from the boats raced up the beach. The familiar sounds of battle began. Elizabeth ran behind the meeting room and closed her eyes. She forced herself to return to her body. It was difficult with all the new information swirling around, and she was terrified. Her breath came in pants and she slid down the rough log wall of the house into a sitting position.

She willed herself not to react to a scream that sounded very near. She slowed her breathing and concentrated on her room, her bed, on the little furry Freya that linked her to her own time.

She felt the bed beneath her, but heard the scream again. Her eyes popped open. It came again, but this time she recognized it as the call of the hawks that nested in the eucalyptus trees behind the house. Freya still lay against her huge baby bump. Elizabeth was glad to see it back.

She stroked Freya until she opened her eyes and rolled over to face Elizabeth. As usual, only a cat was there for a few moments. The ellipsoidal pupils expanded and retracted and human Freya was back.

"Are you really pregnant?" Elizabeth asked her.

Yes. But as when you are in my world, here, now only Thor's soul resides within me. Besides, look how tiny this body is. How could it house a human child, much less a god? Her eyes twinkled. Elizabeth couldn't tell if Freya believed this or if she was playing a massive joke on her human companion.

Elizabeth looked at the tiny kitten and decided, there probably wasn't room for another kitten in there. She didn't let herself get into the fact that Freya here was a kitten herself, and couldn't possibly be mature enough to have gotten pregnant.

You are thinking too much again, I see, Freya said.

"Of course I am. But I do feel better. Time to get up." Somehow with the battle and visit to Volksvang, as she was starting to think of it, she'd let the whole espionage thing slip her mind. She made a mental note to look on a world map and see where the village was. Some day.

She hurried as best she could into her slippers and went to the kitchen for tea. A glance at her phone told her she'd only been asleep for an hour.

She saw Tig watering from the window. He stood next to a strange man she hoped was Bob. She needed her tea. Her nausea and exhaustion were gone. She was a complete lightweight she thought. Let's say, Freya is a figment of some sort, she was still a warrior, so maybe Elizabeth could channel some of her energy and not be so . . . weak.

Freya-kitten had followed her out. *That is not up to you,* she said.

What do you mean?

You and I are tied together, as are our worlds and our children. You are weak, as you say, so I can be strong. It is not weakness, at any rate. You are, how do you say? Taking one for the team. She looked thrilled coming up with this saying.

Elizabeth pondered this while her water boiled. She filled a cup and got out her go-to tea, peppermint. She was about to comment when Tig, who must have heard the kettle, came in with the man.

"Hi, sweetheart. Feeling better?" he asked.

"Much. Fine, in fact." She introduced herself.

"Oh, this is Bob," Tig said by way of introduction.

"It's not really, right?" Elizabeth asked.

"No, but it'll do." Bob was a little taller and thinner than Tig. He looked like an office worker, not like a covert ops guy, or spy, or whatever the term was. Dark hair flopped engagingly over dark eyes and his smile was genuine, although Elizabeth

267

got the impression he didn't smile much in his line of work. "You've got a beautiful place here." He turned to indicate the pond out the window and she saw a bulge in his jacket she assumed was a weapon. Equally she hoped it was and it wasn't.

"So you're staying with us?" she asked.

"Yes, ma'am. We're going to hunker down for a couple days. I've already spoken to the outside officer, who was not happy about it, by the way."

"What? Hunkering?"

"No. That I'm here. But that's neither here nor there." He sounded cheery. Like he'd gotten one over on the boss. Elizabeth decided she liked him. He'd given up whatever he was doing, rearranged his schedule to help strangers. She did know the fire fighters would do anything for each other, so that went a long way as far as a reference went.

"Seems like that little girl asset got her clock cleaned by you folks, so two things are foremost in my mind. She's given up and is pursuing other leads, like Karl, or she's coming back with reinforcements. Let's hope the former."

"What if it's the latter?" Elizabeth took her tea to the table and sat. Suddenly her legs didn't want to hold her up anymore.

"We've run the numbers, and that's the far less likely scenario. You're fine."

"What numbers?"

"Probability. She, and we, feel the back-up isn't here, correct?" Elizabeth glanced at Tig who nodded. "So, she's going after it another way. She probably needs to make up for losing it," Bob finished.

"Is Karl in danger?" she asked.

"No more than he was, and less if he makes it to the safe house."

"If he makes it?"

"He'll make it. He has security, but you never know."

"Sheesh," Elizabeth said.

Bob seemed relaxed. Maybe too relaxed? Didn't they want an agent who might be more concerned? What did they know about him, really?

"How about barbequed chicken for dinner?" Tig asked.

"Sounds good. What can I do?" Bob asked.

"Want grilled veggies, too?" Tig emptied out the vegetable bin in the refrigerator. "Here, cut these into grillable size and we'll marinate them in a foil packet."

Elizabeth was a bit surprised the discussion was over, but she didn't have any other questions at the moment. The men had the meal in hand so she went to Karl's room. She had intended to change the linens for Bob, since Karl would be staying at the safe house until this was over. She was overcome with melancholy and sat on the bed. Karl's stuff was still here as if he would walk back in and crack a joke and smile and he and Tig would pick up some complicated pond conversation like they'd never left off. She wondered if that would ever happen again. He sounded like he wanted a career with the CIA which was much more exciting, and paid better, than pond work. Either way, it looked like Tig would lose his partner.

Elizabeth gathered up Karl's stuff and put it in bags and took them to their closet in the bedroom. She didn't want Bob pawing through it. It wasn't much, but it was Karl's. Some text books, clothes, cards from Stacy. Stacy! How was she going to find out about Karl? Elizabeth didn't have Stacy's number, but she knew where she lived. She was due back tomorrow. Add another thing to the list.

She stripped Karl's bed and threw it all in the washer. The boys knew when someone tried to make a bed and had come to help. They jumped on the mattress cover and lay flat, taking up as much real estate as possible.

"You're too early, guys. I just put it in the wash."

This feels so nice, Edward said.

Something about an empty bed, Teddy added. Elizabeth knew what he meant. A bed with no sheets, pillows or human belongings. She liked to lie on the bed that way sometimes, too.

Freya had not joined them. Elizabeth went through the house calling her. She found her in the bamboo yard, sitting on top of the stone gargoyle, Fluffy's, head. "Why didn't you answer me?" Elizabeth asked.

I have a lot on my mind, Freya said. She sounded forty.

Can I help?

I think I have it sorted. The battle ended much like the one you saw, but the land is less.

Growing smaller. I don't know if my own battle is enough to stop the loss of land. It weighs on me.

I can only imagine. Whether Freya was in her imagination or somewhere in the past, Elizabeth still loved her and wanted to help. She just didn't know how. Certainly her battle skills were not going to serve. What could she do? She would have to think on it, too. Maybe after the money laundering thing was resolved. Man, the things that romped through her brain. A couple weeks ago she was worried about maternity clothes and constructing a crib. Now she was waist deep in a CIA case and a disappearing village that might or might not exist.

She sighed. Feeding the koi always made her feel better. She diced some tofu and grabbed a bit of koi kibble and headed out to the pond.

Us too, said Edward.

Yes, you too.

Feeding us makes you feel better, right Mom? Teddy.

Elizabeth laughed. The cats loved the little dried koi kibbles so she dropped a few on the flagstones. Freya had not had this treat before, but she saw the boys scarfing them up, so she tried a few.

Not bad, she said.

Not bad! Edward said.

It's almost as good as tuna juice, Teddy added.

Dinner proceeded, and although the men seemed to have safety covered, Elizabeth's mind was never far from Karl, or Volksvang.

271

Twenty-Seven

Tig and Bob sat up late strategizing. Elizabeth thought Tig secretly liked this and hoped he wasn't interested in a career change. She couldn't stay awake and took the cats back early for some NetFilms before finally dropping off.

She awoke before Tig. Not surprising since she'd fallen asleep before he'd come to bed. She wondered if Bob stayed awake all night watching. He'd need to sleep today, maybe. Perhaps they were trained to stay awake for days at a time. That would let Tig out. He needed food and sleep in that order. On nights when the department got a lot of emergency calls, or had an especially a big fire, he really struggled after the adrenaline rush. Fortunately they were usually allowed to sleep afterward, but sometimes events coincided with a big training and all was lost for the whole shift. She smiled watching him sleep.

She quietly left the room taking the cats with her. Up until only a couple months ago, she and Tig would not let the cats sleep with them. Now she couldn't imagine them not there. True, the boys had adjusted their sleeping positions to take up less room when Tig was home, but they'd added Freya to the mix. Freya always slept on the long pillow beside Elizabeth's head, so she didn't bother anyone or get squished when she or Tig rolled.

Bob sat in her meditation chair watching the street. It was next to the picture window and had the best view. The blinds were angled so he could see out, but someone outside would have trouble seeing in.

"Morning," she said. "Coffee?"

"Thanks. I tried to make some earlier, but I didn't get the proportions right. Maybe I was just tired."

"Are you hungry?"

"A little, but don't go to any trouble."

"No trouble. We usually eat a big breakfast around here. Anything during the night?" Elizabeth put her kettle on and prepped the coffee maker.

"Nothing. Nice and quiet. They changed street operatives around 5, but that was it."

"I appreciate your coming here so last minute. As you see, I feel pretty vulnerable, and the girl, spy, whatever, showing up with a gun was pretty awful. It feels like a dream now. Nothing like that has ever happened to me before."

"Yes. I know. The first few close calls I had in my career, the same thing happened. I'd replay them in my mind, and my brain didn't allow that they were real. Kept trying to make each one into a dream, something more acceptable."

Elizabeth nodded. Her own 'dreamwalks' caused her to question what was real lately. She brought over his coffee and set out cream and sugar.

She removed her tea bag from her own cup and began to scramble eggs and toast bread.

The smell of toast brought Freya back into the house. The boys returned to see about some scrambled cheese eggs.

"You okay with eggs and cheese?" Elizabeth asked him.

"Absolutely. Free food I don't have to cook? You bet!" Bob smiled, and it was contagious.

As she put the food on serving plates, Tig came out and kissed her hello. "Coffee?" She handed him a cup.

"Thanks. I'm wiped out and I didn't stay up all night. Thanks, Bob."

"No problem. You get used to it."

Elizabeth got the impression their case *was* a problem; he just wasn't telling them everything. They sat at the table, Edward stationed in Tig's lap, Elizabeth's legs stretched onto the extra chair for Freya. Bob was allowed to sit at the remaining chair. Teddy lay dead center of any pathway in the kitchen, whether to the refrigerator or all the way to the laundry/cat room. He was a strategist.

The mountain of cheese eggs was quickly reduced to rubble. Freya got plenty of buttered toast, but the pile went fast, too. "Oh, Tig. I forgot the fruit. Please get it out for me," Elizabeth asked.

Tig retrieved a big bowl of cut fruit salad. Everyone took a little, although Elizabeth could tell they were full. She took a few berries, but didn't have room for much more. "Don't worry, you guys, we can add it to lunch. I just wanted to make sure you got enough to eat."

"She always says that, and I'm always stuffed to the gills," Tig said.

Bob chuckled and began clearing dishes to the sink.

"Don't do that," Elizabeth said.

"Hey, you cooked. I can manage to throw a few things into the dishwasher."

Tig finished the clearing up while Elizabeth sat with Freya and her tea a few moments longer.

"I'm going to check with the street operative," Bob said.

"Isn't it a secret?" Elizabeth asked.

"Not anymore. The bad guys know we're aware you've been targeted. Sometimes it's better to show your hand."

"So the spies won't come in?" She felt weird saying that word, but couldn't come up with a better one.

"We hope not. But if so, we're ready for almost anything."

Elizabeth thought he didn't sound at all sure. With only two officers watching the house, how prepared could they be? She didn't know how many people the bad guys had, but she was sure it was more than two.

She locked the door behind Bob and watched as he crossed the street to chat with a scruffy-looking man in a sedan that had seen better days. She felt better. He did not look like an official anything. He looked like he lived out of his car.

Bob returned and she let him back in. "That's good news," he said.

Tig came back from changing clothes. "What?"

"Bethany was arrested yesterday after she left here, so she didn't get to pass on any information she may have learned from you."

"Great," Tig said. "It kind of threw me, that young-looking student pointing a gun at us and me knowing I might have to go against her. My brain didn't compute it."

"I know what you mean. I have more good news. Karl made it to the safe house. The back-up is in good hands."

"So Karl is safe? He doesn't have to do anything else?" Elizabeth asked.

"He's not a trained officer, so his only job is over right now. He'll have to testify, but that's way down the road."

"When can he come home?"

"Maybe in a few more days, after all the arrests have been made. We want to be sure we've got all the players. Just because someone's arrested doesn't mean they're out of the action."

"What does that mean?" Tig asked.

"These guys have lots of underlings all over. We don't want Karl, or you, in danger as part of a revenge plot for giving evidence." He saw their faces. "We just want to be sure. It's only a few more days."

"You hope?" Tig asked.

"It's hard to be absolutely positive, but yes."

"I thought the CIA couldn't tell you anything. How do you know so much?"

"I was read-in on this after you came to me. I thought it might be tied to something else I was already working on. Turns out I was right and they brought me in."

"What are you working on?" Elizabeth asked.

"Now that would be telling." Bob's smile was back.

"Abramson said the federal government was involved and he didn't mean the investigation. What did he mean? It had to do with Karl and the wildlife rescue center, didn't it?"

"You already know what Karl was doing because he blabbed to you. One of the issues was the bad hackers were moving money from federally funded programs."

"Stealing from the wildlife center?" Elizabeth asked.

Bob nodded. "Among others. See these programs have millions of dollars funneled through them from grants and donations. That's how a lot of them keep afloat. Once you start taking money from either a federal grant or a federally funded program, which is what they did, the stakes get much higher. We get involved, for one."

"So, Karl was fake hacking?" Elizabeth asked.

"No, he was really hacking, but with our consent. He was able to follow the money as it was moved, do some moving of his own, as well as control how much. What he didn't know, but we've been able to find out since with other hackers and our own officers, is who the accounts belong to. All Karl saw were numbers and dollars, account numbers and amounts. He couldn't tell who was doing it or where it was going, but we have teams of people on this. He did almost blow the whole thing, but we were able to salvage it because he made the back-up. But when he did, it was flagged, it still gave us the intel we needed. We would have liked to play this out longer, try and get them all, but that's the way it goes."

Tig and Elizabeth stared at Bob. This was not how *she* thought it would go. She expected something more definitive and secure.

Bob clapped his hands. "I'm going to get some shut-eye. I've got at least one more shift of night watch and I plan to be ready. I feel comfortable grabbing some Zs since Trevor is out there." He nodded to the street where it appeared for all intents and purposes, 'Trevor' was also snoozing. Elizabeth hoped he was really good at his job.

"Sure," Tig said. "I'm going to catch up on some chores around here and paperwork for the business."

"No chores in front, though." Bob looked serious. "Only behind the fence."

Tig had installed a Japanese-style six foot high fence all around the back and side yards. It had been intended to discourage predators, but now it might discourage bad guys. *Or not,* she thought, remembering Freya's account of their last invasion.

"Sure, no problem. I'm going to start with paperwork. I'm pretty wiped anyway. Begin easy."

Elizabeth felt a bit jumpy herself. She had a text from a potential communicator client she hadn't returned because of all the craziness and crime. She decided to take care of it now. She could communicate with animals remotely. She'd been practicing, getting better at it, knowing once the baby was born she'd be pretty housebound for a while. She didn't want to take a newborn to an environment with an unstable animal.

She reread the text. No real information except a phone number. Not unusual. People often found it difficult to say in a text what was happening with animal behavior, especially if they hadn't talked to her, or any other communicator previously.

She went back to the bedroom for privacy and called. "Hi, this is Elizabeth Murphy, the animal communicator. I'm sorry it took so long to get back to you. How can I help you?"

A high pitched feminine voice that reminded her of Bethany answered. "Thank you for calling me back. I didn't know what to do. I don't want to call Animal Services, but I think it's hurt. I'm not sure."

"What's hurt? Can you start from the beginning?"

"Okay. It's like a fox or something. I've seen it behind my house, and I think it's hurt because it stays near the back fence. It's been there off and on for a couple of weeks. Maybe it's a dog. I know we have coyotes here but not, you know, other stuff." Elizabeth did not clarify there was a lot of 'other stuff' in their area.

"If it's a dog, something's going to eat it. It's kind of wild. I started putting out water and then some dog kibble since it stays around so much. I figured if it's hurt, it can't hunt. Or if it's a pet, you know, it needs help. I wanted to catch it, but it disappears when I go out."

The voice sounded younger than Elizabeth first thought. "How old are you?"

"Thirteen. Does it matter?" She sounded scared now.

"Not at all. What's your name? I'm Elizabeth."

"I know. I'm Sammy."

"Great, Sammy. Do your parents know about the fox or dog?"

"I tried to tell them but they said we don't have foxes here."

"Sammy, you are right. We do. We have red ones and gray ones."

"Yeah, but my mom said we don't have white ones. Those live in the arctic or someplace. You know, because of their coloring."

Elizabeth's heart stopped for a moment. This changed everything.

Twenty-Eight

A white fox. Elizabeth had seen one in Volksvang and figured it for an arctic fox. She'd also seen one here, in her dreams, or her mind, but she'd been unable to tell if it was real. As Sammy's parents said, we don't have white foxes here. Something strange about it. Maybe though, Sammy had seen a lost Pomeranian who was too scared to let her near. Elizabeth didn't have much hope for its longevity if it was a house pet. One way to find out.

"Sammy, can you tell me where you live?"

"Oh, near the state park. I can hear the coyotes and we get raccoons. One time I saw one of those giant-rat things! What do you call them?"

"Possum?" No doubt Sammy was excited by the local wildlife. Not unusual she hadn't seen a mountain lion, bobcat or bear; they were very shy.

"Yes!"

So Sammy lived not far from Elizabeth. Maybe that's why she'd seen the white fox in some form. She wondered if it was the same fox she'd seen in Freya's world. That would be weird, but she'd been experiencing a lot of weird lately. Was it a coincidence the university hacking club was called the 'White Foxes?' She'd have to find out the significance of the name. All arrows pointed to the same thing, she just wasn't sure what it was.

"Sammy, I can't come over to you because I'm very pregnant, but I can try and talk to the fox without seeing it. Would that be all right with you?"

Silence as Sammy pondered this. "I guess. Is it the same thing as you talking to it when it's in front of you?"

"Sort of. But you say the fox or dog doesn't let you come near. That it runs away."

"It doesn't run away, I just can't see it anymore," Sammy corrected. "If it's hurt, it can't run, right?"

"It could. It depends on what is hurt about it. I can try and find that out, too."

"Okay. What do I do?"

"You don't have to do anything but be quiet for a few minutes. Can you do that?"

"Why? What are you doing?"

"I call it inside my head, to inside its head and we talk. Sometimes animals don't want to talk, just like people." She wondered if she'd gone too far with her description.

"Then do you tell me what it said?"

"Yes, that's right. If it's a wild fox, it might not talk. Sometimes wild animals are scared of humans, which is good, but I won't get much information. If it's a lost pet, it's used to people talking to it so it's more likely to talk to me, although I'm a stranger."

"Stranger danger," Sammy murmured.

Elizabeth stopped herself from laughing just in time. "Absolutely. We'll just have to find out."

"Wait a second. I have seventeen dollars allowance saved up. Is that enough to help an animal?" Sammy asked.

Elizabeth had no intention of taking allowance from a child, but she heard how sincere she was and didn't want to stop Sammy from becoming another animal advocate. "That's exactly right, but we'll do the accounting after, depending on if the animal talks to me. Okay?" In fact that was not how she did it, but Sammy thought it sounded fine.

"Okay."

"Remember to be quiet for me. It might feel like a long time, but that's good. It might mean the animal is talking. I'm going to put the phone down while I do this, so you won't be able to ask me anything. I'll be back when I have some news."

She set the phone down and grounded herself, this time lying on the bed. She didn't have a chair in the bedroom and sitting up with no back support for any length of time wasn't fun. It took a bit longer, but she was adept at varied situations and soon enough she was virtually wandering the outback calling to the fox.

It answered right away, the way she'd seen it in Volksvang. It poked an adorable face out of some salt cedar. Its white coloring was actually not too bad for camouflage since the calendar was heading toward September and the grasses were all dry and yellow-white. The sand dune under the whole area was also a creamy white.   She immediately saw the issue. It was not an arctic fox, but an albino one, pink-red eyes stared from above the pointed muzzle.

So, yes a fox, and a real one. Why had no one else seen it before Sammy? She didn't think it was a spirit fox and now saw it wasn't the one in Volksvang. That fox had dark eyes, so not an albino, and it could change its coloration for summer. This poor little guy would stand out pretty much all year long.

The local weather changed from dry to rain and back again, but there were no big color changes in the foliage during fall here at the coast. Locals joked the weather was either dry, or super dry. The state had been in an official drought condition for years; hence all the new landscaping since people could no longer water lawns or plants with any regularity.

Hi, little one. Will you talk to me? she asked it.

Yes.

Are you injured?

No.

Lost?

No. I was told to come here.

Who told you to come here?

A lady.

A lady told you to come to the girl?

No. But I couldn't find you, so I came to her and told her to help me. So the little fox was communicating with Sammy, but Sammy didn't know how to read him.

284

Can you show me the lady? She expected Freya and was surprised to see Bethany. Bethany was some sort of communicator? Odd. It wasn't just 'good' people who talked to animals, or rescued them, but that was usually the case. Sometimes people were loners or preferred animals to other people, but that type 'read' differently when she encountered them. She hadn't sensed anything like that in Bethany. Granted, two minutes at Abramson's office and five more at the house where she threatened to shoot Freya were perhaps not the best indicators. Most 'animal people' would never threaten to harm a creature under any circumstances.

Why were you supposed to find me?

I am to stay close and report.

Report to the lady?

Some hesitation. *Yes, but also another.*

Show me. The fox showed her what looked like the fox in Volksvang.

Why? What's going on?

Confusion. *I only did what was asked.*

Who asked you?

Cousin Fox. The picture of the other fox again, with the dark eyes.

Do you live here? Behind these houses?

Sometimes. I move when needed.

Perhaps that was why he hadn't been seen. *So, you have done your job by finding me?*

Yes.

What will happen next?

I go.

Where? Are you sure you are healthy?

285

Yes. The girl provided food and water. I didn't have to leave my post to hunt. However, I wish to hunt.

What was the purpose of you finding me? I still don't understand.

Another connection I helped maintain between you and the other world.

A connection between you and uh, Cousin Fox?

Yes.

Why can't Cousin Fox do it himself if you can?

Cousin Fox has other things to do. She saw flashes of Freya's familiar battle, but now Elizabeth saw the other fox running, darting, and disappearing into a thicket. A man shot out the other side, huge, bearded and well-armed, throwing himself into the fray with abandon, almost joy. Moments later he vanished in the same smoke that revealed Elizabeth, and a small white fox raced up the mountain into the trees. In the vision, Elizabeth was gratified to see the treeline didn't end in nothing where the fox went. In fact, she thought it firmed up the border of the nothing as it traveled. Must be an illusion of the smoke and battle. She remembered this was only this fox's version of events. Perhaps not even as it experienced them, but as they were told to him? She wasn't sure.

What is the purpose of that lady you showed me? She meant Bethany.

Darkness presses in upon her. She does what she needs to protect herself.

Elizabeth had no idea what that meant. Maybe Bethany was threatened into doing what she did? She had no idea how these crime syndicates acted. That a little fox knew of her was more peculiar. Her brain could only handle so much. Perhaps for another day. The two foxes were connected, and she was the target of both. Maybe.

So, you are safe and are leaving the area? Are you going back to Volksvang?

Perhaps. I may see you again. You are all that I was told you were. Your magic is strong, and your baby will have strong magic, too. The fox abruptly severed the connection and vanished from her mind both in spirit and in her vision of him.

Elizabeth roused herself from meditation to find Freya lying next to her head on the pillow. However, Freya was not on duty, she was completely asleep. The cell phone, which she had put on the nightstand for her communication, had little squeaks emanating. She presumed they were Sammy, tired of waiting. She picked it up.

"Hello? Sammy?"

"What happened? That was forever!" Elizabeth glanced at the time. It had been fifteen minutes, so forever in teen time.

"I'm sorry, Sammy. The fox had a lot to say."

"Oh, wow. So great. Is it okay?"

Elizabeth had to pick and choose what to tell Sammy. Nothing of Volksvang, of course, and nothing of the money laundering in which Bethany was involved. She did not have fifteen minutes of reporting to validate. She decided to wax euphoric on the fox's merits and its desire to find Sammy.

"Yes, it's fine. It's very smart and wanted to find you. It is a he, and needed you to take care of him for a while, which you did. And you did a great job. He was, uh, migrating and knew you'd help. Your folks are right, white foxes aren't from around here, but he's not a true white fox. He's an albino, which is unusual. Do you know what albino is?"

"Yeah, we saw an albino python at the zoo. Creeped me out a little. But I felt sorry for it too. No giant white snake, or any animal I guess, is going to survive looking like that in the wild."

"Absolutely." Elizabeth had been correct in her assessment of Sammy's care and concern for animals. "You might grow up to talk to animals, too, one day. The fox wanted to talk to you, but you didn't understand him."

"I'm sorry. I didn't know." Sammy sounded about to cry.

"Don't worry; you understood something because you came to me for help. He got what he needed and we both got a cool conversation, right?"

"Yeah. What's going to happen to him now?"

"He's rested and ready to move on. He has a fox family he's traveling to meet." Complete lie, but no part of the real story was going to be shared with a thirteen-year-old girl at this time.

"Will he be okay? Looking like that?"

"I think so. No one else saw him so he's managed to stay hidden. You're the only one he wanted to see him. He's very smart," she repeated.

"So, how do I pay you?"

"I'm thinking Sammy, maybe you want to start communicating with animals a little?"

"Sure, I guess."

"Talk to your parents and see if they'd let you train with me. Then we'll call it even. If you don't like it, you don't have to continue. Your parents could come over and meet me and my husband at some point and we can work out details if you like."

"Okay. But my parents are probably going to think it's weird."

"You know what, Sammy? Almost everyone does." Sammy giggled. "Call me after you talk to them, but I can't start your training for a while. Remember I said I was going to have a baby?"

"Uh, huh."

"He's coming sooner than later, so I can't do anything for a bit. Hey, maybe you might want to think about babysitting too, to add to your skills. Have you babysat before?"

"Yeah, once, but she was like three, and I was so tired by the end. My parents signed me up for a Safety-Sitter class this summer. I had to learn CPR and first aid, plus, like how to play with babies and kids of different ages. It was exhausting."

Elizabeth laughed. "I can imagine. Think about it. Our baby won't be running around anywhere for a while." *I hope,* she amended. "We wouldn't leave you alone with him until we all felt comfortable. We'd pay you to visit and learn while we're here. Does that sound better?"

"Yes!"

Elizabeth had been on the phone almost an hour. "I've got to go now, Sammy. It was nice to meet you, over the phone."

"You too. Bye." Sammy hung up.

Twenty-Nine

After her enlightening conversation with Sammy about the fox, which turned out to be about both foxes, Elizabeth was ravenous.

She and Freya went to the kitchen. Elizabeth didn't see Tig, so he must still be doing paperwork in his little back workshop where he fixed his equipment and stored tools and pieces of things. It wasn't set up for an office, really, but it did have electricity and a work table and chair. Bob was still asleep in Karl's room, Tig's old office.

She scooped a big serving of fruit salad, turned on the kettle and sat at the table. Her mind drift over the conversation with Sammy and the fox, along with the fox in Volksvang she thought turned into a man. Was that right? Or just an illusion due to the battle and the fires. She supposed she'd have to go back and see. She surprised herself by thinking of it as a journey. *Oh, I'll just go back and see if this place in the past still has the battle playing so I can revisit it for magical beings.*

She hoped pregnant Freya was safe and healthy. How did that work? Kitten-Freya was here much more than Elizabeth went back there. The baby tolerated the visits just fine, as far as she knew. Shoot! She had never rescheduled that check-up.

For sure she'd call later today. Now Karl was safe, she felt better about leaving the house. She checked the calendar for open dates around Tig's work. He liked to go with her. She did not want to have Bob go along. That made her smile, a visit to the OB-GYN trailed by FBI agents. Maybe it would be over by next week. It was already September 1. Summer had flown. The baby's original due date was early January, but she thought he would to be ready sooner than later. Maybe a Thanksgiving baby would be nice. She didn't want to have a Christmas baby. Her grandma had been a Christmas baby and she always felt ripped off when everyone combined gifts. Elizabeth thought if she had a baby that shared a holiday, she'd make sure to celebrate both the birthday and the holiday.

Freya was sticking close to her these days, spending almost no time in the outback with the boys. Even now, when Elizabeth got up to brew her tea, Freya waited on the dining chair to resume her spot on Elizabeth's legs, touching her belly. Elizabeth could feel the comfort Freya and Thor gave each other. Maybe that was why she'd asked if they shared a baby. Yeah, that wasn't weird, but something was going on between the two babies and the kitten-warrior.

Thor began to shift. Tiny contractions rippled across her abdomen. Painful, but tolerable.

It was too soon. Elizabeth froze with fear. *Too soon. I can't have this baby now.*

Breathe, Freya said. *Relax. Call your healer.*

Elizabeth texted Tig: I'm having contractions. Come to the kitchen. I'm calling Dr. Phillips.

She reached the doctor's office just as Tig hit the kitchen. He saw she was on the phone and grabbed a bottle of water from the refrigerator and guzzled.

She hung up. "The office said to come in right away. My water hasn't broken so the doctor doesn't think it's real labor. Something called Braxton-Hicks contractions which is very common. They need to be sure the baby's fine. If they're worried, I might have to stay overnight at Tolosa General."

"How do you feel?" Tig squatted next to her and grabbed her hand tightly. "I'll get the car." Then he stood too fast and knocked over the remaining water.

"It's okay," Elizabeth reassured him. "I'm a bit less nervous. I'm going to get a few things in case I have to stay over."

"Shouldn't we go right now?"

"Yes, but a minute or two for me to get a toothbrush is okay. Really, the doctor's office said it's fine, so I think so too." She gasped and stopped moving.

"I'm getting Bob."

293

"Bob's not coming!"

"I'm not taking my pregnant wife out of this house without security. We haven't gotten the all clear yet from Abramson, or anybody."

Elizabeth waddled down the hall to get a few things while Tig woke Bob.

A few minutes later they met near the door. "Ready?" Tig asked.

"Yes." Elizabeth's worry was coming true. The FBI at the doctor's office. He wasn't coming in, that was for sure.

"I told Trevor what was going on," Bob said. "He'll let the others know. He's staying with the house. I'm driving."

Tig didn't dispute it, but handed him the keys to Elizabeth's car. "I'll sit in the back seat with you, in case it gets worse."

Elizabeth agreed, because the contractions were getting more persistent. She didn't want to show it, but she *was* worried. She had accepted the baby might come early, but not several months early. All the discussion about lung development rose in her mind, and she knew it was too soon. Even for a super baby like Thor. She tried to cheer herself by imagining him in a little cape and flying around, but the pain was worsening.

Tig helped her buckle in and then took her hand. It was so early they hadn't attended birthing classes yet. Something made her look back at the house and she saw Freya sitting in the window staring at her.

"Okay," Elizabeth said.

"Okay?" Tig repeated.

"Yes, I'm okay, and I need to ground myself. Freya wants to stay connected, so I'll do the best I can."

"Connected?"

"For some reason, she has the ability to make me feel better when she's touching me. When I had nausea, she could make it go away. I don't know how, but it worked. She knows she can't come with me now, but if we stay connected she might be able to help. I don't know, but I'm willing to try."

Tig nodded. He understood her connection to the cats, but she hadn't told him about Freya's special abilities and Elizabeth's in-depth bond. Now wasn't the time to argue about it. She saw him accept it like he had so many other things in their life together.

She slouched sideways in the seat a little to take the pressure off her throbbing abdomen. Tig held her hand, and she found herself squeezing it when the pain grew. "Sorry," she gasped.

"It's fine," he said. She smiled recalling Freya's catch phrase.

Elizabeth concentrated on her breathing and in between contractions felt a little weight on her stomach, like when Freya lay there. A warm pressure. Thor felt it too and became less agitated. The ripples continued, but were bearable. Bob followed Tig's directions and they pulled up in front of the door to the doctor's office, which fortunately shared a parking lot with the hospital.

"We weren't followed. Take her up and I'll park," Bob said.

Being followed was the last thing on her mind, and she saw it was the last thing on Tig's too. Thank goodness Bob had been checking for a tail.

"207 Dr. Phillips," Tig said to Bob. Tig helped her out of the back seat and to the elevators. She didn't think she could make it up the one flight of stairs.

The receptionist took her in immediately. They hooked her up to one monitor for the baby's heartrate, and one for her own. They did an ultrasound and the regular check-up list.

Dr. Phillips felt it was nothing to worry about, but told her she was right to come in. The pain was a bit more severe than most Braxton-Hicks, but still within normal range. They had her lie on her side. They also reviewed other options including what was a definite 'come to the hospital' now alert, like bleeding. The baby's size now concerned the doctor. He was almost at delivery size and weight from their estimates. However, he was months from the delivery date. Her body could not sustain this continued growth, they told her. They also said they could not predict lung development from the outside. The lungs were the last to develop, because they were not needed until after delivery. They were concerned about his size versus his development. She was to come in every week now.

"I've been under a lot of stress and I know it's not good for me or the baby. I think that's over now," Elizabeth added. She also remembered warrior Freya pregnant and running uphill, sword in hand, and figured war was stressful too.

She had forgotten to stay connected to Freya. She quickly focused and found her. She was lying on her pillow, panting slightly.

What's wrong? What's happening? she asked the kitten.

I'm not sure. I think it's the same thing that's happening to you.

We'll be home soon. If we are experiencing the same thing, it's fine. It's like you're getting ready for the baby to come, but he's not coming yet. Try not to worry. I'll be home to help you. If you can change position, sometimes that helps. Look at her, the expert now.

Yes. I will wait for you.

Poor Freya. Alone and scared. Having a baby, even if you are a warrior, is scary. And the medical care back in Freya's time, whenever that was. Yikes. And one other thought. Was Freya in her own world experiencing contractions, too? During a battle? Or would it be lucky timing that found her resting on a fur bed of some sort? Elizabeth felt herself getting more anxious and willed it away.

Elizabeth insisted that resting at home was best for her. She became so determined to leave Tig looked even more worried. The nurse gave her literature and reminders, and it was all Elizabeth could do not to scream, "I have to go!" She figured that would get her the opposite result, so she focused on her connection to Freya and her own breathing. She found the small contractions had lessened considerably and in Freya too.

Bob was in the waiting room when they emerged. "False alarm," Tig told him.

"That's good. Everything okay?" Bob asked.

"I just need to get home," Elizabeth said.

"This happened twice with the wife. All was fine then, too," Bob said.

"You have a wife?" Tig asked.

"And kids?" Elizabeth added.

"Yup. But we're not supposed to talk about family, so you don't know anything, capische?" He did the index finger-to-nose gesture from the movie *The Sting* that meant we have a secret together. Elizabeth found it charming and funny. As she supposed he meant it to. It put her at ease, knowing a little bit about him.

The trip home was much less exciting, but Elizabeth kept her focus on Freya.

"I'm sorry you guys," she said at last to Tig and Bob. "Thank you for your help."

"No problem," Bob said. "Maybe I'll get a bit more shut-eye."

"Oh, we had to wake you. I forgot. I'm really sorry," she repeated.

"All part of the service, ma'am." Bob saluted and headed for his room.

Elizabeth went back to the master bedroom as fast as she could. Tig trailed behind.

"You okay?" he asked.

She couldn't say a kitten was in labor too, so she just said, "Freya's not feeling well so I need to stay with her a bit. I should rest, too, I think."

Elizabeth lay gently on the bed, her head on the pillow next to Freya. Freya lay relaxed looking, but Elizabeth knew she was sore and worn out from the contractions. If Freya was synched to her, then her contractions had stopped when Elizabeth's had.

Tig gently ran a hand down Freya's tiny body and she opened her eyes. "Tea?" he asked Elizabeth.

"Yes, thanks."

How are you? Elizabeth asked.

Better. You?

Same. That was exciting. Is this your first baby, too? Elizabeth asked.

Yes. I didn't think I would be afraid, but I am. Women of my village have many children but have never said they were scared. I was never in the room with them, but I could hear the screams. Everyone could. I just thought it was pain.

Does anyone ever die giving birth in Volksvang?

No. We only die in battle.

Interesting statement. Perhaps not accurate, though.

Why are you afraid, if you won't die? Women still die here, in this time, with the best medical care.

I don't know. I have been wounded before, so I don't think I'm afraid of the pain. Perhaps I am, though. This pain was like nothing I've ever felt. She thought for a bit. *Also, maybe I am afraid because of this second life is tied to me. If I am wounded in battle, it is just me, but now there is another person, a part of me who might be hurt, too.*

That's a good comparison. Elizabeth put her finger on Freya's paw and closed her eyes.

Tig came in with a tea cup and a small saucer. "I thought she might want some water if she wasn't feeling good." He held the saucer in front of Freya, and she took a few laps.

"Thank you. You're so thoughtful," Elizabeth said.

"I'll leave it on the nightstand in case she wants more. Is she hungry?"

Not now, Freya answered.

"No, not now, thanks," Elizabeth said. "We're going to nap for a bit. Bob, too, I guess."

Tig smiled. "Don't worry about dinner. I'll get something together. Changing of the guard. Trevor's car is gone, so don't worry. Maybe it's a good sign and the bad guys are under arrest. Or we just got a new guy and don't have him sussed out yet."

Thirty

The battle began like the others. As soon as she got there she checked the ridgeline. It looked stable, or at least not worse. She remembered the white fox running up the hill, and the ridge becoming restored as he did.

This time Elizabeth did not wait for Freya. She climbed the hill, dodged among the trees and searched for the fox. The warriors raced past her and she hid, though she felt invisible to them. Now that she knew Freya was pregnant, she saw the swell of her abdomen under her furs as she ran up the hill. Elizabeth did not stop her or call to her. She knew the fox was related to the rebuilding, or at least stopping the destruction, of the land and she wanted to find it.

She came to the clearing where the wounded had been gathered like the last time. It seemed the same, but Freya did not look for her, or in fact, seem to see her when she crossed the glen. Farther up, the mountain and trees continued, so whatever was happening to save Volksvang was working. Elizabeth struggled up the steeper hill, the trees farther apart the higher she went. It looked natural though, like when she'd been to Colorado and the

301

trees stopped and the snowcapped mountains, bare of green, began.

A small white face peered out of a cluster of boulders near the crest. Elizabeth slipped and slithered upward until she reached the boulders. She had not reached the crest in fact, but an optical illusion of layers of mountains, which reassured her. She was relieved to see Freya's world continue, but hoped she would not have to follow the fox any farther to get answers.

"Wait!" she called as the fox turned away. It stopped, watching her. "Please don't go."

The fox tilted its head but didn't bolt. She closed her eyes and tried to connect with it in her mind, but it was either resisting or just didn't care. She probed gently and heard a deep laugh.

Her eyes flew open and a man stood near the uppermost boulder. Laughing. A big smile. Bearded, covered in furs which were in turn covered in blood, the same man she'd seen before, run out of the clearing after entering it as a fox. Other than Freya, she had never met anyone or anything that transformed before. An animal was an animal, and a person was a person—Freya didn't really transform. She inhabited the body of a kitten in Elizabeth's world. That made sense and was totally different. She shook her head, trying to comprehend this new information.

"Why should I wait?" the laughing man asked.

Either he spoke English, or she understood his language. She'd spoken to the fox in English, she presumed. But maybe not.

"I, uh, I came to help and I saw you," she began lamely.

"I know who you are. You're being here helps, but not by anything you are doing. Just try not to be seen." He smiled again.

"That's right! How can you see me? There's no smoke now."

"This is my land. I know what happens here."

"Freya said this was her land."

"It is. But it is within my land, so it is my land as well."

That made sense. "I have so many questions."

"I know, but as you see, we are at war, so I may not have time to address them all now." He smiled, and it was infectious. She had no idea if she was dreaming, but she should enjoy it, she figured.

"How do you know Freya?"

"She is my wife."

"You're Oor!" Elizabeth was pleased she remembered. "It's so nice to meet you."

He raised his eyebrows and she realized how weird her words must have sounded under the circumstances.

"I have many names, but that is one."

"Like a last and a middle name?" she asked.

"I know not what you mean." He got very formal so maybe she'd insulted him in some way.

"I'm sorry. Nevermind. Am I speaking your language, or are you speaking mine?"

"Does it matter?" He grew impatient. "I don't have much time, and you are wasting it."

"When I was here before, the ridge was disappearing and now it's not. I saw you running as a fox and the land rebuilt as you ran. Can that be right?"

"It can. We are at war but as we succeed, and I am able to run the land, it stabilizes and grows. Not the first time this has happened, and it will not be the last, but it is important I do this each time to save our people and our world."

Elizabeth really wished she'd taken the time to Google Viking history because she was sure she was somewhere in it. She knew they didn't rule the world anymore, but she wanted to know more of what was happening. And why.

"Where am I? Freya said this is Volksvang, but this is part of a bigger country or territory, right?"

"Yes. Volksvang is Freya's part of Asgard. I rule Asgard and she controls many things in Volksvang." He glanced behind him, and she saw mountains fading in the distance.

"I see." She didn't, but she did see danger approaching. "How do I help?"

"Each time you visit, you bring strength and energy. This is what we need. We battle and have been victorious, but the outside world has become more powerful, and it is more difficult to bring back balance. The world cannot forget us!"

Elizabeth wanted to tell him she would not forget, and that the world had not forgotten, but a roaring filled her ears. The ground shook with the sound of many running feet.

"I must go." He whirled and ran over the crest toward the larger mountains. She followed. By the time she reached the top a few seconds later, only a small white fox ran down into the next valley.

She looked back and saw a horrific battle making its way up the mountain. She still could not tell definitely which warriors were Freya's, but got a feeling the ones in darker furs were the enemy. The sound was overwhelming. Not the repetitive chink of metal sword on metal sword the movies were so fond of showing, but the thunk or slither of sword against flesh, occasionally against leather shield, and the moans of the wounded, the grunts of effort, the cries of fear and effort at evading a blow.

Following the noise came the smell. She could *see* the smell, like a fog or mist, accompanying them up the mountain. A tendril of offal, a trickle of coppery blood, a wash of fear.

She couldn't stand it. She sat behind the boulders and threw herself back to her own world. She awoke on her bed, Freya next to her head.

Freya's eyes opened and a moment later, her person-spirit returned.

I met your husband, was the first thing Elizabeth thought to say.

I see. What did he tell you?

He filled in a few gaps, but as you probably know, you were all in a battle. The battle. It seems to be the same one every time. Is that right? Freya nodded. *But it has different outcomes?*

More or less.

305

He said something similar to what you said. The outside world determines what happens to yours. Your land of Volksvang is within the country of Asgard? Freya nodded. *Who is invading you?* Elizabeth struggled to recall anything she might have read or seen. *The English?*

I don't know who that is. Some of our people have gone to other lands, and that has caused our crisis. They have found other gods and taken over those lands, drifting farther away from us. Without them, we are disappearing, and without us, they cannot survive.

Your people are not forgotten. Not now. Try not to worry. It will be all right.

You do not know that. You mean well, but the battle can have an outcome in which we disappear. You have not seen this, not lived it.

Freya closed her eyes in a very human way of blocking out bad thoughts. Elizabeth took one finger and ran it down her forehead between her eyes, the way she liked.

"I'm sorry."

I know. You are human and doing your best.

"You're human too, sometimes."

Freya opened her eyes. *No, I'm not.*

Maybe Freya was more cat than person and had trouble differentiating while in her cat form? Oh, dear. Time to change the subject.

How are you feeling? Have the pains stopped?

Yes. Thor is hale.

Elizabeth's cell phone rang. Caller ID said MOM.

306

"Hi, Mom! How are you?"
"Guess what? We're Vikings!"

Thirty-One

"Vikings? What do you mean, we're Vikings?" Elizabeth asked her mother.

"Our trip ended in Scandinavia. I've always wanted to go there! We didn't have a real itinerary as you know, so when we had a few days I said Sweden first!"

"Where are you now?"

"Back home. We're getting settled, but I had to tell you. It's so exciting."

"So, Sweden?"

"And Norway. We didn't have time for Denmark, but those two countries are amazing."

"How did you find out we're Vikings? And how do you know your information is accurate?"

"We went to some history museums and I paid for an ancestry DNA thing along with a document and background search. You know how I love museums!"

Elizabeth knew. She'd spent a lot of vacations during her youth trailing behind her parents at a variety of museums. It wasn't that she didn't like them, but she'd read the information and move to the next display. Her parents would stay looking at a woven basket remnant for what felt like hours. "So tell me about your discovery."

"Before we left on the trip I sent in for your father and me to have our DNA history. I was the one who was excited about it, but he tolerated it."

"Mmm hmmm." The fastest response to keep her mother talking.

"I forgot all about it until I got the email on the trip! Isn't that a coincidence! Turns out we have Scandinavian ancestors on both sides! So that makes us Vikings!"

Not exactly, but okay. Elizabeth remembered Vikings weren't the nicest people at that time, Freya notwithstanding.

"So, we went to Sweden and Norway, and I immediately sent for a rush family history, with those countries flagged. If you just want a history, they give you everything as far as they can, but that can take weeks or months, depending on how hard documentation is to find. When you go back far enough, sometimes documents are lost or don't exist. A lot of records are in the churches, birth, marriage and death records. But for us it was harder because they didn't have churches there then."

"What do you mean, 'there then?'"

"Vikings were pagans. When you go back far enough, there's no Christianity, no Christ, you know, so no churches. They had writing, but not a lot of documentation lasts a thousand years. Eventually oral history was written down. We met a lovely lady at the university who helped answer some questions, but honestly honey, I could spend six months there doing research!"

"I bet. So is the information specific to our family?"

"That's harder to pinpoint. It's as accurate as I could find, but we really didn't have much time. I'm getting more information sent to me when they have it. Once I get my teeth on the bit, I don't want to let go!"

Elizabeth laughed. Her mother was very enthusiastic once she got interested in something. "What other ancestry do we have?"

"What?"

"Besides Vikings, what else is there?"

"I didn't pay too much attention. But some Irish, Scottish, some Russian, which was a surprise. It seems our family followed wherever the Vikings invaded. That doesn't speak well of our ancestors, but you can't have everything."

"Back up. So, the Vikings invaded other countries, I sort of remember that."

"Of course you do, raiding and pillaging, all of that."

Elizabeth really wished she'd paid more attention in school. She tried to tie it into what Freya and Oor had said. "So, when the Vikings went exploring, they raided and took over other countries or towns, and mixed with the local population, and became part of our lineage?"

"Yes. At the museums they had these great maps of the Viking explorations. One of the main reasons they left their home territories was to look for better farm land. Imagine it being cold and gray and unsuitable for farming most of the year."

Elizabeth didn't have to imagine. She'd been there and remembered how inhospitable the land was. In fact, no one mentioned farming at all, and she hadn't seen any signs of it. The ground that wasn't crusty beach was hard and rocky.

"Where did they go? Eventually they did find Christianity, right?"

"Yes, but nobody likes to be invaded. When they came to England, they went head to head: pagans versus Christ. Quite a controversy. They even came to North America!"

"How come I never heard that?"

"Probably because you didn't pay attention. They came to Labrador off the east coast of Canada. They set up farms and tried to cultivate crops. After a hundred years at the most, they gave up. If only they'd come a little farther south! We'd have had Vikings in Florida! Oh, it's so exciting!"

"Yes, it is." Elizabeth understood a little better what she'd been told. She still didn't understand how it tied to the crumbling of Freya's land. Another thought occurred to her. "How is it now, in Sweden and Norway? Are the Vikings remembered well there?"

"What do you mean by well? Fondly?"

"Remembered at all, I guess."

"Of course they are! I just told you we went to these museums and people were so helpful when they found out I was interested. Your father wasn't as excited as I was, but it was near the end of the trip and I think he wanted to get back to the shop."

Elizabeth agreed it was probably the case. "I guess I want to know, if the Vikings are, I don't know, revered or scorned, because of their violent history."

"Everyone has a violent history, Sweetie. But, no, there are lots of restaurants and bars with Viking themes, tours that talk about the history and some remains of communities. Just some wood foundations really. They rebuilt a Viking village, but it was too far and we didn't have enough time to see it. Next time."

"Sure." Elizabeth wondered what Freya and Oor meant, about being remembered if Vikings were so prevalent there today. Maybe they didn't know that. They were in the past. Somewhere. Oor mentioned their people traveling and finding other gods and forgetting them—their own gods, she presumed. Maybe that placed them around one of the times of the explorations/invasions? Where they met Christians. She knew a bit about the missionaries and how dogged they were in converting native populations around the globe. That didn't really help pinpoint a date, but she supposed it didn't really matter, since Vikings and their history were still around. Look at her; she was a Viking, according to her mother.

"So how are you feeling, hon?" Her mother changed the subject.

"Good. There is one thing. It's fine, but the baby's developing faster than they like. He's really big, and they're watching it now. I have to go in every week. They're concerned about lung development because he can't get much bigger without causing both of us distress."

"But you're feeling all right?"

` "Yes. I got some Braxton-Hicks contractions so I had them check, and other than his size, I feel okay. Huge."

"You said he. Is it really a he, or are you just calling it that?"

"We're calling it Thor, but yes, it's a he."

Silence. "I was mostly kidding about the Vikings."

"I know, but we've been doing some research of our own and it just came up. We're not really going to name him Thor." Elizabeth hoped. "It's just a nickname because he's so big," she hedged.

"I hope so. Thor is a wonderful name if you're a pagan god, but not if you're a middle schooler. That's just asking for him to be slammed inside a locker every day."

"I know Mom. It's been a little stressful, so we're blowing off steam." No way was she telling her mom about anything else; the white fox, Freya's world, the CIA, money laundering. Her mom knew she was an animal communicator, but since she didn't witness it every day, Elizabeth wasn't sure how much she bought in to it.

Freya. "We rescued a kitten, Mom. Her name is Freya and that's what started the name thing."

"Tig is okay with a third cat?"

"Absolutely."

"And the boys?" She had a soft spot for both Teddy and Edward.

"They love her."

"How did you come to name her after a Viking goddess? Don't you think that's a little strange after what I just told you?"

Very. Elizabeth was not going to tell her mom Freya either named herself, or came with the name.

"A goddess?" Elizabeth asked.

"Yes. Freya is the pagan goddess of just about everything. She is a very powerful warrior in her own right and controls her part of Asgard, called Volksvang."

"Volksvang," they finished together.

"What's Asgard? A part of Norway?" Elizabeth asked.

"No. Asgard is the mythical land where the gods live. Freya controls the part called Volksvang, or 'people's meadow.' When warriors die in battle, half go to be with Odin in pagan heaven called Valhalla, and half go to Volksvang and are resurrected to fight again."

"Odin sounds familiar."

"He should. He's the most powerful god and like his wife Freya, he's the god of war and a bunch of stuff. I have pamphlets on all this in my luggage someplace."

"Odin is married to Freya? I thought she was married to Oor?"

"You don't know anything about anything but you know Freya is married to Oor?"

"Uh. I heard it somewhere."

"Oor is another name for Odin, like Freya has other names like Frigg. We're talking way back when the people of the area prayed to Odin and made sacrifices. Lots of variations and versions of the stories, but that's all they are, stories."

The penny dropped. This is what Freya and Oor had been worried about. Not that Vikings would be forgotten, but that they themselves, the old gods would not be remembered.

"And of course, one version of that is they have a son, the god Thor. He had a lot of power, too," her mother continued. "Oh, I could go on, but when we come for the birth, we can talk more. I should have more information from the researchers by then."

"Yes, Mom. Thanks. That's a lot to think about."

"It is, isn't it?"

"How's the jet lag?"

"We're over it. Your dad's already gone back to work. I'm catching up on the house. Restarting the newspaper, collecting the held mail, restocking the fridge. All that stuff."

Elizabeth faded out on the to-do list. "Mom, you might want to be prepared, warn dad, I think this baby's coming early. Really early, so if you want to be here, be ready. I don't think I'm going to get a lot of warning, no matter what the doctor says."

Elizabeth remembered Freya said the baby would determine things and she believed it.

Thirty-Two

When Elizabeth hung up from her illuminating conversation with her mother, Freya still lay on the pillow next to her.

"I understand better what you've been talking about," she told the kitten.

About what?

The battles and the cost to your people. Elizabeth didn't know how to bring it up that perhaps warrior-Freya was not 'real' in the sense that people were. In fact, she didn't understand it herself. Perhaps it was a baby-hormone induced hallucination. If so, then Freya had the same hallucination, so for the purposes of her sanity, she decided to go with it.

She knew Freya was a warrior and ruled her territory, but for all her discussions, Volksvang and Asgard were real, they existed somewhere. They lived there, fought there, died there. What wasn't real about it? The fact that humanity was slowly forgetting them was also real, and the battle for their existence continued and repeated. How could she help break the cycle?

Oor, or Odin had told Elizabeth that her returning each time gave them strength, and Freya had said the birth of both boys would redirect the failing world. When Elizabeth was there, it certainly felt real. The stakes were very high. If the boys were connected in some way, she was terrified that if something happened to Freya or her Thor, something could happen to her baby. Common sense told her this was ridiculous, however, most of what had happened in the last couple months was beyond rational thought. But that didn't make it real.

What kept her from feeling like she was losing her marbles was the human spirit in the little cat. From the beginning, she had sought Elizabeth for help and was like no other creature Elizabeth had ever communicated with, no matter how intelligent.

*   *   *   *

Throughout September, she continued to 'visit' Volksvang and the battles continued with marked success. Elizabeth had done some research on Norse gods, and while interesting and coincided with what her mother had discovered, didn't really provide any ideas or solutions. She still waffled between wondering if she was delusional and being sure her trips were fact.

Each time she saw the land reconstitute. Her mind was always on both 'Thors,' Freya, Oor or Odin and Asgard. Perhaps that's what aided the land; it simply being on her mind. She was careful, never stayed too long, tried to remain invisible, but occasionally a warrior would see her and stand momentarily, mouth agape. At one point Freya told her she'd said to her warriors that a goddess from the people was visiting to bring them luck and strength, so if they saw her, to leave her alone.

Elizabeth still wasn't sure which warriors were whose, so unless they were actually with Freya, she tried to remain hidden.

At home, her belly continued to swell, but had slowed its pace. Freya the kitten had become more lethargic as Elizabeth did, and as she presumed, did human Freya as her birth time approached in her own land. Elizabeth remembered Thor was in charge of timing, but beyond that, she was unable to figure out what else determined the birth. Since the doctor's usual markers were of no use in this instance, she only visited the clinic for her weekly check-up. Dr. Phillip's was pleased the baby's size had stabilized, even though according to scans, he was fully developed. She suggested the growth was because Elizabeth hadn't counted her calories properly. Elizabeth didn't dissuade her since she had no other reason to offer. At least, not one that made any sense and wouldn't get her a 72 hour observation hold in the mental health services wing.

In early October she and Tig received the first update since Karl had gone into official protection. Bob stopped by the house unannounced.

"Come in, come in!" She hugged him. He was a welcome sight after all the help he'd given them. The official guards had only stayed an additional week after Karl had left, and then most unfamiliar vehicle traffic stopped. Nothing roused their suspicions, however, so they felt safe.

Elizabeth's one concern was she hadn't heard from Karl, and tried to follow the 'no news is good news' theory. When she'd called Abramson's office, a voice message relayed he'd gone on sabbatical for the remainder of the semester. That didn't sound good.

Since it was afternoon, she offered up a beer, which Bob accepted. Tig was not on nights anymore, and it was one of his days off, so he joined him.

Fall on the central coast was the best part of summer. Since summer was almost continuous fog, residents joked that summer came during the fall.

They took their drinks to the table near the pond. Elizabeth had her tea, and brought a little blanket to ward off the afternoon chill. It got dark around 6 PM now, but daylight saving time change would be in a couple weeks and darkness would fall even earlier. Then it would really seem like winter.

The boys joined them on the warm flagstones just in case any snacks might be offered. Freya waddled out too.

"Wow, she's gotten big," Bob commented as Freya swayed to where Elizabeth could put her in her extended leg-lap, as per usual.

"Yes, she has." Elizabeth didn't mention the cat carried the soul of a god. She let him think it was due to age and overindulgence.

They watched the koi burble and splash as Bob filled them in.

"I'm sure you've been concerned, but there was nothing I could tell you until now. After your part in the case and the evidence gathering, I was reassigned and I haven't been here. I got back yesterday so I thought I'd catch you up."

"We figured as much, "Tig said.

"Thank you for coming," Elizabeth added.

"The case is scheduled for trial in a couple months. All relevant parties are in jail, without bail since most of them are flight risks and have plenty of resources to skip."

"All of them?" Elizabeth asked.

"Not all involved, but all we could get. You know how that is. Some are so insulated we're never going to touch them, but now they have to pull up stakes and start all over in some other country. Do you know how many bribes that will involve?" he joked.

"What's going to happen to Karl?' Elizabeth asked.

"He'll remain in protective custody until the trial. It's hard on him, but we found his girlfriend and she's with him now."

"She agreed? I thought you had to basically give up your family?"

"In theory, but this is only until the trial's over. We have security on them."

"So, they're here? Can we see them?" Tig wanted to know.

"They are not here. They've been relocated, and no one can see them."

"Stacy's close to her parents. Do they know? They must be worried sick."

"They know she chose to be with him, but they don't know where they are or what they're doing. Stacy wanted to be with Karl, and he wanted to do the right thing."

"I suppose he would. I'm glad my instincts about him were right," Elizabeth said. "Is there any chance they'll be found and you know, something happens to them? So he can't testify?"

"It's always a risk, but few people know where they are—I don't even know. Right now the trial is set to begin after the first of the year."

"Oh! They'll miss Christmas," Elizabeth said.

"They would have anyway, even if the trial started sooner. They'll be protected through the trial."

"I see." Elizabeth was holding Freya for comfort, but it wasn't working like she'd hoped. "How long?"

Bob blew out a breath. "Sometimes a year, maybe more. We just don't know."

Tig and Elizabeth exchanged a glance. They might never see Karl again. Elizabeth teared up. She'd have made sure to give him a real good-bye if she'd known.

Tig took her hand. "It'll be okay."

Elizabeth shook her head. She wasn't sure. She felt Thor shift inside. She looked down at Freya and saw her abdomen mirroring her own. They were getting close to Thors' birthday. She wished she could ask Freya's Thor what his schedule was. That made her smile a little.

"I've got to get going." Bob stood.

"Thank you for telling us. Let us know if there's anything we can do, or if anything changes." Tig shook his hand.

"If I can."

Elizabeth hugged him at the door. "Do you know anything about Abramson? He's gone on sabbatical. Is that normal?"

"I don't know. He's in a completely different area from me. I'll see what I can find out. He is an academic and they aren't really normal, are they?" Bob smiled, and she had to smile back.

Sunset approached and the wind picked up. Elizabeth pulled her blanket closer and returned to the patio to get her tea cup and Bob's beer bottle. The cats had all come inside. A brisk fall breeze was too much for house cats to withstand.

She started water boiling for pasta. Janie, from across the street, had given them a bunch of summer tomatoes she'd canned so Elizabeth sautéed garlic and onions for a fresh sauce. Elizabeth went to the front window to close the blinds. The sky was scarlet. Stunning and blinding. She stood for a moment enjoying it.

We have to go. Freya.

Elizabeth looked down. Freya had waddled out to her and now patted gently at her ankle. *Go where?*

Battle. Freya turned and headed for the bedroom, their defacto battle station.

Elizabeth turned off the water and the sauce and left a note for Tig that she was having a lie down for a bit. Dinner would be fast when she finally was able to make it. She had a feeling this battle would be a defining one.

They were both so used to popping in and out of Volksvang now it took no time for Elizabeth to ground herself and arrive outside the long house. It felt different this time. Vastly different. Freya was with her on arrival, for one. For another, she handed Elizabeth a short sword and oddly, it did not feel strange in her hand. When she looked down at the sword, she was wearing furs like Freya. All other times she had been wearing whatever she already had on, like the time she ran uphill in bedroom slippers. Fun *and* practical. Now she was warm and felt protected, however false that feeling might be. Even a leather shield failed to fully ward off a direct blow.

Freya immediately ran and called out something as she did. Elizabeth risked a look back at the shore where in all other versions, the dragon boats were pulling up to the dock and warriors jumped out and ran for the beach yelling, in full battle mode.

This time, the boats were only halfway into the inlet, oars reaching, splashing, men yelling, angry faces grimacing.

Why had they arrived earlier than usual? Perhaps Freya had something to do with it. She said they'd had to leave, but in previous visits, their leaving Elizabeth's time did not affect their arrival. She had no time to ponder this because she understood Freya's yells. She was calling to the warriors to get to higher ground, to have an advantage. Men and women poured out of the buildings and trailed up the rocky hill. For the first time, Elizabeth saw children. Her heart squeezed. What were children doing here? In a battle? As warriors? She was very confused. The children took off with a smaller group of warriors and ran parallel to the beach away from the boats, then vanished into the trees. Elizabeth prayed they would either be able to hide or get far enough away so as not to be targets.

Elizabeth knew she only carried her baby's soul in this world, and so ran fairly easily up the familiar route. However, this was Freya's world, and Thor was huge which made her ungainly. No way she could fight and protect herself and the baby. Elizabeth knew why she was here. She was not a warrior, but somehow she had to make sure Freya and Thor survived.

Sweat ran down her face and back in the heavy furs. She slowly caught up with the main group, but she heard the thunder of the invaders gaining. Freya's warriors turned to face their enemies. Elizabeth ran to find Freya. More warriors were here than had ever joined the battle before. And they all could see Elizabeth. As shocking as that was, as she ran past seeking Freya, even more so was the quick bowing of heads, murmurs of, "goddess, thank you," and "milady," and "bless us and protect us," that followed her up the mountain.

Thirty-Three

Elizabeth found Freya toward the top of the ridge, yelling strategy unfamiliar to her warriors, by the look of them. In previous battles, Freya was at the fore, and although she managed to escape serious injury, many among her ranks had not fared as well.

"Where did all these new warriors come from?" Elizabeth gasped out when she reached Freya.

"Oor is coming and sent reinforcements." Freya moved down the ridge toward where the two armies would meet.

"He's been here before. It hasn't made much of a difference." Elizabeth followed, remembering the fox.

"His strength has grown with each victory. He was not able to bring his warriors with him until now. He was more spirit than flesh, but things have changed. We have more power and if we win today, victory is ours. The land will be safe."

Elizabeth wondered if 'more spirit than flesh' meant he was here mostly as the white fox and so was unable to fight. Made sense. But he had changed into a human form, at least to talk to her. Maybe that was spirit, too. Like she was to the warriors. Only visible in the smoke, and *like* the smoke, insubstantial.

But even she was different today. She wore furs with a sword tucked into her belt. She was more than smoke. All the warriors saw her.

"Freya, Freya!" Elizabeth pulled on her arm. "You can't fight like this. It's too dangerous. Thor is too big, you can't move properly. You and he could get hurt. Then what would happen to Volksvang? All these battles for nothing?"

"I have to lead my people. They look to me. I have to be here." She glanced at her tribe of filthy, dedicated men and women. Weapons drawn, they hunched, tense, ready to launch at the enemy at a moment's notice.

Elizabeth saw them, too. They looked a little insane, but perhaps it was a good thing. A word came to mind from her recent research. *Berserkers.* So named because of their reputation for going berserk in battle. Suddenly it all made sense. In her own life, there was very little she would fight for, and certainly nothing like this sort of fight. She would die for her family, but that was different, a sort of metaphorical death. But here, in each person's eyes, their own mortality could be minutes away. And they were fine with that. Their deaths were for the greater good.

"Freya, even if you win, you and Thor might not come out of it. You said how important he is to your world and that it was tied to my world. You have to put that first if you want your world to survive," Elizabeth pleaded.

Before Freya could respond, two things happened simultaneously. The enemy, hundreds of them, broke through the lower trees, running, swords up, screaming.

And from behind Freya's people on the ridge, Oor also ran, screaming, sword held high, the sun glinting off it so it looked like a blazing torch. His people surged forward, bringing him and Freya's warriors along. Unfortunately, it brought Freya and Elizabeth along as well.

Elizabeth grabbed Freya to pull her away, but as she did, a calm filled her, followed by deep anger and a surge of power. She pulled her sword while keeping hold of Freya. Freya also held onto Elizabeth and pulled her sword with her free hand.

Elizabeth's primary objective was to get Freya to safety, but she would protect these people too.

Together, the two women fought off attackers. It was counter intuitive to stay attached, and yet, Elizabeth knew that was where her sudden strength and sword skill came from. Perhaps she offered something similar to Freya.

The two armies clashed on the steep mountainside, blood running downhill, making it hard to keep their footing. Oor yelled and pushed, and his men split Freya's group as they ran down the middle. Freya's people divided and began to flank the uphill fighters. Freya had known to change strategy from the flat beach and village to have more of the fight on the steep mountain.

Keeping the uphill advantage, they fought with gravity, and the enemy had to curse and bleed for every inch they gained, which today was not much.

Elizabeth's only goal was to get Freya off the field but Freya wanted to take out as many of the opposition as she could along the way. Elizabeth was becoming accustomed to the noise and screams by now, the sound of bodies falling and wounded crying out. She would never get used to the smell. It was overwhelming as the enemy fell with increasing speed due to the support of Oor's warriors.

Freya refused to hide, but she did allow Elizabeth to guide her up and around to where there was less action. The pitch of the main fight carried it downhill toward the village, both to maintain the advantage of the slope and keep the enemy constantly on the move. From their vantage point, they could see Oor in flashes in the wide-spaced trees since he was so big, and they certainly heard the battle. It slowed and quieted, with Freya occasionally dragging Elizabeth a few paces to swipe at a warrior who got too close.

The sounds of battle stopped and the sounds of the forest resumed, as though nothing had occurred. Moans of the injured could be heard along with the birdsong.

The women slowly made their way toward the beach. Elizabeth was cautious, not wanting to be surprised by another warrior waiting to pick off Freya's survivors. Freya had no such ideas and marched down, finishing off stragglers as she went.

"Hey, you don't have to do that. They're probably going to die anyway," Elizabeth said.

"Yes, I do. For several reasons. One, we don't take prisoners and we don't waste time and resources saving them." Elizabeth thought that was harsh. "Two, they are warriors and fought honorably, they deserve to die an honorable death. And three, they are already dead. You said you knew that? You had learned about my land?"

Elizabeth had forgotten that part. It was all so real. If they were already dead, why did they fight so hard? To die again?

As usual, Freya picked up on her thoughts. "Yes. Our life's meaning is to fight for honorable causes. For our lords and leaders, our land, our children."

"So, here, warriors die to fight and fight to die? Over and over?"

Freya nodded. Then Elizabeth was reminded to ask about the children, but Freya continued. "I rule Volksvang, and Oor rules Asgard, but a true warrior's heart lies in his reaching Valhalla."

"Oh, yes. Heaven. Sort of," Elizabeth added.

"Your Christian god is with you even now." Freya smiled.

"No. I'm not religious. I, uh," Elizabeth trailed off.

"That is what I mean. Your culture of the Christian heaven is known all over the world. So few know of Valhalla and our ways. We, rulers of Asgard and our lands, are fading. But you have helped bring us back. And so will these boys as they become men." She gestured to her belly.

They had reached the village.

"Have you met the Christian god?" Elizabeth had no idea why she asked that.

Freya looked at her strangely. "Of course not."

"Why not? If you're both gods or rulers. You both watch over humans, don't you? Why wouldn't you have met?"

They reached the long house and entered.

"I was thinking of how to explain this to you." Freya took off a layer of furs and Elizabeth did the same. She got them each a drink of something that smelled vile, an ancient ale of some sort Elizabeth guessed, but she was exhausted, hungry and thirsty, so she took the mug. She thought Freya was going to ignore her question, much like the cat she was at home, but she sat and finally answered.

"Our worlds do not, overlap, I guess you would say. For you humans, they do in your thought and philosophy, but we live in different spaces. It is not like we meet and discuss which humans we want to come to our final places. It is a bit more complicated. We were not aware of the Christian god until our people voyaged and met others who worshipped him. There are more than that!" she exclaimed. "I know it sounds unbelievable, but there are many gods and many worlds outside of our own."

Freya took a big gulp of her drink. Elizabeth took a small sip and gagged. *That can't be good for the baby,* she thought. She decided she'd failed Religion 101 and changed the topic.

"When the enemy arrived today, I saw children here for the first time. They were running with some of our warriors. I hope they are safe." Elizabeth realized she'd said 'our' warriors. Freya looked at her. "Oh. They may be safe, but they are already dead," Elizabeth said sadly.

Freya nodded. "It is true. Children are lost in battle. Often the enemy wants to be sure none grow up to be warriors or create more warriors. Those children are here because they were heroes in their lives. The earned the right to be here. They are protected from the battles. It is agreed on both sides. We are warriors but not animals. They have suffered enough."

Elizabeth still felt sad, but was a bit reassured. All her adrenaline had faded now, leaving her with a weariness through to her bones. "I need to go soon. This is the first battle where I thought you won the big one. Did you?"

"The 'big one?'"

"I don't know. Oor came and brought reinforcements; the enemy is gone, at least most of them. Do you get to keep their boats?"

Freya smiled. "We keep whatever we want. We are Vikings."

Elizabeth laughed. Her mother would be thrilled. If she could tell her, which she didn't think she could. Maybe she could formulate it into a story of sorts. Too good not to share.

"Yes. The battle is over, and the big war is done," Freya said. The land is safe and we are not forgotten."

"How can you tell?"

"I know. But more importantly, Oor knows. He controls much of what you see and what happens. You will not forget this, will you?" Elizabeth shook her head. "And as your life passes, you will tell others, in a fashion. Your mother, father and eventually your son, will carry on the stories and so our legend will grow and become secure again, like a tree with sufficient roots." Elizabeth understood. "The last link is the birth of our sons, which will be soon."

"How soon?"

"One more moon."

"How long is that?"

Freya rolled her eyes. "Look it up."

Elizabeth burst out laughing.

Thirty-Four

Elizabeth awoke at home in bed after the victorious Great Battle. Freya snoozed on her pillow, but Elizabeth was no longer fooled. A great warrior and a goddess was housed there. She lay recalling the moments of the fight and the subsequent conversation, but already it was taking on the feel of remnants of a dream—fuzzy around the edges and not terribly clear.

Elizabeth had one piece of business to complete. She called Abramson's office once more. She hoped to find out what happened to him and to Karl, and since Bob didn't know, perhaps he did. If he didn't answer, maybe a department head or someone could at least tell her if he was truly on sabbatical.

She punched in the contact she'd named 'spyguy.' Perhaps she ought to change it.

"Dr. Abramson's office, Barry Fox Teaching Assistant speaking," a voice said.

"Oh. Is Dr. Abramson available?" She hadn't expected anybody else to answer.

"No, he's on sabbatical for the rest of term. Is there something I can help you with?"

"*Barry Fox?*"

"Yes, what can I do for you?"

"Are you part of the White Fox club?" she asked in a burst of sudden inspiration.

"Yes, I am." He sounded pleased. "Are you interested in the club?"

"What do you do?"

"The White Fox is the university cyber security and hacking club. Our mission is to provide the tools, knowledge, skills and resources to make the internet a safer place by protecting personal computers, private data and information systems." He sounded as if he were reading the words.

"Okay. So you're teaching students to be safer on the internet?"

"Yes, that is our club mission statement, you see."

"Why is it named White Fox?"

"The club was founded by me and a friend, George White, when we were freshmen, so we put our names together. And also, because white hats are good hackers, we thought the white part would be a nice addition."

That answered that question, but not about using the club as a recruitment tool. Or maybe they didn't do that. Maybe Abramson just trolled the campus. If that were true, she knew Barry wouldn't tell her.

"Do you know when Dr. Abramson will be back?"

"He's scheduled to resume classes after Winter Break, but beyond that, no."

Elizabeth thanked him and hung up, not much wiser than before.

*   *   *   *

October drew to a close and the days were short, fairly dark, and colder than seasonal norms. Halloween decorations went up all over town, and Elizabeth despaired of getting their own up the way she felt. Tig had offered to do it, but this was her favorite holiday and she wanted to take part. Finally it was the last week of the month. Now or never. She opened the garage and began pulling the bins from lower shelves. Tig found her and helped pull the ones from up high.

They took everything into the house, and for the next few hours, enjoyed hanging decorations and sharing memories of previous Halloweens. Last, Tig pulled a ladder and put the giant inflatable, light-up black cat on the roof; everyone loved the cat.

It took most of Sunday and she was exhausted by the end. Halloween was Wednesday and Tig was working days, so he should be home early enough to see the tiny tots, which were their favorites: toddling Supermen, witches, princesses and ladybugs who clearly had no idea what was going on, but if you stuck to the script, strangers gave you candy! What a great day.

Typically, Tig and Elizabeth shut off their porch light by 8PM. They felt trick or treating was really for young children, and when high schoolers showed up, it was over. They would take the remaining candy—Elizabeth always bought a bit too much of their favorites—back to the bedroom and they all watched NetFilms.

Another aspect of the holiday they loved was pumpkin carving, but with the typical whimsy of California weather, it could be raining, hailing or hot

335

as the dickens, so they'd learned not to carve until the day before. One year the pumpkins had grown a nasty green fuzz one day after carving and didn't make it to the holiday itself. Tuesday would be their carving day after Tig got home from work.

Some years they dressed up for the kids coming to the door. This year Elizabeth didn't think she'd manage it. She might have trouble just getting up and down to answer the door fifty times. But no way was she missing even one adorable two-foot tall football player!

When Tig arrived home on Tuesday evening, she had the dining table covered with newspaper and carving tools and Sharpies out. She had to cheat and use a pattern if she wanted a really cool Jack O Lantern, but Tig was a skilled artist where pumpkins were concerned. He could just draw a face and start, and it always came out fantastic.

An hour later, each had a masterpiece. She had bought a pumpkin with a ghoulish green-gray skin and it looked marvelous. They tested them with candle stubs and dubbed them worthy for tomorrow night. Tig put them on the porch bench to stay cool. The neighborhood was pretty safe and vandalism rare, although Halloween did tend to bring out the 'rascal' in some people.

Everyone settled in for the night and Elizabeth had just gone to the kitchen for a refill on her water bottle when her own water broke. She knew what happened, but it was still scary. And messy. She worried about slipping as she made her way back to the bedroom.

"Tig. My water broke. I think we should go," Elizabeth said. The doctor had said early on they didn't have to rush to the hospital the second her water broke, but she had since rescinded that because the baby was so big and the pregnancy so unusual.

"It's too soon!" Tig said.

"The baby's ready. Don't worry. It's time." Elizabeth knew that in her heart.

"But he's two months early! What about his lungs?"

"I'm ready, and he's ready, but let's get to the hospital and be sure." Elizabeth felt strangely calm, especially compared to Tig's reaction. He did not have the information she did, that Thor called the shots and a small striped kitten functioned as a mid-wife of sorts.

Firefighter that he was, Tig jumped out of bed and threw off his PJs. Elizabeth didn't bother changing out of hers, except into dry pants. They had an overnight bag packed and ready, a 'Go Bag' as they were called in thriller movies and so had adapted the term for their own.

The contractions weren't bad. Like Braxton-Hicks, but now she knew what they felt like, she didn't panic. She also knew they would get worse.

She explained to the boys what was happening. Their main issues were staying on the bed and getting lots of food. Teddy made sure to make that point clear. Janie was already on standby for cat sitting. Tig would text her with news tomorrow.

Elizabeth checked Freya on her pillow. Her abdomen rose and fell and lurched and she panted like she had before. Elizabeth knew kitten Freya was not going into real labor, but she reflected Freya in Volksvang. She kissed her on the forehead and promised to stay connected as much as possible.

Freya's eyes alternated between warrior and kitten as the pain came and went. It was a little disconcerting, but she knew Freya was doing her best at the other end with mid-wives or whatever she had. She wished now she'd taken the time to learn. She wanted Freya to be safe. If something happened during birth, would the kitten die over here? She didn't want to think about either problem. Did goddesses die? If Freya died in childbirth, would she still return to Volksvang, even though she wasn't killed in battle?

These and other pointless thoughts swirled around in her head as Tig shepherded her to the car and they drove to Tolosa General.

The last thing she did before they hit the E.R. doors was to text her mom. "It's time."

Thirty-Five

A woman going into labor was not an emergency like a traffic accident, so the check-in staff and procedure getting her up to maternity was much more relaxed and happy. Everyone loved a baby. Elizabeth did not mention she was two months early. She figured it would come out eventually, but she was not concerned. All was as it should be.

Staff told her Dr. Phillips had been informed. She arrived and opted not to try and stop the contractions. She felt the baby's survival at this point was better outside the womb. Elizabeth had used all her mental skill to will this decision into being. The contractions continued to worsen, and finally she was offered an epidural when it got so bad she literally could not see. She gratefully accepted after being reassured it was safe for Thor. Tig wisely stayed out of the decision. The two of them and Dr. Phillips had gone over all this in detail several times and the consensus was Elizabeth would not have an anesthetic. That was before Thor became the size of a VW beetle and wanted to come out fighting.

Twenty-four hours later Elizabeth knew she'd missed the trick or treat window. She was no closer to having the baby. In fact, the pounding contractions had caused her cervix to begin to swell shut and Dr. Phillips informed her a C-section was called for.

Her parents had driven down from Walnut Creek that morning and had remained at the hospital, mom popping in to offer distraction with tales of their trip. Her dad was extremely uncomfortable seeing his daughter in such pain so he wandered the halls and found nooks and crannies to entertain himself. He brought take-out from nearby restaurants for everyone but Elizabeth. She was not allowed food, once the possibility of a C-section was raised in case more than the epidural anesthetic was required. Food was the last thing she wanted.

Now she understood how women died in childbirth and wondered again for the millionth time how Freya was doing. Unable to keep her promise of a constant connection due to the high pain level, she had to content herself with checking in between contractions. However, the last few hours they had been a minute long and a minute apart, nearly back to back. As best she could tell, Freya was experiencing the same labor she was. One amazing aspect: Once Elizabeth received the epidural, Freya also experienced the benefits.

It was nearing 11PM when they wheeled Elizabeth into surgery for the C-section. Tig was allowed to come, but no one else. Mom and dad camped out in the waiting room.

Elizabeth, now not feeling the pounding agony of contractions, could fret full time about Freya. No C-section for her. She tried to ask Freya how she was coping, what the midwife or healer thought, but her queries went unanswered. She hoped everything was fine. She also wondered if she'd know, or sense, if something happened to her or the real Thor. She sent out all her warm, golden energy, in hopes that although Freya didn't respond, she could receive it.

"It's a prince!" Dr. Phillips had begun the C-section and was far enough along to determine that. Tig's eyes over the mask looked ecstatic. Elizabeth was happy, too, but exhausted. They had rigged up a mirror and sheeting contraption so the surgical field was sterile, but Elizabeth could see what was happening. She felt no pain, just tugging and pressure, so it was a strange sensation to see a big hole in her abdomen with a baby's head sticking out.

"It's a god," Elizabeth mumbled to herself, and one of the nurses asked, "What dear?"

"Nothing. Can I see him?"

"They're going to clean him up a bit first," the nurse said.

"Is he healthy? What does he weigh?"

The baby's strident cries attested to strong lungs. After a quick weigh-in and measuring, the answer was six pounds, one ounce. Much bigger than the estimate.

Dr. Phillips and the internet had gone over all the post labor procedure. The baby was thoroughly checked. While that happened, she got to watch the rest of the show, the delivery of the placenta and then vast amounts of stitching and stapling. Tig gave her a kiss, but then hovered around the newborn area, waiting for his son.

Elizabeth felt frantic without a response from Freya. If the last near 36 hours held true to form, Freya would have delivered too, matching Elizabeth in pain and pace.

At last, the baby was pronounced healthy and placed in her arms and she felt herself relax. His round, red face squinted up at her, and she kissed his downy head. He wasn't crying now, but made adorable snuffling sounds, grunting, with little fists freeing themselves from the swaddling.

"Happy Halloween!" the staff called out in a chorus.

"Thank you," she said. It was her best, and worst, Halloween.

She felt the strength and the weight of him and knew she loved this little being more than she'd ever loved anything in her life. She glanced at Tig. From his expression, he felt the same. Tears leaked and ran down the sides of her face into her hair.

Freya was in her head. Thor had been born too. She felt the way Elizabeth did, lost in love with her son, but her circumstances were different. She projected to Elizabeth a cold, dark night with snow falling. Women clustered around her and lots of blood. No C-section of course, but Freya had had a rough time of it. Freya gave thanks for the epidural, even though she didn't know what it was. Elizabeth was relieved she hadn't decided to tough it out herself, because she couldn't imagine getting through this birth with 36 hours of labor and feeling every crashing pain. She hadn't known Freya would also receive the benefits of the drug, but she was glad she had.

Elizabeth asked her what had happened, if her labor had been delayed similarly, and Freya said yes. The healers had given her a drink and applied a poultice to take the swelling down and allow the cervix to open. This was beyond Elizabeth's imagination and she once again thanked the world of modern medicine.

Freya was exhausted too, but sent Elizabeth a scene of reveling, music, drinking and noise.

What's going on over there?

It is part of the Winternights Festival.

What's that? Is it like a birthday party for Thor and you?

No. It is an important festival that marks the beginning of the winter season. We remember and honor our dead, our ancestors, and there is much divination about the year to come.

Elizabeth wondered at the fascination with the dead among these north people. Even when they were dead, they weren't really dead, she thought wryly.

Is Oor there, too?

He is readying for The Wild Hunt. He knows he has a son and he will see him soon. It is fortuitous that our sons were born this night. I thought they might be. It is one of the most powerful of the year, and that power is passed to our children.

You mean the Winternights Festival thing?

In part, but that lasts several nights. It is also Odinsday and it is forever rich with gifts.

Gifts?

Wisdom, bravery, honor, sacrifice and more.

Those sounded like things that might be more helpful to a Viking, but Elizabeth didn't say anything. Who knew what her own little Thor's life might become and what 'gifts' he'd need?

Odinsday, like your husband? He is Oor but also goes by Odin, right? Elizabeth was trying to piece together an unpieceable puzzle.

Yes, he is everywhere. He travels a great deal, and to your world.

I've seen him as a fox in your world, but the fox I saw here, was not him, right? Its eyes were red.

That was how he manifests on his travels at times. The fox functions as a conduit, and is also him. A duality, if you will.

343

"Okay, are you ready to go to your room?" the same kind nurse asked her.

"Yes." Elizabeth was so tired, but wasn't sure she could sleep. Sometime during her conversation with Freya, the baby had been moved to his own clear Plexiglas crib.

She was transferred to a gurney, and the release of the wheel lock sounded like a gunshot in the relative calm after the birth. Both were rolled to their room. Tig followed. She had requested that the baby stay with her. Some mothers preferred to have the baby stay in the nursery and have it brought to them for nursing and care. Elizabeth wanted him with her.

Once in her private room she was transferred to a regular bed which felt fantastic after the surgical bed. "We know you asked for the baby to room in, but we recommend you start tomorrow," the nurse said. "Tonight might be your last night of sleep for a while. We will feed him tonight and tomorrow we'll help you with breast feeding and some infant care, all right?"

Elizabeth glanced at Tig and he nodded. She didn't know why it was important that he back her up on this. They had talked the procedure through, but right now she only wanted rest. She thought it might be the rougher time of unanticipated surgery that made her unable to think clearly. Maybe it was her connection to Freya, like having two babies, but whatever it was, she needed Tig to be okay that the baby wasn't with her this first night.

He took her hand, then bent and kissed her. "You rest. We'll be back tomorrow. Your parents will see him in the nursery, and we'll all come by afterward. They want you to stay here a couple days because a C-section is a major surgery. Also, they want to be sure you know how to care for yourself and the baby. Elizabeth nodded, disappointed she'd have to stay longer than she'd thought, but a bit relieved she wouldn't be alone with the baby yet.

He took his leave, and the nurse started to roll the clear crib out. "Can I hold him one more time?" she asked.

"Of course. But then you need your rest. And he needs his first feeding." She latched the crib wheels and lifted him out.

Elizabeth cuddled the little bundle, wondering at the tiny features, his miniscule fingers with their microscopic nails. He started to fuss and nuzzle at her chest. She looked at the nurse. "Can you help me?" Although she hadn't planned to nurse just now, the baby did, and her body did. She felt her swollen breasts expand and the pain became severe.

The nurse nodded and went through the process with her. Thor got it right away, which was good since Elizabeth had no idea what she was doing. The nurse said sometimes babies have a hard time latching on or figuring out a natural rhythm, but this baby nailed it.

The nurse had her switch sides and the relief was unbelievable. Thor passed out a few minutes later. The nurse gently put him back in his rolling Tupperware and wheeled him away. Elizabeth fell asleep immediately and barely awoke when they came to check her vitals.

Her next conscious moment was of the orderly wheeling in a breakfast tray followed by Tig and her parents.

Thirty-Six

Elizabeth shuffled to the bathroom while her family waited outside. The baby's clear crib was also brought in and a 'lactation' specialist came to assist with Thor's breakfast. He needed no help. Elizabeth was filled with joy watching her son and thought she could stay like this forever, just the two of them, mother and child. Freya's thoughts drifted to her and she felt the same, wherever she was. Elizabeth sent out love and joy. She hoped she'd see Freya again.

Now that the Great Battle, as she thought of it, was over she knew Freya the goddess-warrior's task was done. At least the task that required Elizabeth's help. She supposed the constant battling that involved the warriors and dividing of the fallen between Odin taking some to Valhalla and Freya taking the rest to Volksvang would continue. That seemed to be their destiny.

She had only begun to research all of this, but from what she'd found, there were pages and pages of mythology woven tightly with Norse history. Fascinating, but lengthy. What she'd experienced with Freya didn't seem to be in the books or on the web anywhere, so maybe this Great Battle was not something that occurred often, or at least when someone was able to keep a record.

As she pondered whether she'd be able to return to Volksvang, or if Freya would still be in the kitten when she got home, her door eased open and Tig said, "All right for us to come in?"

Elizabeth smiled and nodded. She had just finished nursing and inexpertly re-configured the 'burrito wrap' swaddling process. Her parents followed Tig into the room.

Tig kissed her. "How was your night?"

"Pretty quiet. Yours?"

"Cats were mad, but I let them sleep with me, and gave them a wet food bribe, so we're all good. I haven't had the courage to tell them you won't be back until tomorrow."

Elizabeth laughed. "I will."

Her mother came over and kissed her forehead. "Well done, sweetheart. He's beautiful."

Her dad leaned in too and said, "He's got my nose." Everyone laughed because her father's nose was handsome but large. Although it fit his face and personality, it was not a baby's nose by any stretch and so had become a family joke.

"Let's hope not, Dad," Elizabeth said.

The baby opened his eyes and surveyed the room. Elizabeth knew infant vision was limited to fairly close this young, but he seemed to see them. Not exactly track, but an awareness.

"Want to hold him?" she asked her mother.

"I'm sure Tig does," she answered.

"I'm going to have the chance as much as I want, so you two should take advantage," Tig said. Elizabeth handed the baby to her mother who cooed and rocked. Her dad touched the downy head. The baby absorbed it all quietly.

Tig pushed her breakfast tray closer, and she picked up a piece of toast. It immediately reminded her of Freya. "How was Freya last night?" she asked.

"She was quiet. She missed you for sure. She slept on your pillow most of the night. When I got home, I found her in the closet. She'd made a nest out of your tee shirts on the shelf. I guess the door was unlatched when we left in such a hurry night before last. After you had the baby and I got home, I found her there and moved her to the bed. She let me but she looked like maybe she didn't feel good. The boys were fine. She was back to herself this morning. I knew you'd want to know."

Elizabeth knew animals often move to a private place to give birth, or die, so she wasn't too surprised. She was relieved Tig wasn't home to question the whole virtual birth or whatever might have occurred. That would have been more explaining than she felt able to do.

The baby started to snuffle and her mom handed her to Tig who began to hum as he rocked—a non-song comfort sound; the baby responded and settled. Tig glanced at Elizabeth, and she saw his eyes were moist and that made her start to cry, too.

"Well, now, I think you've had enough excitement for now, young lady," her dad said.

"I think so too, Paddy," her mom agreed. "We'll come back in the afternoon for a quick visit, okay?" She stroked Elizabeth's hair.

"I am pretty tired. I think Th—uh, the baby needs to nurse again. I can't really tell yet."

She caught Tig's eye and they smiled, both realizing what she'd almost said.

"Oh! What name did you decide?" her mother asked.

"Liam Patrick Murphy," Tig said.

"As in, me?" her father asked.

"Yes, Dad, you," Elizabeth said.

This time it was her father who had tears in his eyes. He bent and kissed her, then turned and hugged Tig. "Well, now," he repeated.

Elizabeth's mom hugged them both too. "Lovely. Very sweet. You know if you give him that middle name, he might get the nose after all."

The tension broke and they laughed. "We'll wait for you downstairs," Elizabeth's mom said.

"Thanks, Emily," Tig said.

"Wait, Mom. I have a question. When I was in labor, and you were telling me about your trip and the Vikings, I think I heard something. Now that I'm more awake, I just want to be sure I heard it right."

"Sure, honey. What?"

"You mentioned the days of the week and how we get them, and some of our holidays, from the Vikings?"

"Yes, a version of it. Norse means North, but not all Vikings came from Norway. Those were the ones who came to North America, you know, Eric the Red and Leif Ericson?"

Elizabeth nodded. "No horns on the helmets, right?"

This time her mother nodded. "Right! I didn't think you were able to listen. I was just filling time to keep you entertained. The Vikings from Denmark went to the U.K. At any rate, days of the week. Okay, for example Thursday is Thorsday."

Elizabeth and Tig exchanged another look. "Really? That's fascinating," Elizabeth said, "but didn't I hear you mention Odin?"

349

"Oh, yes. Odinsday became Wednesday! Isn't it interesting?"

"Wow." Elizabeth wondered if that was what Freya meant about the day being significant. Both boys were born on Wednesday. At least she knew hers was, and since Freya mentioned the significance of that specific day, she assumed it was the same over *there*. Wouldn't it have been more significant for them to be born on Thursday? She'd have to ask. Anyway, she was really drifting off now.

"You guys came together?" Elizabeth asked.

"They're staying at the house, at least for now," Tig said. "It was easiest. We might take two cars this afternoon if I can stay longer?"

She nodded. "You can watch us both sleep. It'll be fun," Elizabeth teased.

"Nothing I'd like more."

Thirty-Seven

Two days later and Elizabeth arrived home with much ceremony. Flowers and toys accompanied her, and it took all of them to bring the booty into the house. The nursery was set up, but Tig took Liam on a tour of the house and property. Edward knew what was happening, but he looked a little adrift at not being carried.

Elizabeth told him he'd soon be back in football position. Edward cheered up. For some reason, both boys liked the smell of Liam, except when the diaper was full. And Teddy, who was not impressed with Garrett, Janie's baby across the street, took a fancy to his own infant. Teddy was often wherever Liam was—whether the crib in the nursery, the rocker infant seat, or carried around by an adult.

Elizabeth was ecstatic that so far, no jealousy or a vibe of hostility, which would be natural for any animal, had showed. She laughed thinking they assumed Liam would grow up to be another feeding source. Probably right.

Her parents stayed a full week and were indispensable with infant care, chores and errands. Her dad got itchy to return to the business, so the following Friday, they packed up and pulled out of the drive.

Elizabeth and Tig waved good-bye and brought Liam and the cats back into the house. Liam was ready for his mid-morning nap, as was Elizabeth, but when she put him in the crib, Tig watching over her shoulder, she had a momentary wave of panic.

"What do we do now?" she asked Tig. "We're all alone? What are we supposed to do?"

Tig hugged her and she thought he felt the same anxiety. "I don't know. I guess we'll figure it out." He'd taken an extra week off with family leave, only two weeks at this time. He was allowed a month, but they'd agreed to save the other two weeks for an emergency, or if Elizabeth felt overwhelmed later. She didn't think now that she would be.

"Maybe you should nap, too?" he asked her. They'd read the baby literature non-stop and one bit of advice that stuck was to sleep when the baby did. No catching up on chores during naps or you'd be the one who never slept.

Because Liam was so tiny and nursing, Elizabeth was the one to get up at all hours to feed him. She knew eventually she'd pump, and there would be bottles for Tig, but now, she loved those moments with just the two of them.

Tig got more night sleep than Elizabeth, so he'd been great about taking Liam during the day so Elizabeth could get a bit more rest. Liam had been born at six pounds and was growing fast.

They tiptoed out, she to her bed and Tig to water the yard.

One thing that hadn't returned to the new normal was Freya. Elizabeth had tried to check in, but was shut down. Or out. Apparently Freya had a mental door too, the way Elizabeth could prevent animals from just listening to her thoughts and parading through her mind. The kitten did not talk to her, even when she asked direct questions. When she'd elicited Edward's help, with his superconnection to her, he said she wasn't answering. Like someone not picking up a phone call.

Elizabeth managed as best she could with a new infant, her parents, her post C-section health, the animals, so she could not take the time to hunt for Freya. The kitten did not have the same connection with her as the human-kitten presence, and she missed it. She hoped this was not their future. She cared for the kitten and would keep her, but it was not the same.

When Elizabeth lay down to rest, the kitten came with her and lay on the pillow, something she hadn't done since Elizabeth had gone to the hospital. She'd been sleeping on one of the dining room chairs, invisible and aloof.

Elizabeth was worried and tired. She turned on her side to face Freya and stroked the small paw with a finger. Freya was curled in a ball, eyes closed, sleeping, or pretending to.

Freya? Her eyes opened and the kaleidoscope flexed and returned, bringing human Freya with it. *Freya!* Elizabeth scooped her up and cuddled, kissing her small forehead, the tiny mouse-purr vibrating.

I've missed you so much. How are you?

I am healing. We are recovering at much the same rate. I did not know providing food for a baby was such a tiring activity.

I know. It's kind of a miracle, but poor planning to be a one-stop shop, you know? Elizabeth joked.

Freya's eyes squinched closed, and her mouth opened with a tiny squeak that was her laugh.

353

Is everyone okay in Volksvang? Is Thor doing well? Oor?

Yes, they are fine. Thank you for asking.

I feel it's kind of my village too. I spent so much time there. Maybe I should visit it in the real world someday. I wonder if I'd recognize it? My mother got back from Norway and said it's amazing. Is that where it is?

I don't know this place.

I guess not. Sometimes mythology and reality do not cross paths, Elizabeth thought. Kind of a crazy thought anyway.

Since you have been gone, Elizabeth said, *the kitten has been just a kitten. It has no personality, it seems. It won't talk to me like a cat would. Is this how it's going to be?* She pulled Freya close again. *I really missed you.*

I will not be able to visit like I have. This was for a specific purpose, not only to save Asgard and all of us, but to bring Thor into the world. Your Thor, too. Freya had a smile in her voice.

Yes. I figured that out. They were born the same day at the same time. Why not on Thorsday? Wouldn't that be more, I don't know, propitious?

Thorsday did not exist until that moment.

Oh. That makes sense. None of the literature she'd read, or that her mother had passed on, had specific dates for events, except some wars and travel, because much occurred before such records were kept. Since it was based in mythology, which in itself was based on stories, guesses and a primitive people not knowing scientific bases for things like thunder or lightning or eclipses, reasons were created.

I have been busy with Thor and unable to speak to you. However, it is not the kitten, it is me. I

354

took up so much 'space' in the kitten since it was so young, it has not had time to form its own personality or path. I chose it however, because it will grow close to you, but you must do the work and foster the connection.

So, it might connect to me more if I work on it?

Not might. Will. But the window for that is short. If you neglect it, the opportunity will be lost.

And it will be a regular cat, not even with an emotional bond like I have with Teddy and Edward?

Think of it as a cup of ale. I have been the ale for most of its life. When I leave, the ale is poured out. I can't help but leave residual drops of ale in the mug, but it is up to you to fill the mug using those drops and your knowledge to form this relationship.

I see. How do I do that?

I don't know. It is up to you, and her. I must go now. My world needs me. You may find your way back some day; I can't see that far ahead. Once I am gone, you cannot reach me directly—our energies will be diminished. However, Edward can still reach me. He has abilities that he has honed.

Elizabeth remembered him telling her he had a special connection, especially when she was in trouble. He was also the one who connected to Liam early in her pregnancy, while she could not.

Her heart felt as if it was being squeezed. She was not ready to say goodbye to Freya.

Let me go.

I can't.

You must. Freya licked her forehead with her scratchy tongue, a special sort of blessing.

I love you Freya.

355

I love you too, sister. Freya closed her eyes and when they reopened, the kaleidoscope was gone.

Elizabeth held her close and cried. They fell asleep together and Freya stayed in her arms until a mild mewling woke them. Tig stood in the doorway with a bundle of Liam.

"Somebody's hungry," he said and brought the baby to her. "Hey. Freya looks good. Did she sleep with you like that?"

Elizabeth looked closely at the tabby kitten, still in the circle of her arms.

Hi, Mom.

The End

Victoria Heckman's first *Hawai'i mystery series* features officer Katrina Ogden, K.O., of the Honolulu Police Department. Her second series, *Coconut Man mysteries of Ancient Hawai'i* begins with *Kapu-Sacred* and continues with her newest, *Kahuna-Priest*. Her third mystery series (*Burn Out & Wet Work)* starring animal communicator Elizabeth Murphy is set on California's Central Coast. Stand alone mystery, *Pearl Harbor Blues,* begins on Dec. 7, 1941 and uncovers a dynasty of corporate intrigue. *K.O.'d at Banzai Pipeline* sends her to the big surf contests of O'ahu's North Shore. She is also the author of over 75 short stories and articles and the editor of seven anthologies. She is a member of Sisters in Crime-Central Coast Chapter.

www.victoriaheckman.com
Facebook: Victoria Heckman
Twitter: @v.heckman